Praise for Au
Inspect

"Based on *Death in a Bookstore's* memorable characters, clever red herrings, and vibrant backdrop of pre-WWII Milan, it's easy to see why De Angelis ranks this high." ***Publishers Weekly***

"De Vincenzi is an investigator who doesn't stop at the material evidence, but digs with uncommon passion in the psyche of his characters, and the atmosphere in which they live and operate. . . a rare delight." ***Il Corriere Della Sera***

"Compared to the detective stories published during his time, De Angelis is a notable exception, for his literary talent, for his innovation of the genre, for his narrative and for the modernity of the figure of Inspector De Vincenzi, rigorous reasoner, philosopher in his heart, a committed reader, and true master of his clients' psychology." ***Il Giornale***

"De Angelis is regarded as the father of Italian crime fiction. . . Alive with period detail of 1930s Milan, and taut with psychological tension, this is a rediscovered gem that deserves a wider audience." ***The Lady Magazine***

"Inspector De Vincenzi is as humane as Maigret, as romantic as Marlowe, as intellectual as Philo Vance, yet stubbornly Italian." ***Oreste Del Buono***

"The inspector is never excessive: witty but human, intellectual and politely sensitive to feminine charm, courageous but not gratuitously brazen, De Vincenzi reasons, tries to empathize, is keenly aware of his faults. Attentive but not meticulous, logical but not obsessively "deductive", devoted to his work but ready to benefit from every unexpectedly free moment . . . The inspector doesn't go out of his way to charm. But he does." ***L'Osservatore Romano***

Death in a Bookstore

Augusto De Angelis

Originally Published as *Sei donne e un libro* in 1936

Kazabo Publishing

Kazabo books are available at special discounts when purchased in bulk or by book clubs. Special editions of many of our books can also be created for promotional and educational use. Please visit us at kazabo.com for more information.

Foreword

Augusto De Angelis, the creator of Inspector De Vincenzi, is, without question, the most important Italian mystery writer in the first half of the twentieth century. Born in 1888 and beaten to death by Fascists in 1944, his life and times were among the most colorful and active of any writer in the genre, ever.

During his lifetime, De Angelis wrote more than 20 books. While many of them feature Inspector De Vincenzi, he also wrote books on history, the theater, and current events. De Angelis was also a highly-respected journalist who interviewed Mussolini himself on three different occasions.

A young man of solid classical education, De Angelis left law school for a career in journalism, working with the most important Italian newspapers of the first half of the twentieth century. His one-on-one interviews with Mussolini, reminiscent of the interviews that David Frost had with Richard Nixon, were held in 1922, 1929 and 1933 and were published in various newspapers even finding their way into the foreign press. De Vincenzi, a firm anti-Fascist himself, was unsparing in his depiction of "Il Duce." The figure emerging from these interviews is a somewhat pathetic, narcissistic politician with dreams of grandeur who saw himself as the liberator of Italy and Europe, a modern-day Caesar who would restore the Roman Empire to its former grandeur.

De Angelis, much to Mussolini's discomfort, suffused these interviews with references to Mussolini's dependence on Hitler and Germany. At one stage in the interview of 1929, De Angelis asked Il Duce, prophetically: "Do you believe the Fuehrer will be true to his word of a triple Alliance? Or do you believe he will eventually wish to rule as the overlord of Italy?"

"The Fuehrer is a man of honor!" Mussolini bellowed, "Men of honor keep their word. Ours is a New Age, an age in which the value of loyalty surpasses personal ambition!"

History records that Mussolini was infuriated by the "spin" De

Angelis put in his articles and other works. It is reported that in their last interview in 1933 (right after Hitler had been elected Chancellor of Germany), Mussolini told De Angelis to "...tell the truth or the truth will catch up to you." De Angelis did tell the truth, but it was not Mussolini's version of the truth, and it finally did catch up to him in July of 1944 when De Angelis was beaten to death by an agent of the Fascist government in a café in Bellagio, Italy. We cannot be sure that this man was sent by Mussolini himself, but it is almost certain that the official version of his death published by the regime, (that he had met with a young woman in the café thereby inducing the jealousy of an officer in the Italian Army) is a fabrication. This attack did not come out of the blue. De Angelis had only recently been released from a Fascist prison so he was most definitely on the regime's radar at the time he was murdered.

But De Angelis's most enduring legacy is his creation of Inspector De Vincenzi. Before Inspector De Vincenzi, Italian mystery authors had imported stock characters from foreign detective traditions. But De Angelis wanted something unique, something truly Italian. He considered the reliance on foreign tropes to be absurd. "I wanted and I want to create an Italian detective novel. They say that we lack the detectives, we lack the policemen and the gangsters. It may well be! In any case, it seems to me that we don't lack crimes. Don't forget that this is the land of the Borgias, the Popes and Queen Giovanna."

A word must be said here about the Fascist government's attitude towards not just Augusto De Angelis, but the mystery genre in general. When De Angelis says, "They say that we lack the detectives, we lack the policemen and the gangsters." he was speaking of the government's discomfort with – and eventual outright prohibition on – any depiction of society that did not echo their version of perfect order and justice. As explained by Franca De Angelis, Augusto De Angelis's daughter,

Mussolini never loved the police procedural genre, he always looked at it with suspicion, and at a certain point he began to actively persecute it. What are the reasons for this marked dislike? First of all, in the eyes of the exponents of the regime, this literary genre encouraged the corruption of moral conventions, especially those of young readers: in the detective novels, in fact (according to Mussolini) good and evil became moral categories a bit too interchangeable and very frequently authority was mocked and virtue questioned. Not to mention the fact that the culprits were often captivating and likable characters . . . So the detective novels, more or less consciously, ended up sowing the seeds of delinquency in the mind (in Mussolini's words!) and for this reason their diffusion was not to be encouraged, indeed, had to be impeded in every way!

As the Chief of Police of Florence wrote of the detective novel in 1936, "One wonders what are we waiting for to make an energetic clean up of all this ballast made of wasted paper, just like Japan did with jazz music, especially considering that in this case it's not just a matter of carrying on a deserved retaliation against enemies who – even when they were not such – have always disregarded our literature, but rather doing meritorious work for the moral and literary education of our people."

To this end, Mussolini's government imposed ever-tighter censorship. In 1941, the government ordered that all mystery novels be submitted for prior authorization before publication. On June 1 of 1943, the government went even further and ordered that all detective novels be seized and destroyed. The murder mystery had now been banished from Italy.

It has been said that no bureaucrat is ever a match for an artist and that was certainly true in De Vincenzi's case. Forced to work in an ever more constricting environment, he was a master at bending, twisting and subverting the rules. For example, De Angelis decided to give De Vincenzi a romantic life and a Jewish woman became the only woman De Vincenzi had ever loved.

And this may well be the real problem that Mussolini had with De Angelis: that the protagonist of Italy's most famous crime stories of the 20s and 30s was in love with a Jewess. This must have made Il Duce's situation with Hitler rather embarrassing, especially since De Angelis' stories were already being translated in German and distributed by the Jewish underground.

In addition to his artistic talents, De Angelis was something of a philosopher as well. De Angelis believed that any literary genre is the product of its own times, and that the pleasure derived from detective fiction is a form of compensation for the social anxieties resulting from the experience of modernity. He wrote, "Today, man finds terrifying the presence of crime in his everyday life, and immediately created a

God to protect him: the God detective, whose cult is celebrated in the crime."

In his pursuit of the "authentically Italian crime novel," he didn't just invent great characters and write interesting stories, he made those characters and stories applications of his theoretical approach to the detective novel. De Vincenzi envisioned stories where, in the end, all the characters had to be true to their inner motivations. "I am resolved," wrote De Angelis, "to write detective novels where people live according to the laws of nature."

And he succeeded. De Angelis gave his hero, Inspector De Vincenzi, a keen understanding of human nature and the psychology of the human mind. This frustrated and annoyed De Vincenzi's superiors just as much, no doubt, as it frustrated and annoyed the bureaucrats in the Fascist Ministry of Popular Culture who had been tasked with getting people like Augusto De Angelis under control. In the words of Inspector De Vincenzi's Police Superintendent, "You disregard evidence. . . appearances. . . earlier crimes. You disregard motives. You observe people, question them, examine them, judge them with your psychological method and then set them free, having decided that they cannot be guilty, because they lack the moral, intellectual, temperamental, or emotional capacity to commit a murder, this murder. . . Where will we end up, De Vincenzi? Your obsession with the psychology of murder is madness!"

The Inspector De Vincenzi novels are, indeed, a product of their own times. As such, they are a fascinating glimpse of Italy before the war. But those novels are also constructed on a keen understanding of human nature and, so, those novels remain as engaging and as accessible today as they were the day they were originally published. While times have changed a great deal, perhaps our inner natures have not.

Joshua Sinclair

Joshua Sinclair is an acclaimed film director and best-selling author as well as a medical doctor and recognized expert in tropical diseases. He is the grandson of both Upton Sinclair, on his father's side and Augusto De Angelis on his mother's.

The City of Milan

Milan, perhaps the most cosmopolitan city in Italy, is in itself another character in *Death in a Bookstore*. While the story is a work of fiction, the setting is not. De Angelis describes streets, parks, restaurants and cafés, even buildings with meticulous precision.

This adds a spectacular dimension to the novel. Milan has changed surprisingly little since the 1930s and many of the places he describes—including the cafes—still exist and are still exactly where they were 80 years ago. You can follow his characters as they move about the city, capturing the same impressions and moods they would capture as they walk, catch a taxi, follow a suspect, eat and drink. While he often provides only a street name rather than a number, using his descriptions it's still possible to identify many of the buildings using Google Maps.

During the preparation of this work, we often felt we were standing in De Angelis's shoes as he made careful notes precisely describing a building or how standing in a particular place in a particular *piazza* limits your view *just so*. In addition to being the premier pre-war Italian mystery author, De Angelis was an accomplished journalist and it really shows in his fanatical dedication to precise and realistic detail. Of course, you can enjoy this work as just a story, but it is a moving, almost eerie, experience to use Google Street View to step out of police headquarters and walk the streets of 1930s Milan with Inspector De Vincenzi at your shoulder.

About the Author

Augusto De Angelis, born in Rome in 1888, was an accomplished author and respected journalist, publishing over 25 books in his lifetime which included works on history, the theater and current events. But he is most acclaimed for the creation of Inspector De Vincenzi, the first "true" Italian fictional detective and still one of the most popular.

Neither the mystery genre nor De Angelis himself were popular with the fascist regime and both were censored. De Angelis's staunch opposition to fascism earned him arrest and, eventually, death when the fascists had him beaten to death in June of 1944.

TABLE OF CONTENTS

Main Characters

Senator Prof. Ugo Magni, deceased

Mrs. Magni, his widow

Pat Drury, assistant to Prof. Magni

Dr. Edoardo Verga, assistant to Prof. Magni

Dr. Alberto Marini, a friend of Prof. Magni

Mrs. Marini, his wife

Norina Santini, housemaid at the Magni residence

Pietro Santini, her brother

Fioretta Vaghi, a love-sick girl

Wanda Sorbelli, a medium

Tina Sorbelli, her daughter

Chirico, a bookseller

Gualtiero Gerolamo Pietrosanto, a clerk at the bookstore

Francesco Ravizzani, AKA the Worm, a petty criminal

Angelo Panzeri, a sacristan

Harrington, a private detective

The Street Sweeper

The Police Superintendent of Milan

Inspector Carlo De Vincenzi

Deputy Inspector Sani

Sergeant Cruni

Prologue

He contemplated the bundle lying on the steps of the church.

The early light of dawn illuminated the deserted square. Under the entrance corridor, which led to an open courtyard, the sunrise lit up the image of the Madonna. A few minutes before, all the streetlights had turned off suddenly. The air was chilly.

A new day was born in the city of Milan, which remained nearly motionless. The noise of trams could be heard in the distance, on Corso Vittorio Emanuele, and on the other side, Via Cavallotti.

The man in the gray uniform looked at the bundle.

It must be rags wrapped up in newspaper, he thought. Yet the parcel appeared too carefully packaged to contain rags.

He hit it with the broom and the bundle rolled down the stairs onto the pavement. It didn't open. It had to be closed with some pin, because it was not tied. From the center of the bundle, below the newspaper's edge, a white envelope appeared.

The sweeper bent to reach the envelope. It was open. It contained a piece of paper folded in fourths. Upon the paper was scrawled a message in large and hurried script in blue ink. *"Please deliver to the police station."*

In his eyes, the parcel had now gained importance. He looked at it with respect, even a little fear. Whatever was wrapped in that newspaper, now that he had found it, he had the irritating responsibility of going to the San Fedele police station to deliver it. After that would come the even bigger nuisance: being questioned, giving explanations, repeating them in court. . . He knew how it worked! Once he had picked up a bunch of fake banknotes, and, after that experience, he cursed counterfeiters around the world.

So many things had happened to him! In twenty years as a street sweeper, he had found nothing but rubbish and trouble on the ground.

3

He looked around. There was nobody.

He kicked the package, which rolled farther. But it was not so light, because it didn't go too far.

Sighing, he passed the back of his hand over his mouth. Finally, he picked up the parcel. There were two pins, in fact, to keep the folds of the newspaper closed around the parcel. He touched the bundle. It was soft; there were certainly garments inside. Still, there was something hard in the middle of the garments, which weighed more.

He approached the empty cart, and placed the package on the closed lid. He secured the broom on the two side hooks and put the letter inside his pocket. He grabbed the rods and pushed the cart. He started slowly down Via Pasquirolo, toward Piazza Beccaria, the iron cart resonated on the pavement.

When he arrived at San Fedele, it was broad daylight.

He took the long way and stopped in front of the Galleria to buy coffee with grappa from a street vendor. The vendor looked him up and down twice before serving him, as he had never seen him before.

"Are you new here? Who are you replacing?"

"Nobody. I was just passing by."

"Are you taking a stroll with your *Isotta Fraschini*?"

He didn't answer. He didn't want to talk. The story of the bundle to be delivered to police headquarters had put him in a bad mood. He grabbed his *Isotta Fraschini* and left.

At the door of the San Fedele police station, he stopped with the bundle in his hands. Who should he deliver it to?

A *carabiniere* was looking at him.

"Tell me. . . excuse me. . ."

"I don't know anything. There, on the porch, there is an agent."

The sweeper addressed the agent, who was smoking.

"I found this on the steps of the church of San Vito, off Via Pasquirolo."

"And you brought it here?! You should know that City Hall takes care of such things. . ."

"Lost items, yes I know. And you get a ten percent tip, too, when you bring them in. But please, read this!"

He gave him the envelope containing the note.

The agent read it and laughed.

"It's a joke! Have you looked inside?"

"No. I don't want to get in trouble!"

"Why? Is it heavy? You think there's a woman's head cut into pieces inside?!"

And he kept on laughing.

The street sweeper stared at the bundle in his hands in terror. No! It couldn't be someone's head. It was soft. The heavier part was in the middle, but it was too small to be a head.

"Well! Go over there to the Flying Squad. The Inspector is in. The night shift officer must still be asleep."

The sweeper crossed the yard and knocked on a door on which he read: "Flying Squad - Chief Inspector."

A gentle, courteous voice answered him.

"Come in. What's up?"

Inside, he found a brunette young man elegantly dressed, who looked at him with vague eyes. He was still absorbed in some thought or his reading.

"I found this, Inspector. . . on the steps of San Vito al Pasquirolo. . ."

"So?"

"There was this letter too."

The inspector read the letter.

"Ok, give it to me."

He took the bundle, removed the pins, looked at them—they were common pins—and opened the newspaper.

A clean, white coat appeared, like those worn by doctors or nurses. The inspector opened the coat and four surgical instruments fell on the table; they were bright, shiny, and sharp.

Nothing else.

The sweeper stood observing.

The inspector took the instruments and examined them one at a time. He recognized a scalpel and then saw some kind of screwdriver, surgical scissors, and a long caliper.

The scalpel had some brown spots. The other tools seemed new.

The inspector rang the bell and a little later the guard appeared.

"Call Sergeant Cruni," he intoned in his courteous voice.

The guard disappeared.

When Cruni arrived, he was still sleepy. He was short and muscular, and his body was too massive for such short legs.

"I am needed, sir?"

"Draw up a report of found objects and register this man's personal data."

"Yes, sir. Please come with me."

Once alone, Inspector De Vincenzi touched the coat, lifted it, and then looked at the surgical instruments. He took up the scalpel and examined it closely.

"Blood stains," he murmured.

He got up and locked everything in the closet.

Then he sat back at his desk and took the book he was reading out of the drawer. It was the last novel by Körmendi. He read all sort of things.

Almost immediately he looked up from the page and stared at the closet. The piece of paper with the strange request was still on the desk.

Who would abandon four surgical instruments, including a blood-stained scalpel and a white coat?

He examined the handwritten note. It was written quickly with a fountain pen. It didn't look fake: whoever wrote it was serious. At the least, they were in a hurry.

He dropped the note on the desk and glanced at the clock: it was almost seven. He began reading aloud, with a bitter smile, the calendar in front of him:

"At 8:30 AM the sun enters the sign of Aries. . . and at 2:28 PM spring begins."

He tore the page from the calendar and March 21 appeared, completely blank.

"Aries. . ." he murmured again. "If only I believed in horoscopes!"

Then he shrugged. The truth was, he did believe in horoscopes as well as in many more things, including misfortune, telepathy, and premonitions. He was superstitious.

Why did he receive four surgical instruments and a white coat on the very first day of spring?

What should he do? Nothing, obviously. The letter and the bundle could not force him to do anything, neither as a police inspector nor as a man. But he could think about it, of course.

The newspaper in which they had been wrapped was the *Corriere* of March 20th. He read it and found nothing special. He folded it and put it in the drawer.

In the afternoon, when he came back to his office, he would show the instruments to a doctor to find out more about them. And then he would wait. Nothing else had happened, or maybe something was happening or could have happened already.

Maybe a murder?

No! He closed the book and put it in the drawer, then got up, put on his overcoat, grabbed his hat and, when he reached the door, he turned off the light.

From the arch facing the courtyard, through the dirty railing and the closed, even dirtier windows, a pale daylight entered. De Vincenzi sighed. He had become accustomed to going to bed when the sun was already high, for he spent most nights at the police station, working or reading. Yet, he sighed every morning. Because every morning, at the sight of the new day, he thought of the country house, in Ossola, where he was born, and where his mother still lived, with the hens, the dog and the maid. He would have been so glad to join his mother. He was young, not even thirty-five, yet he felt old. He had fought in the war. And he had a contemplative spirit. Some of his boarding school mates called him a poet to make fun of him. He was so much a poet, that he became a police inspector. . .

He was about to open the door to leave when the phone rang. He winced. Why now?!

He went to the phone and lifted the receiver.

"Hello, Flying Squad. . . Hello! Hello!"

No one answered. He said hello again and then hung the receiver back on the hook. Someone had called by mistake. He took a few steps toward the door to finally leave, but he hesitated. He went back, picked up the phone and talked to the police station operator.

"Did you call the Flying Squad perhaps?"

The operator answered immediately.

"Yes, Inspector. Did they say anything?"

"Not at all! There was no one!"

"That's strange! I heard a woman's voice. She asked for an inspector. And she sounded anxious. I connected her to the Flying Squad, because I know that you are usually there at seven o'clock, even though the day shift isn't in yet."

"A woman's voice? Are you sure?"

"Yes, I am..."

"And did she say anything else?"

"She said, 'An inspector please! May I talk to an inspector?' 'What is it about?' I asked. 'Let me talk to an inspector, I implore you!' So I immediately connected the switchboard to your number."

"All right. I will wait for ten more minutes. Let me know if she calls back."

He sat down and waited. He had put his hat on. He looked out at the railing, in the courtyard, at a weak and wretched tree, which was flourishing, almost as if it had begun recovering from a disease. He was thinking. Suddenly he wondered why plants bloom every season, how they find strength, beauty, and youth while men don't.

He remembered the end of the *De Profundis* by Oscar Wilde. He had read it at boarding school and it influenced his thinking ever since: *Expression is as necessary to me as leaf and blossoms are to the black branches of the trees that show themselves above the prison walls and are so restless in the wind.* He had been looking for expression too, and he had ended up becoming a police inspector to find it! But wasn't this room with bars at the windows a kind of prison too?

A quarter of an hour later, he called the operator.

"Nobody?"

"Nobody, sir."

He hesitated, but only for a moment.

"I'm leaving, then. I'll be back at two o'clock this afternoon."

9

"Ok, sir."

De Vincenzi left, and shortly thereafter he crossed Piazza San Fedele and then Piazza della Scala, pausing for a moment to watch the cleaners' water jets flood the square under the rays of the new sun.

Chapter 1

"He came home at eight o'clock and went to bed. It's nine o'clock now, and you're already looking for him! Oh! Where has the Inspector been all night long?"

Cruni smiled, looking at the woman standing on the threshold of the door, almost as if she wanted to prevent his passage.

A good old woman, Inspector De Vincenzi's maid had been his nurse and didn't want to leave him unprotected. Cruni knew that.

"He was at the police station, Mrs. Antonietta!"

"Oh! And now what?" the woman exclaimed in a loud voice, her red cheeks flushing. "Do you want him to die of exhaustion? Not to mention the miserable salary you give him! Such a clever person!"

"Indeed, Mrs. Antonietta, as he's clever, we always call him. He is the best!"

Cruni believed what he was saying. He had great admiration for his boss; but even if he didn't think so, he would have said it anyway just to calm her down. As a matter of fact, she brightened at his words, raising her shoulders and straightening her thin body making her seem somehow elegant in her tight black dress and large white apron.

"But it isn't charitable! What would you do without him, if he died?"

"We won't lose him, you'll see! But he'll get angry if we don't call him. It's a serious matter, do you know? And the Superintendent wants him right away!"

The woman stood aside with a gesture of resignation.

"Come in and call him then. But please do it softly!. . . Never mind! I'll take care of it."

She knocked at the door of her master's bedroom, then turned the latch, and went straight into the dark room toward the window. She

11

opened the window shutters and the room was filled with light.

De Vincenzi opened his eyes, moaned, and quickly sat up in bed.

"What is it, Antonietta?"

"The usual, my son! Sergeant Cruni wants you right now! I didn't want to wake you up, but he insisted."

"All right. Let him in and bring me coffee, please."

Cruni was in a hurry, running on his short legs and moving his hands around his hat's brim.

"Forgive me, sir! But the Superintendent begs you to immediately join him."

"Why? Do you know?"

"He didn't tell me but I can imagine. A dead man was found in Via Corridoni, in a bookseller's shop."

"And there are no other inspectors at the police station in San Fedele? And isn't there any inspector in Via della Signoria?"

"I know, sir. But it seems to be a big deal. Something for the Flying Squad. The Superintendent talked to Deputy Inspector Sani, who gave me the order to come and fetch you."

Antonietta brought the coffee.

"Go prepare me a bath, please!"

De Vincenzi jumped out of bed.

"Go wait for me in the other room, Cruni. I'll be right there."

Twenty minutes later they were hailing a taxi, because De Vincenzi lived in Corso Sempione and Cruni said there was no time to waste.

"No time to waste. . . to go see a dead man!" De Vincenzi murmured.

But meanwhile, he remembered that it was March 21 and the Sun had entered the constellation of Aries, and that that very morning he was brought four surgical instruments and a white coat. *"Please deliver to the police station."*

"Do you know anything else about the murder? And is it a murder?"

"I've heard there were two bullets in the back of the skull."

"Who is the dead man?"

"I don't know. But he seems to be quite important."

"In a bookshop?"

"Oh yes, it must be that bookshop at the beginning of Via Corridoni, to the right. . . where there used to be a typography. . ."

"So you don't actually know anything."

"Nothing, sir. I finished at eight o'clock, too, and I was in the office by chance. Deputy Inspector Sani sent me over here, saying that you prefer me to others."

De Vincenzi smiled. It was true, though, he would always ask for Cruni when he was out working. He liked him and trusted him. He and Cruni had history.

The taxi stopped in front of a large door. De Vincenzi paid and rushed toward the courtyard.

Deputy Inspector Sani welcomed him with a comically desolate smile.

"They dragged you out of bed, eh!"

De Vincenzi gave him a friendly handshake.

"It doesn't matter," he murmured, walking straight into his office.

"Do you want me to tell you?" Sani asked, following him.

"Wait."

He picked up the receiver of the phone.

"Did anyone call?"

"Pardon me? I've already called the Flying Squad four or five times this morning. . ."

"Are you the same operator who was there at seven o'clock?"

"Yes, sir. . ."

"Then the woman's voice. . . do you remember it?"

"Yes, sir. She didn't call again."

"Ok. If she calls again, contact the Flying Squad, all right?"

"Okay, sir."

De Vincenzi turned to Sani, who sat in front of him.

"This morning at about seven, a woman called the police station and asked anxiously to talk to an inspector. The operator put her in communication with me. At that time, you know, I'm the only one here. I answered right away, but I didn't hear anything. She was gone. Do you understand?"

"I see. . ."

"If she ever calls when I'm away, note what she wants and let me know. It's important."

"Is it important because she is a woman?"

The inspector shrugged.

"Curiosity, nothing else. All right. Now, tell me and do it quickly, because I guess the Superintendent is waiting for me."

"Yes," Sani said. "It won't take long. Did you know Professor Magni?"

"The surgeon?"

"Yes, the surgeon."

"Is he the dead man?"

"Exactly. Two bullets in the nape of the neck."

"In a bookshop?!" De Vincenzi exclaimed. "And what was he doing in a bookshop in the middle of the night?"

"That's one of the more mysterious points. But it's not the only one. As soon as the body was discovered, an hour ago, the Superintendent, given the notoriety of the deceased. . . As you know, Magni was a senator, president of many charities, I think he had also been Minister of Education many years ago, when ministers lasted three months at the most."

"I know, go ahead."

"So the Superintendent wanted to call the family personally. Well, the wife answered and as soon as he started speaking, she interrupted him, saying, 'Do you want to talk to my husband? He's still asleep, but I can wake him up.' So then he asked, 'Are you sure your husband is in his room?' 'Of course,' she replied. 'Where else would he be?' 'Err, ehh, didn't he go out last night?' 'Yes, he did, but he came back at midnight.' 'How do you know he came back?' 'Why are you asking me so many questions?' the poor woman said, beginning to get worried. 'I know, because when he came back he came to greet me in the room as he always does.' Then the Superintendent realized that giving the news by phone would have been too brutal—and too confusing—and told her that it could wait and not to call her husband. Now, he's waiting for you and then, of course, he will go to Magni's house himself."

"That's strange!" De Vincenzi murmured. After a pause he said, "I'd rather go myself."

He stared at Sani. He got up, and stood in front of the desk and pensively shuffled a few papers. His eyes glanced over the white envelope and the note, which he had examined a few hours earlier. He winced.

He went to the closet, opened it, and took out the white coat and the surgical instruments. He went back and put them on the desk. "These are Magni's instruments," he said. Sani watched him, astonished.

15

"Who gave you those?"

"Maybe the murderer himself. Or, maybe someone who will help me find the murderer. Now, I'm going to the Superintendent. You leave those instruments on my desk and don't let anybody in here in my absence."

The Superintendent welcomed him, standing in the middle of the room as De Vincenzi entered. He was a short, fat, well-groomed person, with gray hair parted on his head and polished patent leather shoes shining like mirrors. He could otherwise have been a peaceful merchant selling women's accessories if he had not had those two little eyes in the middle of his fat face. They were so lively, blue and penetrating that they seemed to pierce you.

"Ah! Well done. Taking it a little easy this morning, eh? No matter, you're still in time. At eight o'clock this morning, the corpse of Senator Magni was found in a bookshop in Via Corridoni. A murder. But not a vulgar murder, not a crime for money. The deceased still had a full wallet, watch, rings, a diamond pin: everything. It's an unusual situation. Tonight, as soon as the newspapers get hold of it, the public will go mad with curiosity. This case is yours. I'm giving you carte blanche. But understand, De Vincenzi, no mistakes. You're either going to end up as Chief Inspector De Vincenzi or Officer De Vincenzi because of this. Are we clear?"

"Yes, sir," replied De Vincenzi, trying to withstand the gaze of those piercing eyes. "I'll go. But may I ask you to wait for my return before going to Magni's house? I would like to be there from the very beginning. . ."

"All right. Magni lives in Viale Bianca Maria. . ."

"I did not know that..."

"You do now. And Via Corridoni. . ."

"Via Corridoni starts from Viale Bianca Maria, ending in Via Cesare Battisti. . ."

"Exactly. So please wait for me. I'll go with you to visit the crime scene, then I'll go to the late senator's house."

16

The Superintendent put on his coat, removed the ever-present carnation from the eyelet, put it in a glass of water, and donned his gloves.

"Do you mind if I tag along? You won't even know I'm there."

"It's an honor," De Vincenzi murmured.

"An honor. . . but not a pleasure!" snorted the Superintendent. "Don't worry. I won't bother you. I'll just take a look. It's you who have to work." And he went down the stairs.

De Vincenzi followed him speculating, oddly, about the woman who hadn't called back.

And he didn't know why he kept thinking about that unknown woman's voice, a voice he had not even heard.

Chapter 2

That morning, Gualtiero Gerolamo Pietrosanto had left home, in the Loreto neighborhood, at 7:30.

7:30 was really too early for Gualtiero Gerolamo Pietrosanto to leave home, and his wife looked at him with apprehension:

"Do you feel sick, Gualmo?"

Gualmo—an affectionate abbreviation of his two long names—was feeling quite well and gazed at his consort with the sweet eyes of an intelligent and faithful dog:

"Not at all, Rita!"

"Are you worried about something?"

No, no concerns. Or at least not more than on other days. He had had his coffee, had some coins for his daily cigarettes, some more in case of unforeseen events, at home there was food. No, he definitely had no worries.

"So, then you'll arrive at the store at eight o'clock!" the woman exclaimed, almost grumbling.

"Oh well. . ." he smiled, pulling on his new coat. "At least for once!"

And he kissed her on the cheeks.

"Ok! Once!" the woman granted. "You shouldn't rush there, considering how much you get paid."

"No. . . I'm going on foot."

Instead, thinking that fifty cents at that time of day would have allowed him to buy the return ticket too, Gualtiero Gerolamo took the trolley car and, at eight o'clock, was in front of the bookshop on Via Corridoni.

He had been a bookshop owner, and what a bookshop! It was right

18

on Milan's most important street, with all the latest books from France, the rarest volumes, the most beautiful bindings. His business had flourished. And he was an expert in the field, just like a professor. But he was an artist and loved the literati. And he was, alas, unable to say no to anybody, so a few years later he had given away thousands of books to the most illustrious literati and received, in return, great and precious photographs with dedications. He had so many photographs that people envied him, portraying the inventor of a hair lotion or a doctor of sciatica and arthritis. But since those photographs had no actual value, he had to close his shop, with an amount of irrecoverable debt bordering on that of the United States after the European War.

So he had become the only employee of the antiquarian bookshop on Via Corridoni. It belonged to a small and dried-up man, who didn't give any credit to anybody, except in exchange for promissory notes.

When he was in front of the store's rolling shutter, Pietrosanto stopped to look at it, amazed. It was the first time he saw it lowered like that in the front. Of course, it's eight a.m. and he's the one who closed it last night. But it had never occurred to him to open it, not at eight o'clock in the morning nor at two o'clock in the afternoon. Giovanni took care of it. That morning Giovanni, perhaps because his bicycle's brakes were broken, hadn't shown up yet.

"Huh. So how does this work?" Gualtiero Gerolamo wondered.

But he remembered that the key was always delivered to the porter so, when he entered, he asked for it with his usual restrained and dignified courtesy.

"Could you give me the store key, please?"

"Oh!" the porter said. "Are you opening this morning?"

"Yes, I am." he half-apologized almost adding, "I won't do it again!"

He took the key, went back to the store, opened the two locks and lifted the rolling shutter. The store was full of books, with the counter in the middle, the owner's desk, and a table buried in paper, forms, and catalogs. Here he spent at least eight hours a day looking at volumes and preparing a quarterly catalog, which was always late for the printer and was never-ending—because when it was over, it started again.

He went in happy, for it was such an unexpected and mysterious novelty being able to enter it first on a new day.

He turned on the light in the hallway, and, passing through two bookshelves, he went into the back of the shop to take off his overcoat and hat.

The back of the shop consisted of two rooms, one next to the other, with a third smaller room to the right of the first. And those three rooms, with ceiling-high windows with bars facing the courtyard, were also full of old books. Many books. Too many books. The rooms, with their dim, swampy light, smelled of dust.

He stopped next to the telephone, where the light switches were, and turned them on. The three rooms lit up, and the great mass of books lined up against the walls, piled on the tables, and stacked on the floor, acquired consistency, showed their spines made of skin or parchment.

Gualtiero Gerolamo began to take off his coat. He did it carefully, because it was new and, with spring beginning that very day, he would need it again in the coming year.

He held it by the lapel and headed for the closet in the room on the right. But he paused, staring with his short-sighted eyes at the edge of the door connecting the first room to the third one. He leaned a little. Then he threw his new coat onto the dusty books and ran through the corridor with a strangled cry.

He reached the glass door at the street, and collided with Giovanni, who had just arrived. Almost knocking him over, Gualtiero staggered into the street, ran halfway through Via Cesare Battisti, and when he saw a traffic officer on duty at the crossroads, fell on him, gasping in a strangled voice:

"There's a corpse!"

As he was wearing a hat, the policeman knew he was not drunk. He considered whether Gualtiero might simply be insane, but the policeman knew that, even among the crazy, such an outburst was something that happened rarely, unless the patient showed up naked in the square.

So he took him by the arm and said,

"Calm down! Where is this corpse?"

Shortly thereafter, there was a large group of people in front of the bookstore, which another policeman, called there to help, was keeping at bay. In the meantime, Giovanni, long and awkward as he was—he had spent sixteen years of his life eating bread loaves without assimilating them—was telling everyone:

"I don't know anything! My bicycle had a broken brake!"

Inside the store, Pietrosanto, sitting in front of the table, stared into the void, slowly recovering, just like a fish that has been out of the water and then is thrown back just in time to prevent it from dying.

After seeing the corpse, the first policeman—who now had not for a moment doubted its existence—had hurried to call the police station in Via della Signoria and was now waiting. In the middle of the store, he contemplated all those books, with a sense of haughty astonishment.

"Do you know him?"

"Who?" Gualtiero Gerolamo asked, shaking.

"The dead man."

"I didn't look at him!"

"You will shortly."

Pietrosanto swallowed.

"Was he the owner?"

The bookstore clerk jumped to his feet. He hadn't thought about that possibility. Yet it should have been the first hypothesis to come to mind.

"What are you saying?" he shouted.

"Hey! Don't yell. There are people out there!"

And the policeman looked at the street with concern, where the group of nosy people was growing and getting more and more anxious.

"The owner!" Pietrosanto repeated in a lower voice. "Do you mean Mr. Chirico?"

"I don't know. Do I? Is that the name of the owner of this store? You should know it!"

"Look, sir, I don't think so. Mr. Chirico is an old, short, thin, ugly and pale man. . ."

"Well, he's certainly pale now. And not all that attractive, either!" And the policeman went to the back of the shop. When he came back, he was serious.

"You said he is short?"

"A little taller than that counter."

"This man is about six feet at least. And he's very elegant. A real gentleman."

"It's definitely not him!" Pietrosanto shouted again.

"I told you not to yell. Here is the inspector."

Gualtiero Gerolamo sat down again. He had recovered somewhat but he felt as if he was going crazy! Who could that six-foot tall *true gentleman* be who had entered the store at night and was found dead by him at eight o'clock in the morning? Inspector Maccari, (the elder colleague of De Vincenzi, close to retirement) came in slowly, looking around, two police officers in tow.

"Is there really a dead man?" he asked, pulling back his hat a little.

"Eh! Yes, there is," the policeman said.

"But is it really a murder?"

The policeman shrugged.

"How did he get in?" Pietrosanto exclaimed abruptly, obsessively thinking of the deceased. The inspector turned to him.

"What did you say?"

"Ah! Sorry. I thought. . ."

"What?"

"I wondered how that corpse made it in here!"

Maccari looked around.

"Hmm! Maybe he was a bookworm!"

He couldn't help himself. After thirty years of service, his sense of humor woke up instinctively and unknowingly in the face of macabre and terrible events.

"Let's see the corpse!" he said with a sigh, and his hat slipped down on his neck again, shaping a sort of halo around his round head and round face.

"This way, Inspector."

Maccari followed him.

The corpse lay supine through the doorway, which connected the first room in the back of the shop to the second one.

He was a handsome man of about forty years. He had a noble face, that the stiffness of death made even finer and more aristocratic. He wore a perfectly-tailored light overcoat. He wore gloves. His head was bare. Maccari looked around for a hat but didn't see one. He saw, instead, a large dark spot of blood behind the head of the deceased, highlighting his silver-blonde hair.

"But how did he die?"

Maybe hit on the head by a hammer or a club, he thought. But then he leaned over the corpse and saw a round hole in his cheek. A gun, obviously. But no blood came out. Must be the exit wound.

"Is he the owner of the store?"

"He says no," said the policeman. "The owner is old and short."

"Bring me that person in the other room. Who is he, a sales clerk?"

"He's the clerk of the bookstore. . ."

"Did he find the dead man?"

"I assume. He ran up to me in the street. He must have been terrified."

Pietrosanto walked in. He was still wearing his hat and was pale.

"Look at him and see if you recognize him."

Gualmo swallowed and exclaimed:

"But how did he get in here?"

It seemed this was the whole mystery to him.

"Do you know him?"

"No. . . Yes. . . I have seen him. . ."

"But do you know who he is?"

"I should know. . . I think I know. . . But I don't remember! Now, I can't remember! Sure, I've seen him other times. Perhaps, I also know him from speaking to him."

"A customer?"

"No! I don't think he ever came to the store."

Maccari leaned over the body and unbuttoned the overcoat and jacket. He took the wallet from the chest pocket. He opened it and quickly found a few business cards and an ID card. He read the name and compared the photograph on the ID with the corpse. He whistled.

"Unbelievable!"

"Who is it?" Pietrosanto asked.

"Senator Magni."

"Ah! I was sure that I knew him!"

The inspector pulled them back, away from the corpse.

"Come with me. Is there a phone?"

Pietrosanto pointed to it.

About twenty minutes later, Sergeant Cruni came out of the San Fedele Police Station to go wake Inspector De Vincenzi, who had just had an hour's rest.

Chapter 3

The policeman had gone back to obstructing traffic and Maccari sat in the shop next to the counter. Stretching out his hand, he selected a random book and began to read it.

Pietrosanto thought of the ways the corpse could have entered the bookshop as he looked through the cards of the book catalogue without reading a single title. This was not going to be a good day.

Half an hour later, Giovanni woke up from napping against a shelf. He went to a corner, by the window, and started sweeping.

"What are you doing?" Maccari asked, looking up from the book.

"I'm cleaning!"

"Well, don't!"

"Pardon me?"

"I said, stop it! Don't you know that by sweeping you're destroying evidence?"

Giovanni did not know, but he left the broom in the corner and then pulled up his pants leg to scratch his calf.

Maccari didn't care about the evidence. And not just because he knew that they would take the case away from him because the deceased was so important that the case would be handled by the main police station. It was also because he just didn't really care. He was about to retire and, at that point, he had had enough. After thirty years of such a life, he wasn't about to start crawling around on the floor looking for dust and footprints. However, if his colleagues from the flying squad found their crime scene excessively tidy, there might be questions.

He went back to reading. The book was *The Betrothed,* an annotated edition with lots of comparisons and many illustrations. And he was having fun. He was enjoying it. Yes, maybe he had already read it. But now it appeared to him new and surprising. He had opened the chapter of the corpse-removers. How terrible! How many corpses! In the other room, too, there was a dead man. But not because of a plague, thank God! He thought of the famous words from that book:

"Passing the threshold of one of those doorways. . ."

The Superintendent came in, followed by De Vincenzi and Cruni, and Maccari jumped to his feet, wishing the broom were out of sight. With one hand, he took off his hat, with the other one he kept holding the book, putting his finger across the pages as a bookmark, just as many years earlier Don Abbondio, the hapless priest in *The Betrothed*, had done shortly before being stopped by the *bravi*. Maccari respected and feared authority but he knew what was important.

"Good morning, Sir!"

The Superintendent greeted him warmly.

"Tell me, Maccari. . ."

De Vincenzi stood behind him and looked at Pietrosanto, who stood up as well.

"Here, Superintendent," said Maccari. "The corpse is in the other room. This is his wallet."

"Who are you?" interrupted the Superintendent, turning to Pietrosanto.

"The bookstore clerk."

"The director?"

"If you like. But it's just me."

"And the owner?"

"Mr. Chirico? Do you want me to call him?"

"Later. In the meantime, tell me what you know."

"What should I tell you? An hour ago. . . at eight o'clock, I opened the store. . ."

"Do you always open it?"

"Never!" Gualmo exclaimed almost indignantly. "It's the first time. . . Even my wife didn't want me to come so early! She was right!"

"And why did you come *so early,* as you say, *this very morning?*

"What?" Pietrosanto said, opening his eyes wide.

"I am asking you why you came so early this morning?" he repeated. "Why, tell me, why?"

He was upset. He stuttered. Then he blurted out:

"Because I am unlucky! Because if a tile falls from a roof, it hits me! How should I know? Why did I wake up early this morning and come here? It was destiny!"

Those words were so desperately sincere and, at the same time, so comic that the Superintendent and De Vincenzi smiled.

"All right. And what did you find?"

"A corpse! And before you ask, I have no idea how the hell it got in here."

"I am asking you." said the Superintendent.

De Vincenzi internally rolled his eyes. He had known this would happen.

"Me? Again, how should I know? Last night, we locked up at seven o'clock and there was no one here."

"No one?"

"No one!" Gualtiero Gerolamo exclaimed, exasperated. "Do you think I'm in the habit of locking Senators up in the bookshop overnight?"

The Superintendent turned to Maccari.

"Are you sure that this is Professor Magni?"

28

In answer, the inspector showed his boss the wallet he had found in the pocket of the dead man. The Superintendent looked at the ID:

"The ID card certainly belongs to him!" he said.

Then he went on removing things from the wallet. There were papers, notes, addresses. There was money in an inside pocket. He counted out three thousand lire and glanced at De Vincenzi.

Maccari intervened:

"Yes. I told you on the phone. He wasn't robbed. You'll find his watch, rings, pin. . ."

"Did you call the doctor?"

"Yes, Superintendent. He just came. He's still here."

"But then he touched the corpse!" De Vincenzi exclaimed.

Without smiling and with quiet irony, Maccari turned to his colleague:

"If he examined him, he must have touched him! But I told him not to erase the evidence."

"The door of the store. . . this one here. . ." asked the Superintendent, pointing to the street door, ". . .was it closed?"

"That's what he says," Maccari said, pointing at the clerk.

"It was closed!" he confirmed. "That's precisely why I don't understand. . ."

The Superintendent ignored him.

"Were there any signs of burglary?"

"None. I examined it. You can look at the rolling shutter yourself. "

De Vincenzi approached the door where Cruni and the officers were standing.

"No sign," Cruni said. "Certainly, there was no burglary. . ."

"Are there other doors?"

Before answering, Maccari looked at Gualtiero Gerolamo interrogatively.

"The door to the courtyard," Pietrosanto said.

"And was that one closed as well?"

"Of course," poor Gualmo said, not having had the courage to actually examine it.

"Are you sure? Don't bother. We'll take a look ourselves."

The Superintendent put a hand on De Vincenzi's shoulder: "Let's start. As soon as we finish here, we'll go to our next appointment and leave Sergeant Cruni in the store. And you, Maccari, if you don't have anything else to tell me, go back to the police station."

"Yes, Sir. Good day, Superintendent."

Maccari walked toward the door.

"Should I leave my officers?"

"It would be better, yes," De Vincenzi said. "Cruni will take care of replacing them and sending them back to you."

"Fine."

He was about to leave, when he realized he still had the volume of *The Betrothed* in his hands. He looked at it with regret, and went back to the counter to leave it.

"Were you reading?"

"A good book, Superintendent!"

He set the volume down, letting his finger slide out of the book with a sigh. Who knew when he would ever pick up the story of Renzo and Lucia again?

Once in the street, he saw the crowd of curious people getting larger, shrugged his shoulders and pulled his hat down over his eyes in his usual way.

"They have time to waste!" he murmured, moving away. "Think how happy they would be if they could see the corpse!"

Inside, the Superintendent sat in front of the American desk—with the lid lowered and locked—and De Vincenzi went into the back of the shop.

"What did you find, doctor? Ah! It's you!"

It was Dr. Sigismondi, of the medical on-call service of Via Agnello, the thin and sickly looking police surgeon whom he had met in Via Monforte, in his friend Aurigi's apartment, when the banker Garlini had been murdered.

"Good morning, Inspector. The professor was killed with two bullets in the skull. One came out of his right cheek and the other must still be inside him."

"How long has he been dead?"

"Ah," the doctor smiled. "The usual question. And you know my answer. Approximately, you mean? Well, a few hours. Maybe just four or five. Or maybe a bit more."

"Since two or three o'clock last night, then?"

"More or less, yes," he shrugged. "Poor professor! If they told me I had to see him like this and in here!

"Did you know him?"

The doctor smiled again.

"He was my university professor of anatomy. He was the youngest professor in Pavia, the most elegant. . . and if I may add, the most gallant. All us students were envious of him."

"Envious?"

"There was no female student who was not in love with him!"

31

De Vincenzi looked at the man, who lay limp on the dusty floor of those gloomy rooms. A corpse among books! And he had been a handsome man, a magnificent example of a human being, a lover of beauty, a passionate and sophisticated playboy.

Why was he killed? Why was his skull pierced with two bullets and treacherously, from behind?

Was it vengeance? The revenge of a husband or a jealous lover?

De Vincenzi remembered the white coat, the surgical instruments, the blue ink note from someone who was sure of their untouchability.

He didn't want to draw any conclusions yet. He was still trying to bring together all the elements as they appeared to him. Only later, he would reason and deduce.

He used to always proceed mainly by intuition, guided by a hidden and unknown sense, which enabled him to give weight and value to the most marginal facts, microscopic clues, while disregarding what others considered to be the most clear and blatant evidence. He didn't trust clues, no more than he would trust their certainty. No piece of evidence was certain and all of them were. No offender signs his crime. Chance signs it for him.

On his knees, he looked carefully around the corpse. The floor was dusty. But from the door—connecting the room on the right to the courtyard—to the body, the dust had disappeared all along a wide strip, as if the corpse had been dragged on the ground.

Why there?

Was there a connection between the "person" of the deceased and the place where his corpse lay?

The inspector went slowly into the room on the right and approached the black door, which opened onto the courtyard.

The two sides of the door seemed to be closed, but he could easily see that the old shaky lock was pulled. The door was just ajar.

He opened the door and went out into the courtyard. It was a wet hole, with a latrine in a corner; in front of it, there was a tub for washing and a covered room where a staircase started.

To the left, after the latrine, there was a passage to the entrance corridor, from which the street could be accessed, past the porter's lodge.

It was an old house, a beehive for poor people. It was a miserable hovel full of bedbugs and smelled unhealthily of wet or dry dust, depending on the season.

De Vincenzi approached the porter's lodge.

"What time do you close the main entrance door?"

Two hasty, anxious voices answered: a hoarse voice and a thin, sharp one.

"Who is it?"

The inspector, who had opened the glass door from which two or three signs hung, entered the room.

The husband was sitting at a cobbler's bench. He had a huge head, a shaved and yellowish face, and bulging eyes, all the typical signs of Basedow's disease. The woman was still charming and probably did not exceed the age of thirty. She was sitting at the table, with a newspaper in front of her. She got up and asked arrogantly:

"Who are you?"

The hoarse voice was hers.

"A police inspector."

The woman remained silent, staring at him. The man put the shoe he was holding between his knees on the floor and remained with the shiny skiver in his hand.

"Who closed the door last night?"

"I did," he answered with his sharp voice.

"At what time?"

"At ten."

"Where do you both sleep?"

"There," said the woman, pointing toward a reddish floral curtain which covered a door.

"Did you go to bed right away?"

"She was already asleep. She must have gone to bed at nine. I went to bed shortly after midnight."

"And from ten to midnight?"

"At the inn, in Via Battisti. There are witnesses. I have an alibi."

"You're talking too much! No one asked you for an alibi. When you came back, were you drunk?"

"I never get drunk. Everyone can confirm this."

"All right. And, coming back, did you find the door closed?"

"Maybe. I closed it, anyway."

"Does it stay closed all night?"

The man raised his scrawny shoulders.

"What can I say? It should stay closed. But considering the tenants we have . . ."

De Vincenzi looked around.

He was about to leave but he paused to ask:

"Did you hear any noise last night after one o'clock?"

"Uh!" the woman said with her deep voice, which did not sound like hers "Every night there is some noise: drunk people going home, someone who quarrels. We don't even pay attention anymore."

"How about two gunshots?"

"No," the woman replied promptly, not at all surprised by the question.

"When they slam the door to close it," the cobbler added "it's like a gunshot."

De Vincenzi stared at him.

"So did you hear them?"

"No," said the man, with a grin. "I don't think so. Last night nobody slammed the door!"

And he laughed.

"Which doesn't mean that a man did not die here last night."

The two remained silent, without any sign of surprise.

De Vincenzi felt a sense of oppression. Their cynicism was repulsive. Even if they had known something, they wouldn't have told him. So he went out. He had a sudden conviction that Senator Magni's murder was the act of a delinquent. But that wouldn't do. Evidence first.

But there, in front of the porters, listening to them, looking at them, he had that impression.

An ambush in the dark street. Two shots. The burglary of the corpse, which they had first dragged into the courtyard and then into the back of the bookstore.

He imagined the sinister couple spying on the murderers' moves and going back to bed when it was all over.

"Tonight, I will put officers around the house and clean up everything!" he thought, and smiled. He could do that. But it certainly wouldn't help him find the killer. Even if someone in the building had seen him, they wouldn't say anything.

The killer didn't live in that building, he was not a thug, he had the calligraphy of a literate man and. . .

Suddenly, he was wondering whether that woman had phoned again, the one who wanted to talk to an inspector at seven o'clock in the morning and who had disappeared as soon as she got connected to him! He couldn't stop thinking about it.

He went back to the bookstore and found the doctor who, having moved a pile of books, was sitting on the counter of the front room, with dangling legs and feet almost touching those of the corpse, so tight was the space.

"So?" the doctor asked.

"So. . . Hopefully, the instructing magistrate will arrive soon for the removal of the corpse. In any case, I will have an ambulance take care of its transport to the Monumentale cemetery. I would like the autopsy to be carried out today. But first..."

He leaned over the corpse and began to rummage in all the pockets, taking what they contained. He had laid down the silk handkerchief taken from the pocket of the dead man, and put there anything he found.

When he finished, he picked up the objects and papers in the handkerchief and rose.

The doctor had closed the black leather bag with the instruments inside and had put it under his arm.

"I'm leaving. What time will the corpse be at the cemetery?"

"Noon. At the latest."

He called Cruni and told him to call the ambulance and warn the King's Public Prosecutor.

"So?" asked the Superintendent when he saw him enter the bookstore again.

"We can go, if you want. Cruni will remain here until they take the corpse away and I come back. The instructing magistrate can take care of it. Perhaps, it would be better not to delay our visit to Magni's house. His wife might hear the news from someone else. There was quite a crowd outside."

The Superintendent got up.

"Did you find out how he got in here?"

"Through the courtyard door," replied De Vincenzi, looking at Pietrosanto, who had lifted his head.

"But it was closed!" said poor Gualmo.

"No, it must have been open. But we will soon see. Cruni, don't touch anything!"

The Superintendent and the inspector left.

On his way out, the doctor had stopped to read the titles of the books on the shelves.

"Can I sweep now?" Giovanni asked plaintively. Gualtiero Gerolamo looked at him without understanding.

Chapter 4

This was a different world.

Three hundred yards away from where Senator Magni died, the world was different.

The senator was found dead in Via Corridoni, among the books, but he had lived in Viale Bianca Maria, his natural environment. And when De Vincenzi was under the marble entrance hallway, brilliant with brass, mirrors, and crystals, when he felt the soles of his shoes adhere to the rubber floor, he understood the feelings he had earlier. It was the sense of the *illogical* that had struck him in the bookstore, that the corpse was *too elegant, too noble and too refined,* lying in the dust of the small rooms as gloomy as the bottom of a swamp. Muddy rooms. The contrast was clear. A golden spoon in the mud. And he wondered again why the dead man was out of his natural habitat. Why the figure came out of the painting.

Nothing of what had happened in the last few hours made any sense. But every subsequent fact showed that strange and heavy contrast: the parcel with the coat and the instruments had been picked up by a sweeper and put on a garbage cart; the crime had all the appearances of the most abominable vulgarity, yet nothing had been taken by the murderer, not even the three thousand lire that could have been easily spent.

There was only one thing missing: the hat. And De Vincenzi, standing next to his boss, in the elevator leading them to the third floor, began to think of that. The hat might have fallen from the senator's head at the time of the killing. But if the murder had been perpetrated on the street, as was plausible, why didn't the killer take care to pick it up just as he had taken care to drag the corpse into the shop? For now—only for now, alas—it had to be admitted that whoever committed the murder wanted to delay the discovery of the corpse as long as possible. Otherwise, they would have abandoned him on the street.

The inspector made an involuntary motion of denial. No! That was not the reason. But rather they wanted to mislead the investigation, confuse things as much as possible.

He felt the piercing gaze of the Superintendent and turned to face him. His boss looked at him and smiled.

"What is it that you don't find natural, De Vincenzi? I can almost hear your brain working, and yet, you still can't match your theories to the facts!"

"That's right, Superintendent! But don't talk about theories yet. We are still in the realm of fantasy. And mine—I can't hide it—is very creative."

The elevator stopped suddenly.

They stepped onto the landing. There were two doors next to each other. On the first was a large brass plate with the name of the deceased surgeon, Prof. Magni, on the other door, nothing.

The Superintendent stood in front of the brass plate and rang the bell and, after a few seconds, the other door opened. A very pretty maid appeared, dressed in black, with a white apron, a starched lace-loop on her neck and another on her head. She had blonde hair.

"Are you here for a consultation? The office is still closed. The professor starts at eleven."

The Superintendent stepped forward, followed by De Vincenzi, who was appreciating the young lady's harmonious and curvy lines. A beautiful woman, no question about it. He looked into her face and saw two bright, gray eyes. But she had dark circles under them, and her cheeks were pale, the typical amber-color pallor of a blonde.

"We would like to speak with the lady of the house."

The maid lifted her lashes and her eyes glared. It seemed to De Vincenzi that she was afraid.

"Now? The lady receives no one in the morning."

"Yet, she will need to receive us. Tell her I phoned a little while ago, and spoke with her."

The maid drew back. The two men entered a spacious, luxuriously furnished anteroom filled with predominantly black wallpaper, golden carvings on all walls and carved-wood overhangs. The furniture was antique and the paintings were obviously by famous artists.

But against those dark colors, the left wall boasted a glass door from which an almost dazzling brightness entered. The interior of the glass panels were covered with white curtains which blocked their view of the interior but allowed the light to enter.

The young lady opened a door and let the two visitors into a small, majestic Empire-style parlor.

"Please wait."

With a look of concern, she closed the door behind her.

The Superintendent looked at the inspector.

"Where shall we start? They know nothing here. Is it possible they still believe he's sleeping in his bed?"

De Vincenzi shrugged. He never thought Magni's wife had actually believed he was still in bed. In any case, there was something strange here. That's why he had asked to attend the first interview.

The door opened and the two men saw a tall, beautiful lady with ebony hair, a naturally pale face, and a sweet, penetrating look. Her mouth was too bright, as if she had put lipstick on in a rush and without looking into the mirror; or perhaps she had exaggerated it on purpose.

She stopped for a moment in the middle of the room, after nodding a greeting, and staring at them.

"Please forgive me, Madam. I phoned you a while ago asking about your husband. I am the Superintendent."

The woman winced.

"You came yourself? My husband…"

The Superintendent didn't help her. She searched for words. Her eyes became almost imploring for a moment. But immediately her face stiffened, her jaw clenched and her eyes became hard. She stood proudly.

"My husband is not home."

"But you, Madam, told me by phone you were sure he was still in his room."

"Yes, indeed. So I thought. But the maid later told me he went out very early this morning, unusually early."

"Ah."

There was a pause. She was obviously lying. But she didn't try to hide her lie, asserted with certainty, almost with violence; she didn't try to be believed. She seemed to say: I'm lying because it's necessary.

The Superintendent stepped forward.

"Madam, I must give you sad news. . ."

She stared at him and immediately forced herself to assume an even greater, glacial coldness.

"I don't understand. Is it really necessary that you tell me? Can't you wait for the senator to return?"

"The senator . . . will not be returning."

The sentence slipped out of his mouth and he stared at the woman to see her reaction.

De Vincenzi for his part didn't stop looking at her for a moment. Everything about this woman interested him. He felt that the mystery began with her.

"What did you say?!"

Now, the lady shuddered and pronounced that question with violence rather than with terror or apprehension.

"Why should he not come back? At eleven o'clock his consultations will begin and my husband never shirks his duty."

"A misfortune has happened, Madam!"

The pallor on the woman's face deepened.

"A misfortune!" she repeated, and leaned back on the armchair next to her, in order not to fall.

The Superintendent stretched out his hand. She raised hers to reject any help.

"It doesn't matter. It's done. Go ahead. But tell the truth."

"Your husband was taken ill. . ."

"No!" the woman cried, and her voice again became imperious. "I asked you to tell me the truth. *What did they do to him?*"

Now it was the turn of the Superintendent and De Vincenzi to wince. So, she knew that the senator was threatened. But what and whom did she mean to allude to, exactly?

"Yes," said the Superintendent, bowing his head. "Yes, that's right. *They've done something.* They hurt him."

The woman shuddered again but she managed to recover. The effort was clear and seemed almost heroic.

"Tell me everything," she murmured. "Is he dead?"

The two men were silent.

She looked at them. Her eyes had filled with horror. Her red lips trembled. A groan came out of her mouth and she would have fallen if De Vincenzi had not caught her in his arms.

They laid her on the couch.

The Superintendent ran to the door and called out:

"Someone help! Is anybody there?"

The maid suddenly appeared from the corner of the anteroom. It was as if she were there waiting, and the Superintendent saw her upset and trembling.

"What is it? My God!"

Meanwhile, the glass door was opened, the white and dazzling door, and another woman appeared on the scene. Dressed in white, she was probably the nurse.

"You, come, please!"

The lady still lay on the couch, but she had recovered somewhat and aimlessly surveyed the room with lost eyes.

De Vincenzi withdrew to let the young girl dressed in white come closer. She advanced slowly, and without anxiety. She stood right beside the couch and took the lady's wrist.

She was beautiful too. Only beautiful women lived in that house!

A lover of beauty, and a sophisticated playboy . . . *All the female students were in love with him. . .*

De Vincenzi watched her with growing interest.

She wasn't very tall. She was a totally different type of beauty from that of the woman lying on the couch. Mrs. Magni could be said to be that classic type of noble, matronly Milanese lady, who asserts herself right away, attracting all gazes. The nurse, on the other hand, had marked cheekbones, deep eyes and provocative lips, slightly open. Her little chin was marked by a pretty dimple. Her golden-brown eyes and her short hair were somehow youthful. Her rather full body, with soft lines, moved harmoniously, uncovering a hint of curve at every movement, even under the white coat, tightened around her hips with a belt.

Her face, her whole person emanated something voluptuously perverse, like a strong, intoxicating scent.

She stared at the lady on the couch with an almost ironic coldness.

The lady raised herself on the couch.

"It's over. Forgive me!"

And she immediately added:

"You may go, Miss. It's nothing. You may go back."

The nurse smiled and turned around to leave. But as she looked at the two men she didn't know, a wrinkle appeared on the white forehead underneath the halo of her silky hair.

When she disappeared, the lady continued to look at the door from which she had left. De Vincenzi went to lock it.

"Is he dead?" the woman asked, staring at the Superintendent.

He remained silent. There was a sob, but when the two men turned to her, they saw a petrified face, as white as wax.

"Did they kill him?"

Finally, the Superintendent found the words.

"It's an irreparable misfortune, Madam. A brutal crime that we will punish. The poor senator was killed with two gunshots, treacherously, from behind. He was not robbed. Vengeance, maybe. . ."

The woman remained motionless. She was listening.

"You have to find all of your courage, Madam, to withstand the terrible tragedy that has befallen this house. And also to help us in our task, which is serious and urgent. Perhaps you can give us some precious clue..."

"I am at your disposal. But, I don't think..."

She paused. Again her eyes blinked boldly.

"No, I don't think I can help you."

The Superintendent made a gesture of regret. He turned to De Vincenzi, who was standing by himself near the doorway.

"I have charged Inspector De Vincenzi with carrying out this investigation. He has to ask you some questions. Please forgive us if we carry out such a terrible task right away, but every moment is important."

De Vincenzi seemed absorbed in his thoughts and didn't move from the door. The Superintendent stepped toward him and he returned to the present.

"Yes," he said, his voice ringing strangely high and loud. "Senator Magni was found this morning. . . in a bookstore. . . with two bullets in his skull. . ."

The Superintendent stared at him astonished. Oh! What made him behave so inhumanely, so roughly? To what purpose did he give all those details? And why was he shouting at this poor woman?

Suddenly, there was a loud thud in the anteroom, and the inspector swiftly turned and opened the door wide. On the carpet, there was a black and white body over which a woman all in white was bent.

"Uhhh," said the Superintendent.

De Vincenzi went out quickly, closing the door behind him.

"What is it?" he asked vigorously, leaning over the maid who was unconscious on the floor.

The nurse straightened up and, staring at him, spoke sarcastically:

"Maids have a bad habit of listening from behind doors!"

The woman's accent was foreign.

"And do these habits also include fainting?" asked the inspector, opposing irony to sarcasm.

"Apparently! Italian maids, at least."

"Are you not Italian?"

"No."

Then she leaned over the maid, lifted her head, gave her smelling salts and helped her to her feet.

"Was it dizziness? Norina, it would be better if you went to your room. Madam will do without you."

The maid walked, swaying, and De Vincenzi did not detain her.

Now they were the only two people in the antechamber.

The inspector turned to the nurse.

"Are you alone in there?" he pointed at the empty room, which was supposed to be the professor's consultation area.

"Yes. Dr. Verga won't arrive before eleven o'clock."

"Who is Dr. Verga?"

"The professor's assistant."

There was a pause.

"Did you know that the senator has been killed?"

"How could I know?"

But she had turned pale. De Vincenzi saw anguish in her face.

"Was he killed?"

"Yes, unfortunately!"

"It's awful!" the girl murmured, and her foreign accent became even stronger.

De Vincenzi felt that dueling with her would be tough. Was she merely pretending to know nothing? Of course, she was pretending. He saw that she was looking at the door through which Norina had gone. Then she looked at the parlor door. If I could read her mind, the inspector thought, it would be much easier. He looked toward the parlor as well. How could they split up? He didn't want the Superintendent to speak with Mrs. Magni without him. She had her own secrets! And this one, here. . . Then he made a decision.

"I'll need you soon, Miss. Would you have the courtesy to wait for me in the other room?"

The young woman bowed her head and moved toward the white room, with her soft, yet firm footstep. De Vincenzi returned to the parlor.

"Well?" the Superintendent asked, more with his look than with his words.

De Vincenzi grimaced.

"Nothing. Later, if you don't mind."

And he turned to the lady, who seemed to no longer notice their presence, so absorbed she was in her thoughts and in pain, a sealed, dark pain. She had a blank look, and her lips were contracted; covered with that red lipstick, her mouth looked like a bleeding wound on her white face.

"If you feel like answering some of my questions, Madam. . . I will be very quick."

The woman roused.

"Go ahead."

"What time did the senator leave home last night?"

"He didn't dine at home last night. But I think he left his office at about seven pm. . ."

"And did he return at midnight?"

"I don't know."

The answer was assertive, although it came after a short hesitation.

The Superintendent started.

De Vincenzi's voice became gentle, filled with moving depth.

"Pardon me . . . earlier, on the phone you told the Superintendent here that you had heard your husband come home last night."

"I lied."

"Yes, but why?"

"Lately, my husband has taken to coming home very late, at four or at five o'clock in the morning. Some nights he didn't come back at all. Of course, I couldn't say this to some random stranger calling on the phone, and certainly not to one asking to talk to him personally. I preferred to lie."

"So, when the Superintendent called you, did you already know that the senator was out of the house?"

"Yes. But I didn't wish to say so."

De Vincenzi bowed his head. Up to that point, everything was simple. That woman was too proud to confess, except when she had to, that her husband betrayed her, that he had a lover. Ignoring what had happened, she had hid behind a lie.

"Can you tell me where your husband spent his nights when he was gone?"

"No. I don't know!"

She straightened, proudly.

"Forgive me . . ." De Vincenzi insisted.

"I did not wish to know. My husband was free to do what he wanted."

"Not even a suspicion?"

"No."

She answered quickly, in a hurry, with a vibrant voice.

"You should understand that your husband was killed and if we knew where he was last night, perhaps our task of tracking down the killer would be much easier."

"I am sure. But the truth is, I don't know anything about my husband."

She paused.

"For a long time, we have lived like two good friends. He didn't tell me anything about his life. I assure you, no matter how great my sorrow, I can't help human justice in any way. And God's justice doesn't need to be helped."

She got up. She took a few steps toward the door and stopped.

"Where. . . where is the corpse?"

The Superintendent replied:

"It will be transported shortly to the Monumentale cemetery. It's necessary. It's required by law, but if you think we should have him brought here tomorrow, to have the funeral start from his house. . ."

"No! Thank you."

Her voice softened, her eyes filled with tears.

"Thank you," she repeated in a tone of gratitude. "It doesn't matter. Not any more!"

And she hurried out of the room, sobbing.

Chapter 5

"Now we're getting somewhere!"

"You think so?"

De Vincenzi thought the mystery was becoming more and more dense. He felt as if he was walking on treacherous ground; any mistake, any misstep, would mean a fall. There were no reference points, yet. No clear evidence to start from.

The Superintendent idly examined the room. They had remained alone in the parlor, ignored.

"What do you plan to do now?"

De Vincenzi winced.

"I would like to remain here."

"What happened earlier when you went out?"

"Oh yes. The maid was eavesdropping. I knew there was someone behind the door. That is why I raised my voice, so that whoever was listening could hear. And when that girl found out about the murder, she fainted."

"That's strange!"

"Quite."

"What do you think of it?"

"Nothing yet, of course."

"She's a pretty girl. . ."

"They're all beautiful here."

The Superintendent shrugged.

"I'll leave you alone, then. As I told you, I'm just tagging along. This is your investigation and I'm giving you carte blanche. And please, keep me informed as you make progress."

He went out into the anteroom, followed by the inspector. There was no one. The whole apartment seemed empty. The Superintendent put his hat on and headed for the door. When he was on the doorstep, he waved goodbye and disappeared, quietly closing the door behind him.

De Vincenzi went straight into the consultation room. He found himself in a clear, bright environment. The professor's office consisted of two adjoining rooms. He had entered the room used for visits and operations. He saw a white lacquered wardrobe with opaque glass panels. There was a marble table against the wall and another larger one in the middle of the room. In front of the window, there was a steel bed that could be lifted in every direction. Above that bed and the marble table, there were two large spotlights and a tangle of electric wires, lamps, and steel arms. There was an exam chair and a large washbasin.

The inspector looked around. On the table against the wall, a number of surgical instruments were aligned. He remembered the ones he'd left on his desk, at the police station, with the white coat. Here too, a white coat was on a hanger next to the door, next to a light ladies cloak and a black cap.

"Did you wish to speak with me?"

The nurse was standing on the threshold of the second room and had certainly been watching him for a few minutes.

"Are any of these missing?" De Vincenzi pointed to the instruments aligned on the marble.

The young woman advanced quickly.

"What do you mean?"

"Did the professor have other surgical instruments besides these?"

The nurse seemed puzzled. She looked at the instruments.

"Besides these? Certainly. There are more there, inside the closet.

51

There are the cases that the professor carried with him when he went to the hospital. I couldn't say if any instruments are missing."

"When was the last time you saw the professor?"

She hesitated briefly.

"At five o'clock yesterday, when he left the hospital and came here. He stayed in this room. He read the appointment agenda and exchanged a few words with his assistant. Then he told me to cancel his remaining appointments for the day. I told him there were still two patients in the parlor. He told me he was tired, he had performed a very tiring operation at the hospital and instructed Dr. Verga to see them. Then he let me go."

"And did you go?"

"Naturally. It was hard not to obey him. And then. . . well, I was tired too. . ."

"You haven't seen him since?"

"No, that was the last time."

"What is your name, Miss?"

"Patience Drury. But no one calls me Patience, just Pat."

"Even the professor?"

"No," the girl shrugged. "He called me Miss."

"Are you English?"

"American. Do you want to see my passport? I've been in Italy for seven years now. . . I studied in Pavia. I have a university degree."

"Were you a student of the professor?"

"Aren't you the clever one!"

De Vincenzi posed his questions without looking at her. He was absorbed in the contemplation of those shining instruments. He seemed fascinated with them.

The young woman had leaned back against the table in the middle of the room and stared at him, glancing through her half-closed eyelids. An ironic smile was on her lips. Her deep blue eyes had darkened. Her hands steadied her against the marble table, she arched her back, her straight legs firmly planted, her head slightly forward; she really seemed capable of upsetting a man. The effect, however, was lost on De Vincenzi who kept staring at the instruments.

"Are you alone in Milan?"

"Just me, yes."

"No relatives?"

"At Lanecliff, on the banks of the Hudson. . . there is still an old man who can be proud of having given me life. But, perhaps, he's not bragging about that, anymore."

De Vincenzi turned around suddenly and stared at her.

"Where do you live, Miss. . . Miss?"

"Pat."

"Miss Drury. Where do you live?"

"In a small apartment, with two rooms, that is, a bedroom and a bathroom, in Via Boccaccio."

"At what address?" asked the inspector, who had pulled out a notebook and a fountain pen from his pocket.

"Thirty-five. Second floor."

"And what's going to happen now?"

"What do you mean? Aren't you supposed to be telling me?"

"I mean now that the professor is. . . that he is no longer here, what will you do?"

"Are you interested in my fate? How sweet. I don't know. We'll see. Meanwhile, I suppose I'll stay here as long as they don't send me away."

"Last night, when you left this house, where did you go?"

The young woman shook her head. She had lost some of her ironic imperturbability. If De Vincenzi's purpose was to exhaust her self-control, he was apparently about to succeed.

"Why are you going on like this? What do I have to do with the professor's murder? If you want to find the killer, you can do something better than questioning me. I'm not the fainting type."

The inspector pretended not to hear. He wanted her to talk, and he was only hoping to make her lose her composure.

"Where did you go last night?"

"To the Klondike region, to look for gold."

"Be careful, you might find something less enjoyable!"

"What?"

"Miss Drury, in the United States, your police have ways to make reluctant witnesses talk. We don't do such things in Italy. On the other hand, there is no law forbidding us from putting witnesses in jail for a few weeks."

The girl turned pale, but she kept smiling.

"So, are you questioning me as a witness?"

"Until I'm forced to change your status, as far as the law is concerned."

"Well, the private life of a witness can't be of interest, can it?"

"You're wrong!" said the inspector coldly. "I'm very interested, for example, in knowing where you've been and what you did last night. . . and during the night."

"During the night, I've been sleeping."

"What time did you get home?"

"Maybe at ten, maybe at eleven. . . I don't remember."

"Did the porter see you come back?"

"You'd have to ask him."

"And before then?"

"Nothing special for me or interesting for you. Maybe I went to the cinema. Maybe I met the Duke of Aosta for a cup of coffee. Imagine anything you like. On the other hand, I could have stayed home to study up on the new electro-hemostasis techniques. I'd bet on the latter, if I were you."

"I'll remember," De Vincenzi said, determined not to let her have the last word. The truth was, he felt he was getting nowhere. She didn't want to talk to him any further and, despite his threats, he had no means to force her. It was better not to insist for the moment.

He changed tactics.

"Anyway, you may be right! I'm not interested in you, but in others. How long have you been with the professor?"

"Two years. Since I graduated."

"And the maid, Norina, I think, how long has she been working in this house?"

Pat gave him a glaring look.

"Why don't you ask her mistress? I met her here."

"So more than two years," the inspector said patiently. "Does she faint frequently?"

The girl smiled.

"That, too, you can ask her mistress. I don't go to the other part of the house often. When I am finished here, at the end of the day, I go home."

A few moments earlier, De Vincenzi had begun to feel someone's presence in the room. He turned to see a young man on the threshold, where the two rooms of the surgery joined. More than the man, he saw his eyes, intensely fixed on him.

"You are Dr. Verga."

"Precisely!" he answered in a tone of wonder and came forward. "What's happened? Why are you questioning Miss? Who are you?"

His questions followed one another very quickly. The young man was now looking at Miss Drury with anxious astonishment. He was clearly nervous and didn't try to hide his anxiety. He was a handsome young man, too. He was strong, robust and yet agile. He probably attended gymnasiums and riding centers. Though his face was not particularly interesting, it was full of intelligence. His dark eyes, beneath his thin eyebrows, gave off a lively light.

The girl looked at him and shrugged.

"He's a detective, Edoardo."

"What are you saying?!"

The inspector observed them. They were addressing each other informally.

"A detective" stuttered Verga. "So you are from the . . ."

"The police, yes." De Vincenzi completed.

Suddenly, all agitation in the young man disappeared. The transformation was immediate, wonderful. He smiled and became absolutely serene. One would have thought he hadn't a care in the world.

"And why are you here?" he asked indifferently. What an extraordinary actor! But was he merely playing the part of ignorance? De Vincenzi was sure of it. All his reactions were wrong. Despite his acting skills, the young doctor couldn't be have gotten very good marks in his psychology classes. Was he playing him for a fool?

56

"I'm questioning the lady and not you . . . yet! You'll be next."

"So the Madonna at the top of the Duomo got stolen and you think Pat—Miss Drury—or myself have it in our pockets?"

"I am not accusing Miss Drury of theft... nor of murder."

The young man stepped in, positioning himself between the nurse and the inspector.

"Don't joke! What does Pat have to do with it?"

"You are the one who is trying to joke, but you can't do it very well! Why did you say that Miss Pat doesn't have anything to do with it?"

"How could it be possible?"

De Vincenzi's frowned and, looking the doctor in the eye, shouted, "With *what* doesn't she have anything to do?! What do you think she has done?"

He hit the bull's eye. Edoardo turned pale, his eyes anguished.

"You spoke of murder," he murmured to De Vincenzi.

"What murder?" De Vincenzi urged.

"Be careful!" cried Miss Drury in English. "The professor is dead!"

"Thank you, Miss," De Vincenzi said immediately, speaking English as well. "But since I understand your language, we all might as well speak Italian, don't you think?"

The American woman stiffened.

"What do you think you have found out, with your English? Edoardo doesn't know that the senator was murdered!"

"Murdered!" Edoardo exclaimed, his voice trembling not with horror, but with fright. His eyes were wide open and his lips trembled. "Murdered! Is it true? Where? When?"

"Last night. And as for the place. . ."

De Vincenzi paused, then tried another blow:

"Maybe you can guess."

"Me? What are you talking about?" said Verga.

"What time did you last see the professor last night?"

"I left at seven o'clock."

"And Miss Pat?"

"Shortly earlier."

The answer was given abruptly and the nurse startled.

"Much earlier. He doesn't remember."

De Vincenzi felt he was gaining ground. The young woman had lied, saying she had left the surgery at five o'clock.

The doctor looked at the girl with amazement as she stared at him intensely.

"Yes, Edoardo. You are confusing yesterday with the day before. As a matter of fact I leave every night at seven o'clock. Yesterday was an isolated case. The professor was tired and. . ."

"I know," the inspector interrupted. "You've already told me!"

And he turned back to the man.

"So, you went out at seven and Miss Drury had left a little before. And the senator?"

"He stayed here."

"And at what time did you meet him again last night?"

"But . . . I didn't see him again, I told you."

"Are you sure?"

"What are you insinuating?"

"Nothing, so far. We'll see later. And, once you left here, where did you go?"

"I went home, in Via Leopardi."

"Via Leopardi is close to Via Boccaccio. . ."

"Indeed."

"Ok. And then?"

"And then. . . nothing. I was home all night. "

"That's all?"

"Yes."

"Are you sure you are remembering correctly?"

The doctor remained silent, shrugging. He was trying to regain a bit of his lost self-confidence, but without success.

There was a long silence.

Pat tapped her fingers on the operating table. The doctor carefully watched De Vincenzi who again seemed fixated on the instruments on the marble table.

"When the professor came back from the hospital, yesterday afternoon, did he have a case with his instruments?"

The nurse responded:

"Naturally."

"And where did he lay it?"

"I couldn't really say. He may have put it on that table. The professor emptied the case after each operation, pulled out the tools and put them on that ebonite tray so that I could sterilize them by boiling. But I don't think he did it yesterday. At least, I didn't sterilize them."

"And did he usually bring a white coat with him?"

"He did when he went to the hospital to operate."

"And yesterday?"

"I don't know."

De Vincenzi entered the first room, leaving the two young people alone. It was a sitting room. There was a sofa, some armchairs, and a desk in front of the window. After a brief look, he returned to the treatment room. The doctor was anxiously muttering to the woman but move quickly away when De Vincenzi entered. The inspector pretended he hadn't noticed. He moved through the room and opened the door connecting it with the apartment.

He turned suddenly.

"Dr. Verga, please, come to my office at San Fedele at 3 p.m." The young man bowed.

"And you too, Miss Drury."

The American woman smiled.

De Vincenzi stepped into the hallway and closed the door behind him.

The anteroom was still empty. He stood there for a few minutes and was summarizing in his head the main points of the interview he just had when the doorbell rang. No one came to open the door. The bell rang again.

Finally, Norina appeared. She was very pale, but she seemed to have recovered. She gave the inspector a frightened look and moved to open the door.

"Good morning, my dear. Is the senator already in the surgery?"

The voice was warm, musical. The voice of a healthy, jovial man. The maid stepped aside and tried to speak, but no sound came out.

"So? What's wrong? You look as if you've seen a ghost . . ."

The visitor came forward. He was about forty years old and rather short, but well proportioned and almost elegant. He took off his hat and put it on the coat rack. He moved as a man who knew the house, and would be welcome at all times. He started to pull off his gloves.

"Go on, tell him I'm here. Two words and I'll leave. I won't even take off my overcoat. With the flu and the measles at their peak, I don't really have much time." He paused, staring at De Vincenzi.

De Vincenzi took a few steps toward him and held out his hand. "Inspector De Vincenzi. . ."

The visitor was obviously surprised. He didn't understand. "What?" He gave the maid an enquiring look, while she, increasingly pale, still couldn't speak.

Reflexively, he shook De Vincenzi's hand and introduced himself. "Dr. Alberto Marini. But what's wrong? Has something happened?"

"Yes. Are you a family friend? "

"Indeed I am! Ugo. . . Senator Magni, I mean, and I were fellow students. Did something happen to Ugo?"

"Unfortunately!"

The doctor remained silent, waiting.

"Last night, Senator Magni was killed!"

"No! Impossible. Killed? Did you just say he was *killed?*"

"Yes."

"And his wife? Is she alright?"

"His wife is fine. Yes, well, she's as fine as anyone can be after such a shock. But I was just leaving..."

De Vincenzi looked at the maid and gestured as if he wanted to speak with her. Then he changed his mind and walked to the door.

"Wait, Inspector. If you don't mind, I will go with you. I may be useful. And also I would like to know. . ."

De Vincenzi looked at him.

"After you," he said.

And the door closed behind them.

Mechanically, Norina returned to her chores.

The apartment fell silent.

In her room, Mrs. Magni, abandoned in an armchair, was staring out at the void with her eyes full of tears.

Chapter 6

De Vincenzi was walking fast with Dr. Marini was by his side. Both men were silent.

De Vincenzi was thinking about Pat Drury. She was an odd one, there was no doubt. Of course, she knew more than she let on. Something must have happened in the evening or during the night, that the girl knew about and that would help him explain the mystery. It was also certain that between her and Dr. Verga there was a relationship of sympathy, perhaps intimacy, or even love. Were they engaged, lovers? Nevertheless, it was premature to conclude that they were accomplices, and that the young man had killed Senator Magni. He was strange, too! He was visibly upset when he first arrived and then, as soon as he knew he was in front of a police officer, he had controlled himself to the point of appearing indifferent and sarcastic. What did he fear at the beginning? What did he fear later, when he was first told that the senator had been murdered?

Though a skillful actor, he was always just out of step. The American woman, with all her coldness, ambiguous cynicism, and taunting unscrupulousness, had much more self-control.

And that maid, who fell to the ground like a rag upon hearing of his death—apparently a surprising piece of news. And listening behind the door meant she was worried about something!

And the senator's wife, who lived with anguish in her heart, lying to hide it!

There were so many people and so many puzzles yet they were all part of the same mystery. What kind of man was the deceased who had created an environment of morbid tension, subterfuge and intrigue around himself?

De Vincenzi turned to Marini, the deceased's friend, who had wanted to accompany him and was now walking at his side, worried but clearly ready to talk about the victim and anxious to know more details.

"Poor Ugo!" he whispered when he realized that the inspector was looking at him. "It's awful!"

De Vincenzi nodded and slowed his walk.

"Tell me about the senator, you were friends."

"Ugo was a successful man, and a lucky one. He succeeded at everything he undertook, in his profession as well as, back in the day, in politics. Both women and men found him charming, most treated him almost with awe. And as far as love is concerned . . . Women loved him . . ."

There was no envy or bitterness in his words, but rather admiration.

"Did he have enemies?"

"Enemies? I don't know. Maybe. Of course, you don't go through life with such exuberant passion and energy, with such self-confidence, without stirring envy and jealousy. But I don't know of any enemies."

He seemed to reflect and then repeated, as if to himself, "No, I really don't know who could have hated him enough to kill him."

He stared at the inspector:

"But why are you asking all this? Was he not killed by some common criminal? Wasn't he killed because someone wanted to rob him?"

De Vincenzi replied, passing over the subject, "No, it doesn't look like a robbery. Nothing was stolen from the corpse. You and the senator were fellow students?"

"Yes. We were boarding-school mates. Back then, Ugo was successful, too. He was always the first in the class, the smartest, the strongest, the most agile of all of us. And all the female students were crazy about him. They called him Handsome Ugo and were at risk of being punished by the professors because of their impudence in passing him notes. I remember! One day. . ."

The inspector interrupted him.

"But his wife?"

"Meaning?" Dr. Marini raised his eyebrows.

"Was he cheating on her?"

"Bah! No doubt he was cheating on her. But he was always full of care for her, correct and deferential."

"Did his wife know that he betrayed her?"

"Well..."

He took a few steps more quickly, wanting to disguise his reactions to this line of questioning.

De Vincenzi did the same.

"You're right to run! I'm also in a hurry."

"Are you going to the police station?"

"No."

"So, could you give me some details?"

"Would you like to see your friend?"

"Sure. If it's necessary. . . actually, no, I prefer not to see him. I can't do anything for him and seeing him would be too upsetting for me. My wife would reproach me, she knows I was very much attached to Magni."

"You have a wife?"

"Yes."

"It was a pleasure. I have to go now. But please come to my office at San Fedele today in the afternoon."

"Certainly."

The inspector held out his hand.

"Goodbye. I want you to know that I count very much on your help to find the senator's murderer."

"Well, you can count on me! I'll help as much as I can. However, though I was very familiar with Ugo, I'm far from knowing the details of his intimate life. We saw each other often, in recent times, because we had found a very interesting medium and the sessions were frequent."

The inspector, who was about to leave, stopped suddenly.

"Did you say a medium? Sessions?"

"Ah! Don't you know that Professor Magni was a fervent spiritualist as am I?"

"And who do you think would have told me that?"

"I thought you knew. It's widely known. Ugo made no secret of his beliefs. He had also written articles about spiritism for scientific journals and was a member of the Circle of Psychic Studies in Via Broletto. I am too."

"What about the sessions?"

Dr. Marini smiled.

"What are you thinking of? Are you thinking of white ghosts, dead people appearing, skulls, bones dancing and all the romantic legends about the subject?"

"I am not thinking anything!" the inspector abruptly interrupted. "But we'll talk about it later today. Goodbye, for the moment."

He left. When he was at the corner of Via Cesare Battisti and Via Corridoni, he looked behind him and saw that the doctor had stopped and was following him with his gaze.

He was another link in the chain! De Vincenzi thought, as he reached the bookstore as quickly as possible and smiled to himself, for any spiritualist session is based on a chain. In any case, that ambiguously elusive friend had given him some great detail and the story about the spiritualist sessions bore keeping in mind. Was it possible that the senator went home late at night or sometimes didn't go at all because he spent his nights at the Circle of Psychic Studies?

This detail could be easily verified, but if he was impressed with the senator's spiritualist practices, he had to admit that it depended on the mysterious nature of such practices in the eyes of the uninitiated. And though he was not entirely such, because he had already dealt with magic and spiritism—naturally only in books—he had always felt a sense of utter astonishment in the face of those who believe in practicing magical rites or attempting to bring forth and question dark forces of another world.

One thing seemed undeniable: occult philosophy had been the nurse and godmother of all religions, the secret lever of almost all intellectual forces, the key to every divine mystery, the ruler of many human beings.

He remembered the prophecy of Ezekiel and the Apocalypse, which the infallible Christian Church had not even tried to explain. But now the matter had nothing to do with magic, yet, thank goodness! If anything, it was about something similar to Taylor's experience, of whom he had once happened to read about in a psychological journal.

He was so absorbed in those thoughts that he didn't even notice he had arrived in front of the bookstore, among the people who were still standing in the street, gossiping.

He shrugged and made his way through the curious throng.

As soon as he entered, he saw the bookstore clerk, who, having climbed up a staircase, was looking at the top rows of books near the ceiling. Giovanni was leaning against the counter and Cruni was sitting in front of the door, smoking. When he saw the inspector, the sergeant stood up.

"Well?. . ." De Vincenzi asked.

"The magistrate has come, he gave the authorization and I immediately had the corpse taken away. I recommended that the clothes be put aside without being shaken, so that you could examine them."

"You did well."

De Vincenzi addressed him informally as he always did when he was distracted or he had to act quickly.

"And what did the magistrate say?"

"That you take care of it and then inform him."

"Did you question anyone?"

From the top of the staircase, Pietrosanto's voice could be heard, strangely moaning, almost broken by tears.

"He interrogated me. He wanted to know why I had not closed the yard door last night. But I did close it, or at least I had made sure, when I left, that it was closed. Usually, Mr. Chirico closes it when he goes around the rooms to see if all the lights are off."

"By the way, when does this Mr. Chirico come here? Does he have a phone at home? Did you call him?"

"Me? No! How could I tell him that there was a corpse in the shop by phone?"

"You could tell him that his presence is required and nothing else."

"I suppose I could. I didn't think about doing that. Well, you are accustomed to dealing with corpses! I'm not, and I'm still upset. . . Do you think this is a something to joke about?"

He kept talking from the top of the staircase and De Vincenzi looked at him from downstairs, unable to conceal a smile. The poor man was comical, and he couldn't really blame him for being upset. He still had his hat on and he had obviously taken refuge up there to pretend he was doing something.

"What are you doing up there? Come down."

"Yes, sir."

And he descended so quickly that he almost fell, saving himself, barely, by clinging to the ladder.

"Careful!"

"Just what I needed. When misfortunes begin. . .", he snorted.

"Sit down. Or rather, no. Come with me in the other room."

Pietrosanto winced.

"Are you afraid?"

"Afraid? No!"

But he had turned pale. De Vincenzi looked at him with sympathy. He was an intelligent man, probably well-educated. It was clear that working in the shop, among those dusty, untidy, overturned and scattered books, he was suffering, accustomed as he was to his old shop, where the best-known literati and scholars met, accompanied by elegant wives and lovers.

"I'm not afraid. I don't think so. But surely it's somewhat upsetting to go to the other room and I don't even know if I can still work here after what has happened. Although I don't know how else my wife and I could earn money if I left!"

"Well, you can stay here. I'll go alone."

And Pietrosanto quickly closed the ladder and went back to take a seat in front of the catalog cards.

De Vincenzi entered the hallway and stopped in the center of those three small rooms.

The corpse was gone now. On the ground one could see the trail that the dragged body left in the dust. De Vincenzi bent to observe that trail and immediately noticed a strange peculiarity: it was not uniform, not continuous. In two places the trail was interrupted and the floor looked untouched.

He looked closer and saw this: in those two points, the body had not been dragged in the dust. He raised his head and looked around. He was puzzled. If they had dragged an inert body, it would not have been possible to leave traces of that sort. De Vincenzi looked at the ground searching for an explanation for the mystery. There were books, magazines, newspapers, a few rolls of wrapping paper, ropes, nails, and dust. Under a counter, lying near the wall of the room on the right, he saw a bag. Without knowing why, he bent to look at it and lifted it with two fingers. The part touching the floor was dusty, but in a strange way, as if it had been used on purpose to collect the dust from the ground. The inspector went toward the corridor and called:

"Giovanni!"

Hurrying in the clumsy, disjointed way of a person who has grown too fast, Giovanni came in and, as De Vincenzi pointed to the bag, he immediately answered:

"No, it was not there. It's the bag used to collect the waste paper. I have never used it to collect dust."

"And where was it?"

"In the back room, over a chest."

"I see," De Vincenzi said.

And he understood, in fact, that this was an essential element in explaining the mystery.

The criminal he had to deal with was indisputably sly.

He returned to the shop and asked Pietrosanto:

"Are you sure that Senator Magni was not a regular client?"

"Absolutely. I've been here for two years and I've never seen him come in through that door. I said I knew him, because he was a famous person in Milan. But I'm sure I never talked to him."

"Uhm!" said the inspector, and sat on the counter among the books.

He was thinking.

Pietrosanto stared at him, astonished. He had never seen anyone sit on the sacred book counter! De Vincenzi took stock of the situation.

A classy criminal, no doubt! A diabolical, sharp spirit, not lacking a certain mental elegance. All the details of the crime appeared premeditated.

He reviewed them mentally, for he never took written notes.

- The corpse lacked a hat;

- nothing had been stolen;

- the trail in the dust showed two interruptions;

- the surgical instruments and the professor's white coat (provided those objects really belonged to Senator Magni. That was a point to ascertain), had been left on the steps of a church, wrapped in a newspaper with a letter: *"Please deliver to the police station"*;

- the professor practiced spiritism;

- the professor had one or more lovers.

Of course, there were more facts to consider, but so far these were the most important ones to keep in mind.

And then there was the phone call of the woman he could not forget, which he stubbornly continued to connect to the crime.

His musings were interrupted by Gualtiero Gerolamo, who had approached him without being noticed. One of Gualmo's specialties was to walk quietly as a cat, with velvet steps. When De Vincenzi saw him, he started.

"Eh! What are you doing here?!"

"I was thinking. . ." the poor man said shyly.

The inspector burst out laughing. Gualmo stared at him, speechless.

"Are you laughing?" Gualmo eventually stuttered.

"Of course. . . Do you always wear your hat in here?"

Pietrosanto exclaimed, "Ah!" and then took it off quickly.

"You know? I don't understand anything today!"

"What were you thinking?" asked De Vincenzi.

"Well. . . I should. . . I should go in the back to pick up a volume. . ."

"Well, go ahead."

"Yes, thank you. . . But please have your... accompany me. . ." and he pointed to Cruni, who was waiting in a corner.

"I'll go with you," said the inspector, no longer laughing.

In the back of the shop, Pietrosanto went looking on the shelves. Suddenly, he uttered a little cry.

"Ah! Look here, Inspector!"

"What's there?"

"Ask me, rather, what's missing! A book is missing. . ."

"Pardon me?"

"Last night there was a volume here, which has disappeared."

"Are you saying that it was stolen?"

"I don't know. The fact is, it's gone."

"Was it a rare volume? Of great value?"

"Of great value? Considering the current prices, it certainly was of great value. See? On this shelf there are only rare books, those volumes that we only show to qualified bookworms, to customers who can spend money. The price? Maybe two thousand lire, maybe more. . . I can't tell you yet, because I don't know which volume is missing; but I'll tell you."

"Bravo! Let me know shortly."

And De Vincenzi went back toward the front of the shop.

A volume was missing! Whether it was rare or not, for the purpose of the investigation, it didn't matter.

Was it possible that the killer—who had not taken a cent, not a jewel or any other valuable thing from the corpse—had stolen a book? No

72

matter how rare, it was not easily convertible into money. Anyway, why would one take an object that would get you in trouble if you tried to sell it if three thousand or more lire were at your fingertips and nobody could associate it as belonging to the deceased?

When they entered the shop, Pietrosanto began feverishly looking through cards and lists to find out what volume was missing from the shelf of rare books.

De Vincenzi began to look at a large atlas. Cruni was silent, as he was accustomed to long waits which anyone less patient would find irritating. Giovanni cracked his knuckles and every now and then the noise of crossed tendons could be heard.

"What the hell happened? Why is there a crowd of people out here? And why are you quietly sitting while there are customers in the shop?"

A little, dried-up man had come in wearing a long coat down to his heels and a floppy hat on his head; he was very angry.

Gualmo looked at the newcomer with his big, blue, gentle eyes. He asked sarcastically:

"Customers? What customers?"

"How about these gentlemen?" The little man pointed at De Vincenzi and Cruni, who watched the scene in silence.

"That gentleman is an inspector and the other one is a police sergeant."

"Ah," said the little man, turning pale. "And what. . . what do they want?"

No one answered him.

He got more worried under the inquiring gaze of De Vincenzi.

"What is going on? What is it, Pietrosanto?"

"Actually. . . actually. . . this morning, when I opened the shop. . . I found a corpse. . ."

"What are you saying?" the little man screamed.

"I said a corpse!" Gualmo repeated seraphically, with cruel satisfaction. He was now taking revenge for two years of tyranny.

"A corpse!"

He looked around, as if in search of help.

"A corpse!"

And Mr. Chirico, owner of the bookstore, took off his hat and scratched his head hard. He had white hair, short and straight up like a brush.

"You are joking!"

"Your clerk is not joking! There was a corpse in your shop."

"But then. . . then. . ." Chirico said, breathless. "Was anything stolen?"

"What do you think they would to steal?" Pietrosanto exclaimed. "The books?!"

"Why not?"

"Actually, a book *was* stolen. But it doesn't matter at the moment," De Vincenzi interrupted.

The owner of all those books thought that even only one of them was important to him, but he didn't dare to say anything. He started as if he would scratch his head again, but he stopped.

"Did you know Senator Magni?"

Chirico widened his eyes.

"You don't mean. . ."

"Did you know Senator Magni?"

"Of course!"

"Was he your customer?"

"No. But he was a member of the Circle of Psychic Studies, of which I am the secretary."

"Ah! You are the secretary of the Circle in Via Broletto?"

"Precisely."

"Do you believe in spiritism?"

"Why do you ask?" answered the little man, who didn't want to make a profession of faith at that precise moment.

"Tell me about the senator."

"A scientist. An affable and humble man. He participated in all our sessions.

"Are they held at night?"

"Oh no! Rarely in the evening. Usually in the afternoon."

"And last night, did you hold one?"

"No. I told you, it happens very seldom. Only if some members request it because they are busy during the day."

"And when was the last session the senator attended?"

"Three days ago. Yes, that's right, last Saturday. . . today is Tuesday."

"And who else attended that session besides the professor?"

"I don't remember now, but I will be able to tell you later. There were eleven of us."

"Dr. Marini?"

"He was always there when the senator came. But how do you know that?"

"And who was the medium?"

"A woman."

"Who?" De Vincenzi asked, stressing the monosyllable with impatience.

"A woman I saw for the first time that night who had been brought by a member."

"And did the senator know her?"

"I don't think so."

"And Dr. Marini?"

"Neither."

"I want the name and address of that woman."

"I'll give it to you. I must collect some information at the Circle. I will try to remember who brought her."

"No. You will go now with Sergeant Cruni. You will collect the information. You will find her and you will bring her to me at San Fedele at 2:00 p.m. today. Cruni, please go with Mr. Chirico. . . and don't let him out of your sight."

Cruni stood up.

The little man looked around at a loss. He scratched his head and murmured:

"A corpse. . . the senator's! In my shop. . ." and he went back to scratching his head.

He looked desperately at Pietrosanto, as if asking for his help.

"How can I do this? I have so many urgent matters to attend to. . ."

"None more urgent than this. Do I make myself clear?"

From the corridor came the insistent ring of the phone. Gualmo was about to run.

"No!" De Vincenzi stopped him. "You go, Cruni."

76

The sergeant returned immediately.

"It's for you, Inspector."

De Vincenzi went to the phone.

It was the police station.

"What's up?"

The operator answered.

"De Vincenzi, is that you?"

"Go ahead! What's up?"

"Thank God!" I was looking for you at Senator Magni's house too, but I was told that you had already left. . ."

"And?"

"Deputy Inspector Sani begs you to come to the police station right away. There is a lady on the Flying Squad's premises, who must speak to you."

"Is she the same one who called this morning?"

"How did you know that? Mr. Sani told me just that."

"I'll be right there!"

He hung up the receiver and rushed to the front of the shop.

"Go ahead Cruni, and do as I told you."

He went out on the threshold and called the two agents left by Maccari, who were smoking on the sidewalk.

"You, over here."

They rushed to him.

"Go inside and stay there. Don't leave, no matter what."

He ran off to find a taxi. While entering it, he saw Cruni and Mr.

Chirico arrive from Via Corridoni. The sergeant was holding the little man by one arm, who was agitated and making wide gestures of despair.

Chapter 7

This new woman was also beautiful!

As a matter of fact, the most remarkable feature of the entire investigation into the murder of Senator Magni was the incredible number of beautiful women connected with him.

Sani had her sitting in front of De Vincenzi's desk and explained, "This young lady phoned this morning at seven o'clock, because she wanted to talk to an inspector. A little while ago, she called again and was connected to me. I told her to come to the Flying Squad and I called you."

"Well done. Thank you."

Sani retired.

The girl looked at the inspector with lost eyes. They were bright, almost fluorescent. She was trembling. She looked to be a young lady from a good family, though her lips were too red and she wore eye-liner. She was elegant, distinct. Nothing was particularly gaudy about her, except for the great mass of copper hair, flaming under her black hat.

"You wanted to talk to an inspector?"

"Yes."

"Well, I'm an inspector. Go ahead."

"Perhaps, it won't seem very interesting what I have to tell you. I myself wonder why I came. But I had to. I couldn't sleep all night. Yesterday, as soon as the bar in front of my house opened, I called. Then, when I was about to speak, I lost my nerve and hung up. But that's it! I couldn't resist anymore. Maybe I made a mistake."

She was about to cry.

"Calm down, Miss. You didn't make a mistake. You will see that you've done well to come here. Please tell me everything!"

"Yes, I'll tell you everything. But you must promise that you will never tell him that it was me! He wouldn't forgive me! I'm not hoping that he comes back to me, but if something bad should happen to him, I'll go mad! Tell me you won't let that happen? That you will protect him? But without him knowing it!"

She stared at De Vincenzi.

"Oh! If he should kill him!"

And she covered her face with her hands, as if she had had a horrible vision.

"Calm down," the inspector repeated. "Of course, we will protect him, but I need you to tell me what it is about. . . and especially *who* it is about. . . ."

The girl sobbed.

"Forgive me! I'm so agitated. I've suffered so much! And I always had to pretend, while in my own house, so that my mother wouldn't notice. Even this morning, to make the phone call, I had to go out, because my mother doesn't want me to phone him and she always keeps an eye on me."

"Yes, of course, I see. But here you can rest assured. And *he*. . . who is he?"

"I met him at a girlfriend's house. He made advances to me right away. I liked it. I loved him. He also seemed to be in love with me, he talked about marriage. He was waiting for his graduation, before meeting my parents. I've been happy for a year. He graduated and. . . he became Professor Magni's assistant. From that moment on, he began to neglect me, to be distant. He told me that it was all because of his work, the visits. . . the surgeries. . . the hospital. . . All excuses! Instead. . ."

She sat up straight, proud, full of hate.

"Instead, it was for a woman! For that trollop! An American woman,

80

who has been everyone's lover,　even the professor's! Do you understand?"

De Vincenzi understood all too well but listened carefully, trying not to show the enormous interest he had in these seemingly incoherent and trivial revelations.

"I understand, Miss. And you have all my sympathy, trust me! Don't be afraid to talk. Try to explain yourself better. If you came here to the police station it means that something serious has happened. Is the man you loved threatened?"

"Oh! Yes! The other man is deadly serious, and last night he shouted in his face: "If you dare threaten me again, I'll give you the lesson you deserve, and I guarantee I don't do things by halves." Because—you should know—Edoardo had struck him. . . yes, he slapped him. . . and the professor grabbed a chair and if the American woman hadn't been there—that　trollop—who knows what would have happened! I, too, rushed there, but Edoardo had closed the door behind him and when he came out he was with her. . . with the other woman, and I had to leave. . . I couldn't face him him. . ."

She sobbed again. Tears flowed down her cheeks.

De Vincenzi let her cry. He must let her talk without having the impression she was pressured and, above all, without sensing how important her story was.

"All right, Miss. I understand your pain. You will see that nothing, however, is irreparable."

"Do you believe it?" she asked with anxious hope.

"Of course! One always goes back to their first love when it's pure and virtuous. A love affair doesn't count. It's a momentary misstep. You'll see!"

"Ah! If it were true! I love him so much. . ."

"So, you met him at a girlfriend's house. And what is *his* name?"

"Edoardo! It's Dr. Edoardo Verga. . . Assistant to Senator Magni."

"I see."

"And the woman who has bewitched him, who took him away, is called *Patience*. . . Drury. . . or something like that, but last night I heard Edoardo call her Pat."

"So, Miss. . . last night?"

"Yes. . ."

She hesitated.

"Don't be afraid," said De Vincenzi cordially, to give her confidence. "You spoke of a quarrel. . . of threats. Perhaps I can intervene."

"Yes, that's why I'm here. I don't want Edoardo to risk being the object of revenge. If it all came down to him losing his job with the senator, it would be a good thing for both of us! But I know Edoardo. He's violent, and the senator could push him to do something foolish. . ."

She covered her face with her hands again.

De Vincenzi made a gesture of impatience, but he immediately regained control.

"Come on, Miss, to despair for what hasn't happened yet, and may never happen, especially if you trust me, is useless and childish. Calm down and tell me exactly what happened last night. Only then can I help you."

The young woman showed her face, wet with tears.

"You're right. Yesterday, I had decided to ask Edoardo for an explanation. As far as I knew, he was by now that woman's lover, and I was hoping to bring him back to me. What can I say, I needed to see him, to talk to him! I told my mother I had been invited to dinner by a friend, because I imagined I wouldn't be back until very late, and before six o'clock I was in Viale Bianca Maria, in front of the senator's house. At seven, Edoardo came out."

"With that American woman, as you call her?"

"No. He was alone. I was about to cross the road and approach him, but at that moment some cars passed by, a truck. I had to stop and he had time to reach Porta Vittoria and get in a taxi. I started running, I jumped into another taxi and told the driver to follow the first one.

We drove all the way to the Sempioncino restaurant. When I saw his cab stopping there, I realized that Edoardo had an appointment, something unusual. I told myself that it was not possible for me to approach him, at least not before I knew what he was going to do and with whom he was going to meet. So, when he got out of the taxi in front of the restaurant, I decided to stay hidden in mine. I had asked the driver to stop some distance away. Edoardo sent his taxi off, and started walking back and forth in front of the restaurant. I didn't understand, I was afraid he had noticed that I was spying on him, that he'd yell at me, and that he'd get very angry. I regretted having followed him. Suddenly, after about half an hour waiting, I saw him jump behind a tree. A car had appeared. It, too, stopped in front of the Sempioncino restaurant and Professor Magni came out, and then that woman. They entered the restaurant. It was then that I understood and I got scared. Certainly, Edoardo had known that they were going there for dinner and wanted to surprise them. I wanted to stop him. But how? All I could do was to stay where I was and wait."

She paused. She was shaking all over, poor girl!

But how lucky for him, having that girl in love and jealous!

"And then?"

"And then I saw Edoardo come out from behind the tree. After standing in the middle of the road for a few minutes, he decided to enter the restaurant. I couldn't stand it any longer. I felt horribly anguished, I thought something terrible would happen. I rushed from the taxi and ran after him. When I entered, I saw Edoardo in front of me climbing the stairs. I followed but I couldn't catch him. I wanted to call out, but I didn't have enough breath. He went up to the second floor and headed toward the door of a private lounge. He opened it and walked in, locking it behind him. I heard the key in the lock and a shiver of terror ran down my spine. I reached the door and threw myself against it. It was hopeless! I stayed right there, then, and the noise of their voices reached me. Edoardo's loud, violent voice and the cold, lashing voice of the senator."

"And the woman?" De Vincenzi asked.

"She was silent, or at least I didn't hear her. Edoardo's voice became louder."

"Was he threatening?"

"Yes! He insulted the senator, calling him an old *Don Giovanni*. He accused him of having forced the woman to go there using black-mail."

"And Magni?"

"He was sneering! He ordered Edoardo to leave. He threatened to kick him out of his house and have the hospital expel him. Their voices became even more angry. I heard the sound of a slap, of a fight. . . I was trembling, I put my eye to the key hole and saw the senator raising a chair and swinging at Eduardo's head. The American woman stopped him. As they rushed to the door, I just had time to withdraw and hide around the corner. Edoardo went out with that woman, they ran down the stairs and disappeared."

"And the professor?"

"He was still in the dining room. He called the restaurant manager. I think he was paying the bill, I don't know. But soon after, he left. And I took a taxi back home. Oh! I feel so terrible!"

So this is what had happened. Was it possible that the young man had later coldly, cruelly, awaited the professor in the street, killed him and brought the corpse into the bookstore of Via Corridoni? If things had gone that way, Senator Magni must have stayed out of the house for several more hours, since the crime had been committed around two or three in the morning. Where had the senator gone once he left the Sempioncino restaurant? And how did Dr. Verga meet him again, if indeed he was the murderer?

There were many unanswered questions, at the moment. Although the evidence against the young man had become quite consistent, De Vincenzi was far from being convinced of his guilt. He was passionate, even violent. He was an emotional person with excessive and ill-controlled reactions—but the characteristics of the crime were such that anyone could have committed it—anyone, apart from someone who was not in control of his passions.

The girl stared at the inspector, who was deep in thought, having completely forgotten her presence, and she didn't understand the reason for his silent, almost threatening concentration.

"Will you do something to help him? Will you prevent the senator from taking revenge on him?"

De Vincenzi came back to reality with a thud.

"Oh, I think I can guarantee that, Miss."

"What do you mean?" the woman asked, widening her eyes.

"Last night, Senator Magni was murdered."

"No!" the girl shouted, standing up, her hands raised in front of her.

De Vincenzi ran toward her and caught her in his arms just before she fell.

Sani rushed into the room. It was necessary to sprinkle her face with water and open the window to let in some fresh air.

She recovered slowly.

At first, she didn't understand what had happened or where she was. When she remembered, terror seized her once her again.

"But it wasn't Edoardo! Please tell me it wasn't him. It wasn't him who killed the senator!" she pleaded, addressing De Vincenzi.

"Of course not! It wasn't him. We can't even begin to guess who committed this terrible crime. The senator was shot treacherously, from behind."

The young woman sighed with relief and the color returned to her cheeks.

"In that case, the murderer can't be Edoardo!"

"Of course," said the inspector, to reassure her.

The girl got up.

"Forgive me, if I caused you trouble."

Then she was struck by a sudden thought and her face darkened. She frowned and clenched her lips.

"But why did you let me talk if you knew the senator was dead?"

"Why shouldn't I let you talk?" replied De Vincenzi, innocently. "Come now! Don't think about this anymore and go home. Time heals all wounds. But before you go, will you tell me your name?"

"Fioretta Vaghi."

"And where do you live?"

"You'll never come and look for me at my parents' house!" she exclaimed with fright.

"Why do you think I should need to?"

"You shouldn't, I guess. It's Via Carlo Pisacane, number 42."

"Thank you."

And she left, not completely reassured.

De Vincenzi thought that, at least, the mystery of the phone call was solved.

Chapter 8

It was about 2 p.m. when De Vincenzi, who had eaten a quick lunch in a small tavern next to the police station, saw Cruni entering his office.

"They're out here, Inspector."

De Vincenzi had been caught while reading. He turned his head.

"Excellent. And who are "they?"

"The bookseller and two women."

"Two? Why two?"

"We went to the house to pick up your medium, who's really more of a large . . . anyway, the one who communicates with spirits. And her daughter insisted on coming with her."

The inspector didn't even smile at the sergeant's attempt at humor.

"What sort of people are they?"

"Simple but honest. Her daughter is a teacher and she's the widow of a railway clerk. She has a house with beautiful furniture in Via Cosimo del Fante."

"Bring them in."

Although the sergeant had been reasonably accurate in his description, De Vincenzi could not suppress a start of surprise when he saw the two women for himself.

While the daughter was a slim, insignificant person with a pale complexion and inexpressive eyes, her mother was about fifty-years-old, though already rather obese and flabby for her age. She had black hair, with no silver strands, and her teeth were healthy and brilliant. They presented themselves with sophistication; their severe and tasteful elegance was superior to their social class.

They advanced toward the inspector's desk in serene dignity. Next to them, Chirico appeared smaller and even more yellow, all clumsy movements and restless gestures.

"Please have a seat," De Vincenzi said immediately. As there were only two chairs in the room besides that of the inspector, the bookseller looked around, scratched his head and remained standing.

The mother spoke at once, as she was pulling up a chair to sit. Her voice was sweet but strangely deep.

"I really don't understand why your officer forced us to come here. If he did so because sometimes—since my doctor discovered that I have strange and remarkable gifts as a medium—I agree to facilitate a séance, I'll tell you right now that I didn't do it for money and I never used any trick or manipulation."

"I told you, Mother, you should never have agreed. Now look where it's gotten us!"

And the young lady turned to the inspector.

"Apart from everything else, it hurts her health, you know? When she comes back from one of those sessions, she has a headache and is extremely weak for twenty-four hours. That's all she gets out of it!"

"Yes," her mother continued. "The fact is, I don't earn anything. And the gentleman here can confirm that I have never asked for anything. He never gave me any money for the few times that I facilitated the sessions of the Circle." Chirico nodded emphatically in agreement.

De Vincenzi listened to them without interrupting. They spoke quickly, although choosing their words carefully and giving them a slight emphasis. It had to be a professional habit learned from the daughter, who was a teacher.

"Nobody blames you, Madam, for these practices," the inspector finally said.

"But I don't *practice* anything!"

"I will say then, for the gifts you possess. As for your daughter, she has nothing to do with this."

"In that case, I can't explain why. . ." the woman murmured and stared at De Vincenzi with her big black eyes.

"Did you take part in a séance held a few days ago in Via Broletto?"

"Maybe. Actually, I did. I remember perfectly. Mr. Chirico came to urge me to attend that session."

De Vincenzi turned around and looked at the little man with a stern gaze.

"Why did you lie, telling me that this lady had been introduced by a member?"

Chirico looked worried.

"But . . . I was upset. . . a corpse. . . Senator Magni. . . How could I think clearly? How could I remember? I said it just to say something."

"Very well!" the inspector cut Chirico off and turned back to the lady. He winced. The woman had turned mortally pale, she seemed about to faint.

Not this one, as well! De Vincenzi thought. She would be the fourth woman to faint in front of me within a few hours. But why would she?

"Do you feel ill, Madam?"

"Mother! Mother!" the young woman exclaimed, leaning close to her.

"I'm ok!" she murmured, making a visible effort. "Could I have some water?"

Chirico filled a glass, pouring water from a carafe which was next to him, on a wooden tray.

The woman drank.

"He spoke of a *corpse!*"

"She gets upset when she hears about such things!"

De Vincenzi thought this odd in someone who made a hobby of chatting with the dead.

"No. It's not that. But I would like you to tell me what this is about. . ."

And she added quickly, with real anguish:

"It can't be! Surely, we are not speaking of the senator!"

"Why do you think the senator might be dead?" De Vincenzi asked at once.

The woman looked at De Vincenzi with feverish eyes.

The bookseller looked around, lost. He seemed almost terrified. Finally, he was able to talk.

"There have been other cases, recorded by scientists above suspicion. Clairvoyance is a recognized gift in certain people. It's terrible, though! There is a whole world around us that we know nothing about!"

"What are you saying?" cried De Vincenzi, oppressed by a strange malaise. "You're all crazy!"

Then he smiled to himself at his attack of nerves.

"You be quiet now, please. Let the lady talk. What do you fear may have happened? What do you mean, and what is this story about the corpse?"

"Tell him," she said, turning to Chirico. "You tell him. . ."

The bookseller looked increasingly agitated.

"It has nothing to do with this crime. It's awful, but it has nothing to do with it. The inspector can't be interested in such a thing!"

"Actually, I'm very interested. Speak. Now."

"Well, the other day the session took place as usual. The lady fell into a trance, the expected phenomena occurred. There was levitation of the table. There were loud noises, violent movements of the curtains, a cold feeling on our skin. The unknown force manifested itself clearly. . . so much so that all the members subsequently told me that these were the clearest and most plausible phenomena they had ever experienced."

"Well, go on."

"Among other things, the lady mentioned the presence of a spirit with which she had established a true communication. And the spirit, at one point, spoke by knocking on the table, thus predicting the violent death of Senator Magni."

Chirico fell silent. He had only been able to finish his story with visible effort. And now he was looking at the inspector as if he had suddenly been relieved of a great weight.

De Vincenzi was deep in thought. He had never had a case involving spiritism, though he thought often about the awesome magnitude of death and the other world. He remembered a summer night in the Ossola countryside, after hiking to the top of a mountain, he had let himself fall on his back onto the grass and had long contemplated the starry sky.

A deep, almost religious, rapture had taken him, and he had concluded that the universe must have a balance that transcends all human imagination. Being able to cut yourself off from time and space meant getting close to understanding that balance. He had also concluded that life is a force of which death is but a stage, and that *after death* there can be no other manifestations of life.

And now he was listening to that withered, pale little man say frightful things such as *'There is a whole world around us that we know nothing about!'*

And that woman, too fat and too flaccid, who chose her words so carefully, had predicted the death of a man a few days before it happened!

Was it a scam or the manifestation of something that lay beyond mortal life?

He had to force himself not to be dominated by the morbid and awful malaise which had clearly contaminated the others. He had a

91

murder to solve.

"Is this why you were so upset, a little while ago?" he asked the lady.

"Yes. But is it really true, Sir, that Senator Magni is dead?"

"It's true. But please, answer my question. How did you remember that prediction if you were in a trance and, therefore, in a state of unconsciousness?"

"It was the senator who revealed it to me when the session was over. He approached me and said to me, smiling, 'So, it appears that I'm scheduled to die in a few days?' I was about to ask him what he meant by those words when one of the attendants approached him and, dragging him away from me, murmured in haste: "Don't you know you should never let the medium know what she said and did during her trance?"

"And what did Senator Magni do?"

"The senator tried to smile again, but he seemed to me very upset."

"Was it the first time you had spoken to Senator Magni?"

"I had seen him maybe a couple of times, always during the sessions of the Circle."

De Vincenzi turned to Chirico.

"And what do you have to add? The truth, this time!"

"Nothing. The senator left almost immediately with his friend, Dr. Marini."

"And who had hypnotized the lady to make her fall into a trance?"

"Dr. Marini. He has a real power of suggestion."

"Very well," De Vincenzi said.

He got up.

"I don't need anything else for now. You may go. But you, Madam,

92

should leave your name and address with the deputy inspector. I may have need of you."

"But aren't you going to tell us why you had us come here?" asked the young woman.

"Not to have your mother predict the future, anyway!" the inspector said, smiling, as he accompanied them to the door.

Chirico was also about to leave, but De Vincenzi held him back: "Stop please. I need some explanations."

The bookseller, for the twentieth time, scratched his head.

The inspector went back to his desk and sat down.

"Tell me! Do you absolutely deny that in that session and in the other ones before it there was some sort of manipulation going on? Do you deny that the table 'talked' only thanks to somebody's conscious and fraudulent actions?"

He asked his questions staring Chirico squarely in the eye.

Chirico smiled. In spite of his fear, he was able to assume an air of compassionate indulgence.

"Please forgive me. You are uninitiated. Whatever I told you now, you wouldn't believe me!"

"I'll need an answer, in any case."

"There was no trick! There couldn't be. All the attendants of that séance were scientists and scholars, like Senator Magni and Dr. Marini."

"Did the doctor and his friend sincerely believe in spiritism?"

"Of course! Dr. Marini even more than the senator and I think it was he who introduced the poor departed to psychic and spiritist practices. He is also an occultist and he knows about magnetism and hypnotism as well."

He smiled as if he were trying not to give weight to his own words— almost as if he didn't want to appear convinced—but it was clear that he was only humoring the skepticism of his listener.

"In other times, one would have called it magic."

"Interesting!" De Vincenzi murmured.

There was silence.

The surgical instruments glittered on the desk and Chirico gazed at them, fascinated.

"Do you believe that the dead come back?"

The question sounded sharp and sudden as a blow.

The bookseller shuddered. He pondered his answer.

"What can I tell you?"

"What you believe."

As the bookseller started to speak, De Vincenzi interrupted him with a gesture of his hand.

"Beware! You ought to answer me as if you were under oath, before the judge. Your answer is strictly connected to my investigation."

"Do you believe, then?"

"For now, I don't want to believe anything and forbid myself to formulate any hypothesis. That's why I'm asking you."

"If you think the prediction of the medium can be related to the crime. . . in the sense of a trick used by the murderer or an accomplice..."

He shrugged, as if to reject that hypothesis, which seemed monstrous to him.

"I believe in the existence of another world around us, which under certain conditions is within the reach of each of us; a strange force compared to which any physical force is weak. And this force can be used by a perverted mind to do evil just as good people can use it to do good. It is a terrifyingly powerful force, because it is the very essence of life. Men can sometimes dominate it but only by endangering their own life, for it kills those who can't dominate and use it!"

Mr. Chirico had become very pale, but he was no longer the insignificant little man he appeared to be. As he pronounced those words, he seemed to rise and grow along with them.

Despite himself, De Vincenzi was impressed.

"Very well," he said, softly. "You may go."

As Chirico reached the door, De Vincenzi abruptly commanded.

"And don't let anyone touch anything in the back of the shop. In a couple of hours, I'm be back to continue the investigation."

Chirico felt the threat hidden in those words and left hurriedly.

Chapter 9

"Sani!" De Vincenzi shouted.

He had suddenly come back to himself after almost half an hour of meditation.

The deputy inspector came in.

"You called?"

"Yes. Close the door. Now listen. Soon two young people will be here, a man and a woman. They are Professor Magni's assistants. They, both of them, are the most likely suspects we have. There is much undeniable evidence against them. Anyone else in my place would arrest them immediately. . . But not me!"

Sani listened to him with respectful attention. He had learned to admire his boss. He felt bound to him by that solidarity which only an unreserved esteem can create.

"If you believe leaving them free is the right thing to do, you are probably right. Trust your instincts."

"I don't know! This time, I don't know. The case is very serious. Not that I make any distinction between the murder of a poor man and that of an important person. To me, a crime is a crime, regardless of who is killed. But this time, I consider it serious and exceptional, not because of the personality of the victim. I don't care if it's a senator. On the mortuary table, all corpses are equal. What concerns me is the personality of the murderer. This crime has all the characteristics of *perfection*."

Sani smiled.

"Do you believe in the *perfect* crime?"

"Yes, I do. And I want to find the perpetrator, using his—or her!— own means. But this makes no sense to you. When everything is over, I'll show you that the only way to come up with something, this time, is to act as if the crime were a clock to disassemble. The perpetrator has created an impeccable machine. . . all the wheels are in their place. . . the balance wheel is on the jewels. . . every little gear matches, tooth against tooth. The murderer is an artist! An inventor, even a genius! Well, in order to find the factory brand, we have to disassemble the device, going back over the work of its author and removing wheel after wheel. . . gear after gear. Do you understand?"

"Not a word. But anyway, I believe you."

"Yes, thanks."

He got up and started walking around the room.

Sani looked at him in silence.

Finally, De Vincenzi stopped.

"Forgive my digression. Sometimes I let my imagination take over and my mind runs away with it. Well, as I told you, these two people are coming. One of them is Dr. Verga, the other one is Miss Pat Drury. What a character, Miss Pat!"

"Beautiful?"

"There are no ugly women in this case! There couldn't be. Senator Magni demanded the best of everything, especially women. The personality of the deceased is playing a major role in this. The senator had to die in the same environment that he created for himself and in which he lived! So, keep the doctor with you, in your office, and send the woman to me first. I'll question her. Then at a certain moment, I'll open our door a little—leave it ajar. Let the doctor hear what we are saying. I'll raise my voice. You'll have to gauge the reactions of the man, but leave him the freedom to act as he wishes. Even if he were to run into this room, don't stop him. Do you understand?"

"Simple enough," Sani answered, about to leave. "I'll go wait for them."

De Vincenzi called to him again.

"Did you send Paoli to Via Boccaccio and Via Leopardi?"

"Yes. He brought a man back with him. He's in his room."

"Good. When I tell you, send him to me."

Sani left, closing the door behind him.

Shortly thereafter, he reopened it to let Miss Pat Drury enter. De Vincenzi, sitting at his desk, was pretending to play with the surgical instruments in front of him.

"Oh! Very good, Miss Drury!" he exclaimed, lifting his head and smiling. "You are exactly on time."

The American woman stepped forward with a self assured and rhythmic grace. She was agile and harmonious. Her slightly-irregular face was unreadable, despite the studied smile on her red lips. Her cheek bones were pink and her eyes had golden specks.

"*Okay!*" she exclaimed, showing her white, small, and even teeth in a big smile. "In America, we say *okay* meaning that it's all right, that people agree. What do you want from me?"

"Take a look at these instruments. You are an expert, tell me what they are for."

The woman picked them up one after the other.

"Scalpel. . ." she said. "It's a tool to cut and incise. This one with a screwdriver shape is a Doyen's helix knife. This, which you probably believe to be a scissor, is a special caliper for electro-hemostasis."

"Ah," said the inspector, as he remembered that the woman had already mentioned this that morning. "It's a tool that must be familiar to you."

"It's a high-end tool, not all doctors use it. And this one, with a wheel at the tip, is a Berger clamp, which allows the operator to make sure a foreign body is taken out and to measure its size."

"So it's with a similar tool perhaps that, right now, they are pulling the bullet out of your employer's skull?"

"Maybe."

"Thank you for the explanation. And now tell me, do you recognize these instruments as belonging to Professor Magni?"

The American woman was firm.

"I never saw them. The professor had some similar ones, of course, but he didn't usually carry them in his case. Anyway, this scalpel couldn't possibly belong to the professor. All the scalpels he owned had an onyx handle. Using precious materials in his surgical instruments was one of his conceits."

"So you're saying for sure that they didn't belong to the professor?"

"I believe they did not."

"And what about this white lab coat? Look."

Miss Drury took the coat and shook her head. "Cotton! No. The professor's lab coats are all made of pure linen."

De Vincenzi knew she wasn't lying.

"So it is impossible that last night Senator Magni had these instruments and this lab coat when he went to the Sempioncino restaurant with you?"

The girl bit her lip and looked upset for a moment.

"To the Sempioncino restaurant?"

"Didn't you go there with the senator last night?"

De Vincenzi expected her to deny it.

"I'm not saying I didn't go. I'm saying it would have been strange if he had come with me carrying four surgical instruments and a white lab coat!"

Indeed. This time it was the inspector who bit his lip.

"Good! Do you always tell the truth, then?"

"When it cannot be avoided. Why should you *always* tell it?"

"Be careful, it's dangerous to play with lies!"

The girl didn't reply, as if that possible danger didn't concern her.

"Sit down, please."

She sat down, crossing her silk-stockinged legs.

"Why did you lie to me this morning saying that you had not seen the professor since yesterday at 5:00 pm?"

"Do not speak evil of the dead."

"It is evil to have invited you to dinner?!" exclaimed the inspector.

"To oblige me to accept his invitation knowing that I had no interest in consenting to his desires is close enough."

De Vincenzi knew he was about to venture down a tangled path. Before judging the dead, he wanted to have a closer look at the living.

"Anyway, now you admit that you were with the professor last night. So you went to the restaurant with him. And then?"

"And then, nothing!" answered Miss Drury, raising her shoulders.

"What time did you take your leave?"

"Almost immediately."

The inspector expressed disbelief.

"Didn't you eat there?"

"No."

"This, in fact, I already know. But I want you to tell me about it, adding some plausible reason. One usually does go to a restaurant to eat."

"We were interrupted."

"Ah."

"And I knew I wouldn't have eaten with the professor and that I wouldn't stay with him more than the time necessary to make him understand the uselessness of his insistence."

"Did you know that Dr. Verga would intervene?"

The girl didn't seem surprised by his words.

"*I didn't know for sure*, of course. But I had some suspicions, because my boyfriend had realized that the professor wouldn't leave me alone, and he spied on us."

"Hold on!" De Vincenzi exclaimed."Slow down. Explain clearly, since you must tell me everything. You agreed to go to the restaurant with Senator Magni. . ."

"I had to! I either went there with him or he would have made a scene in the surgery!"

"Very well. Your boyfriend. . . Dr. Verga is your boyfriend, isn't he?"

"Yes, he is."

"How long now?"

"A couple of months."

"Did he say he'll marry you?"

The girl nodded. "Why are you interested in this?"

"Because I know Dr. Verga is engaged. . . to another woman."

Pat smiled.

"I know that too! And this woman still loves him! And she's right. She has good taste!"

Well, that had gone nowhere, mused De Vincenzi to himself. If he had hoped to arouse her jealousy, he had clearly failed.

"How did your boyfriend know that you would be there?"

"I didn't tell him. But yesterday, when the professor returned from the hospital at five o'clock, we had a very, ahh, lively conversation, and Edoardo could have heard us. In fact, it was to prevent Edoardo from intervening on the spot that I consented to that dinner."

"So, Dr. Verga came in while you were in the restaurant?"

"Yes."

"Was there a violent scene?"

"Yes."

"Did your boyfriend strike the senator?"

"Yes."

She was dully monosyllabic. She seemed to be having fun. De Vincenzi felt irritated.

"It will be more difficult to answer, in a few moments!"

"Why?"

"What did you and Dr. Verga do when you left the restaurant?"

"Edoardo took me home."

"In Via Boccaccio?"

"I only have one home!"

"And did he accompany you inside?"

"No."

"Did he leave alone?"

"He went to his house."

"Was he upset?"

"What do you mean by upset? Of course, he didn't shout and punch the air. He was more worried than anything else. The professor had threatened to hire another assistant and we knew he would do it. And he could also harm Edoardo's reputation, if he wanted, at the hospital. We both risked losing our jobs, because I wouldn't have stayed with Magni if Edoardo had to go."

"So Dr. Verga was still upset when he left. What time did he leave you?"

"The front door of my building was about to be locked when we arrived in Via Boccaccio. It must have been around ten."

"And Senator Magni was killed at two in the morning," De Vincenzi said conclusively.

Miss Drury looked at him. A shadow of fright passed over her eyes but she remained silent.

The inspector walked to the door, opened it, checked what was going on in the other room and then returned to her, leaving the door ajar.

"Do you understand the significance of this fact?"

The girl shrugged.

"Any supposition is valid, after what happened in the restaurant."

"What supposition?"

"Are you sure you have never encouraged the professor in. . . let's say... his desires?"

From the nearby room came the squeaking of a chair, as if someone moved violently on it.

"There was no need for it!" Miss Drury answered with a smile. "The professor was. . . easy to encourage! It was enough to be a woman!"

"And your boyfriend was jealous!"

"I don't like jealous men. In America we don't have any use for jealousy. The only thing is that Edoardo found it unbearable that the professor stubbornly bothered me, persecuting me with his solicitations. And if he was spying on us, he did so only to be ready to protect me."

"Do you believe Mrs. Magni had noticed her husband's attentions toward you?"

"Oh! Mrs. Magni..."

"What does that mean?"

"She was used to it."

"Tell me about Norina," De Vincenzi said.

The girl got up.

"Do you want me to tell you about all the professor's loves?"

"Ah! So was the maid one of his loves too?"

"I don't know. I don't care! Ask her. The girl faints easily and will talk."

"Now I want to know what kind of relationship you, Miss Drury, *really* had with the deceased. The Sempioncino restaurant is not a place a woman would go with a man without being intimate."

De Vincenzi felt uncomfortable in being so brutal. But he had to. He had judged Dr. Verga as a violent person and could not but hope for an angry reaction on his part.

He suspected, in fact, that he was about to achieve his purpose. In the other room, the young man had got up and was very upset. He heard him say a few excited words to Sani.

"Do you think that I killed the senator after being his lover?"

"But someone could have killed him, precisely because you were his lover."

The door swung open and Dr. Verga burst into the inspector's office.

His face was red and his eyes sparked with fury.

"When will you stop insulting Miss Drury? What do you want from her?"

"Why did you come in here? I didn't ask for you yet!"

"I came in without waiting for you to call me! You are not being a gentleman!"

"Perhaps. But I am a Public Safety Inspector right now. And I'm asking, what did you do, Dr. Verga, from eleven last night to this morning?"

"I was in bed."

"We'll see! What time did you go home?"

"At eleven-thirty . . . at midnight. . . the time needed to get to my house. . ."

"Watch out! You told me you live in Via Leopardi. From Via Boccaccio to Via Leopardi it only takes, at the most, two minutes on foot!"

"I went to the park. I was still upset and wanted to calm down."

"Are you sure you went to the park?"

"Yes!"

"And that you went back home at midnight?"

"Yes!"

"Who lives in your house?"

"I'm subletting a room in a sort of guesthouse. My family lives very far from Milan."

"Is there a hostess?"

"Naturally. And her husband too."

"I know!" De Vincenzi snapped loudly and stepped to the door.

"Bring me the man that Paoli brought here," he ordered Sani, and returned to the couple.

The young man had turned mortally pale. Pat kept close to him and was holding his arm. She was staring at De Vincenzi with intensity. They didn't have long to wait.

Sani introduced Dr. Verga's host. He was a big man with a chest like a wardrobe and a round head on his squared shoulders. In spite of his boxer's body, he had a chubby, infantile face, a little nose and the mouth of a shy young girl.

He looked at De Vincenzi, then saw Verga and greeted him with a friendly smile.

"Are Dr. Verga's landlord?"

"Yes, I am."

"How long has the doctor been your tenant?"

"For exactly six months."

"Does he usually come back late at night?"

"Like all the young men. Sometimes he doesn't even come back. It's because of his age and the fact that my wife forbids inviting women over."

The man was talking in a thin voice that didn't sound like his own.

"And what about last night?"

"Pardon me?"

"I asked, what time did he come home last night?"

"But he didn't come back at all, last night! I thought he had told you. Maria. . . my wife. . . found his bed intact this morning."

The young man was silent. He hadn't even moved. Pat looked terrified.

There was a heavy silence.

"All right. That's all. You may go."

The man realized that his simple words had, somehow, massive implications and he looked around, astonished.

"Perhaps I shouldn't have said that?" he asked, addressing the doctor. Edoardo, in spite of everything, smiled at his naïveté.

"Go!" the inspector repeated.

The man left, more and more astonished.

De Vincenzi sat down at his desk.

The silence lengthened.

That's De Vincenzi 1, Dr. Verga 0, thought De Vincenzi.

Should exploit his advantage immediately and question him thoroughly? Certainly, anyone else would have done so. But he wanted to gather more evidence. He was not convinced that the young man had murdered the senator.

He looked up at the couple. They were silent, clinging to each other. Then, suddenly, the inspector waved them away.

"Nothing more from you, either, for the moment! You may go. Tonight at 10 o'clock I'll be waiting for you here. Please be prompt."

Edoardo started. He believed that he was being set a trap. He started to speak, then shook his head and shrugged.

"Come on," he said to Pat, and they left.

Sani appeared at De Vincenzi's door.

"Do you want them followed?" he asked in a whisper.

"Of course," replied De Vincenzi. "Send Cruni and somebody else. Cruni will take care of the man."

And he added with some concern:

"Make sure he doesn't lose track of him even for an instant!"

Then he slowly went back to his desk, pensive.

Chapter 10

He stayed in his office for a long time, with the door closed. Sani could hear him pacing back and forth, as he always did when working on a difficult problem. The motion made it easier for his brain to work. As De Vincenzi paced, the phone rang. "Hello?" A long silence followed. Evidently, he was listening. Sani heard him say: "Alright! I'm coming." The sound of the receiver being replaced ended the conversation.

Shortly after, the door opened and the inspector appeared wearing his overcoat and hat.

"If anyone's looking for me, I'll be back in an hour."

"Do you want me to go with you?"

"No. It doesn't matter."

He went out into the courtyard.

He walked with his hands in his pockets and his hat over his eyes. A colleague greeted him, but he didn't see him.

One more problem! Yes, this way, everything would be clear; but he felt it wasn't. That woman had to be hysterical and the fact that she had fled from the senator's house didn't prove anything. And anyway, why did she run? She had simply left. There was nothing strange if she had really been the senator's lover. His lover? The whim of an hour! She was beautiful, nothing in her reminded him of a maid. He had probably wanted her, if he ever did, because he was not a man who would have missed an opportunity, while she, instead, had believed who knows what.

She had fainted when she heard he had been killed. Moreover, that house probably seemed now unbearable to her. Perhaps, she really loved him. And she had disappeared. Nothing could be simpler than that.

When he was behind the Duomo, he waited for the tram car. He got on and remained standing on the deck of the second car.

So far, things were not clear to him.

Anyone else in his place, would have arrested Dr. Verga, passed the file to the instructing magistrate and never thought of it again. That would have been the safe thing to do.

But his inquiries were too important to him and he couldn't act that way. He wanted, he needed, to find the truth, examining the various characters in the play. It was an exclusively psychological work. He believed that everyone acts *as they are capable of.* To him, the material clues were only reference points for the character's internal motivations. And, as all good dramatists know, it is the characters' motivations that drive the story.

When he arrived at the lobby of Magni's house, he tried to find his center and clear his mind from any prejudice.

He rang the bell and a young man opened the door. He was wearing the bottle green uniform of a driver.

"Please tell the lady of the house I am here. I am Inspector De Vincenzi."

The man let him pass and De Vincenzi again entered that severe anteroom, which the door of the surgery illogically illuminated with clear light.

"Is the nurse here?"

The driver looked at the door.

"I don't know. Miss Drury always passes through the other door."

Then he left.

Moving quickly, the inspector went to the door of the surgery and opened it silently. He looked inside and saw no one. But from the second room he could hear the hushed yet excited words of two voices. Pat had to be in the parlor with Dr. Verga. De Vincenzi closed the door.

Mrs. Magni entered and made her way slowly to De Vincenzi. Her ivory pallor seemed more evident due to the black dress she was wearing. More than ever, she looked matronly and beautiful.

"I asked for you because the girl's disappearance doesn't seem normal to me."

"You did well, Madam!"

"Would you like to sit down?"

She pointed to the parlor where De Vincenzi had already been that morning.

"I'd rather have a look at the maid's room."

"Come with me."

They crossed a very elegant dining room, with sideboards full of silver dishes and flower paintings on the walls. Then they passed a bright living room, a wardrobe, and a hallway with three doors. The first one was the kitchen, the second one was the maid's room. Passing in front of the kitchen, De Vincenzi saw an obese, elderly woman, probably the cook.

Norina's room had an iron bed, a dresser with a mirror, a closet, and some chairs. The bed was made up. On the chest of drawers there were two or three photographs of a man. It was always the same: a young man with a beautiful face and a deceitful, fleeting glance. One of them showed him dressed like a sailor, and in that costume the feminine beauty of his body seemed even more evident.

"Do you know who this man is?"

"Norina's brother."

De Vincenzi took a photo from the frame and put it in his pocket.

"What's your maid's full name?"

"Norina Santini. I know she was born in Livorno. . ."

The inspector wrote the name on the edge of a newspaper he had in

110

his pocket.

He looked around. There was no trace of a planned departure. He opened the drawers of the chest. They contained fine linen, a pack of illustrated postcards, a few letters. Everything was in order. In a corner of the room, on the floor, there was a suitcase. In the closet, some dresses and a heavy coat.

"She didn't take anything with her. She'll come back."

"It's strange, however, that she left the house before midday without saying anything, knowing that she should have served at table."

De Vincenzi continued to look in the small drawers. He began removing the parcel of letters and postcards. Suddenly, he picked up a newspaper clipping, reproducing the portrait of a man, and slipped it in his pocket.

"Did you find anything?"

"Uhm. . ." said the inspector, moving to the closet. He pretended to look closely at a dress, to avoid answering.

The portrait in the newspaper clipping was that of the senator.

"There is nothing else to see here, Madam."

They went back to the anteroom.

"How long has Norina been in your service?"

"A couple of years more or less. . ."

"Were you satisfied with her?"

"I can only say good things about her. Respectful, skilled, hard-working. . ."

"Did her brother come to visit her?"

"Never, until last week. It was Thursday or Friday. Hearing an unknown voice in the anteroom, I came in and saw Norina with a young man. She told me he was her brother. I had already noticed the photographs and recognized him. Then he came back again. And yesterday Norina asked me if she could go out for a couple of hours, because her brother had to leave and wanted to say goodbye. So she told me."

De Vincenzi headed to the door.

The lady plucked at his coat to hold him back.

"Have you nothing to tell me? Did you find anything?"

The inspector shook his head.

"Who killed my husband?" the woman asked in a flat voice that made the question sound even more dramatic.

"I promise you that the crime will not go unpunished, Madam!"

The woman's eyes were full of tears, she was trying her best not to burst out sobbing.

"It's terrible!" she murmured, still with that flat voice.

"Yes, it's terrible," De Vincenzi repeated as an echo.

He approached her.

"Don't you have any suspicions? Can't you imagine who could hate your husband to the point of…?"

"No!" the woman answered, and her voice became sharp. "No! I can't imagine it. I don't know my husband's enemies, any more than I know his friends."

Maybe she meant his girlfriends, thought De Vincenzi.

"What do you think of Miss Drury, the nurse?"

The lady's eyes became hard.

"What would you like to know, exactly? Do I really need to answer this question?"

"No. Forgive me."

More silence. The inspector moved to leave, but when he was at the door, he turned.

"We'll look for the maid, of course. . . but if she comes back, I'd be grateful if you would let me know."

The lady nodded.

As soon as he reached the street, De Vincenzi turned to look at the windows of the senator's apartment. They were all closed, with the curtains lowered. Yet he would have sworn that, behind one of those windows, someone was observing him.

He went down Via Corridoni quickly and entered the bookstore. In front of the main entrance of the building, he saw the good-looking porter surrounded by a group of people. They were obviously talking about the crime, while her ugly husband was probably sitting at the cobbler's bench, unless he was at the bar to gossip too. And inside the building, up that funnel-like yard, the odors of a mass of putrefying bodies and souls continued to rise, eternally.

In the shop, Pietrosanto was browsing a large illustrated volume right in front of Maccari's two officers.

"Haven't they sent anybody to replace you?"

"No, Inspector," one of them replied.

"But it doesn't matter," said the other, with a smile. "Here or elsewhere, it's the same to us. . ."

"Yes, you're better off here, after all."

Pietrosanto closed the volume.

"I was showing them the illustrations of *Don Quixote* by Doré. . ."

"The owner?"

"He hasn't come back."

"Has anybody entered the other room?"

113

"No, Inspector," one of the officers answered immediately.

De Vincenzi headed toward the hallway, but he stopped before entering.

"Are you sure you didn't notice anything unusual in the rolling shutter, this morning when you opened the shop?"

"No. . . I don't think so. . . I told you, I never open."

"Was it locked?"

"I think so."

De Vincenzi noticed Pietrosanto's hesitation.

"What struck you? Tell me."

"Struck me? Nothing. But, thinking about it, maybe one of the two locks was not closed, while last night both of them were. . ."

"Are you sure of that?"

"Sure? No."

"Who had the keys?"

"The porter, next door."

"Are they always delivered to him?"

"Either to him or to his wife. And there's never been a book missing."

"Yeah. . . That rare book that you said is missing. . .?"

"Ah! The book! Do you want to know the title?"

"Of course!"

Pietrosanto picked up a card from the table.

"I found the inventory card. . ." and handed it to him.

De Vincenzi read it:

La Zaffetta - Venetia, 1531 - no. 8° - This small, indecent work is falsely attributed to Aretino, but it is instead by Lorenzo Veniero, a noble Venetian who by means of it sought to revenge himself on a Venetian courtesan named Angela, whom he here designates by the Venetian word "Zaffetta", which means, in Venetian dialect, daughter of a policeman. The volume, written in large Roman letters, does not show place or date of publication. It contains a sonnet by Veniero to Aretino. It consists of 114 octaves. It was sold for 48 fr. in 1805.

The inspector looked up at the clerk.

"Strange! How much is it worth?"

"A few hundred lire. . . It's up to the customer. It's an erotic work."

"Pornographic?"

"That would be up to the reader."

"And it was stolen!"

"Yes. And there were rarer and more expensive volumes on that shelf."

"Do you have any idea why?"

Pietrosanto, although he had recovered from the morning's fright, had, of course, no idea.

De Vincenzi put the inventory card in his pocket and entered the corridor.

He stayed in those three rooms for half an hour, and when he came out, he seemed satisfied.

"Does your boss ever come back to the store, in the evening or at night?" he asked Pietrosanto.

His blue eyes opened wide.

"Mr. Chirico? No, not that I know. . ."

"And the porter, could she have given the key to a stranger?"

"She shouldn't have done so, of course!"

"No, she shouldn't; but she *could* have done it."

"Did you find something?"

De Vincenzi didn't reply and left the store, saying:

"I'll be back."

As soon as he got to his office, he called Sani. He gave him the photograph and the maid's details.

"Search for her everywhere. Call the other inspectors and police stations. Then go to the Bureau of Vital Statistics and see if there's any information about him."

Sani looked at the picture.

"This guy looks pretty dodgy to me."

"Me, too."

Sani left.

De Vincenzi pondered. Slowly, he pulled a small lead bullet out of his waistcoat pocket. It was only a little deformed. He looked at it and put it next to the surgical instruments.

Then he picked up the phone and asked for Dr. Sigismondi, saying that he could be found at the cemetery, at the Via Agnello emergency room, or at his home.

Shortly after, the phone rang.

"Hello, is it you, doctor?"

"Yes, it's me," replied the doctor. "What's up? I would have come in an hour to bring you my report."

"Did you carry out the autopsy?"

"Yes."

"Did you find the bullet?"

"Yes. Just one though, while there are two wounds. It's a 25 caliber. A very small automatic pistol, perhaps the smallest on the market. Like something a lady would carry in her handbag."

De Vincenzi smiled.

"It was not a woman, Doctor!"

"I wouldn't know."

"Me neither," laughed De Vincenzi.

"Anyway, I'll be there shortly."

"Sure. If you don't find me, leave the report here."

"Yes. . . Ah! Listen. Just a detail. Inside his body, we found plenty of alcohol. And I'm convinced that, if he hadn't been shot in the head, we would have found a hyperemia in the cerebral membrane."

"What does that mean?"

"That the senator had been drinking a great deal of liquor before he was killed."

"Ah! Good job, doctor!"

He hung up. It was not strange that the senator had been drinking. From 8 p.m., when he left the Sempioncino restaurant, till about 2 a.m., at which time he had presumably been shot, he must have been somewhere, possibly a cafe or a bar.

He pressed the bell and asked the officer to call Sergeant Padovani for him.

An elegant young man entered, who looked more like a dancer than a policeman.

"Sergeant, you must ask your inspector to leave you free tonight. I need you."

Nothing would have pleased Padovani more.

"Yes sir, Inspector. I'm off tonight, so it's very simple."

"Good, go to Bertolò, the photographer on Corso Vittorio Emanuele, and pick up a photograph of Senator Magni. He will certainly have some ready, because the newspapers will have asked him for them. Once you have the photo, go to all the venues, cafés, bars, and restaurants that are open after 1:00 a.m. and ask if last night the senator was in one of them and at what time and with whom."

"I understand, Inspector. I'll take care of it."

And the sergeant went out, moving gracefully and wearing a jacket that, for anyone else, would have been a size too small.

De Vincenzi smiled. For one evening, at least, the unhappy women of the night on Padovani's beat would be left in peace!

Sani came back.

"I transmitted your orders about the girl. As for her brother, I found this file."

He handed it to him along with the photograph. It was thick. The inspector took a look at the summary. "Theft; theft; criminal possession of a weapon; insult and violence against police officers; another conviction for insulting a public official; theft; pimping; violating parole; rape; use of counterfeited money; violating parole. Well, our friend *has* been busy! He was sent to Ustica's prison and was released on March 5, 1917, because his redemption application— fighting for his homeland—was accepted. From 1918 to 1924, he had two convictions for pimping."

"A nice guy, eh?" Sani commented.

"Not bad at all," De Vincenzi replied. "Have him arrested, if we can find him. Take care of it yourself."

"Tonight, I'll go out with the patrol. Do you want me to organize a round-up?"

"Yes. I'll ask the Superintendent for the order."

"I would also carry out a search in the apartment building of Via Corridoni. I know it well, and we'll find there all the good customers of the San Vittore prison."

"No. Not there. I don't want to scare them off. I want them to talk."

De Vincenzi stood up and sighed:

"Now, I'm going upstairs to the Superintendent."

As he slowly climbed the stairs to the second floor, he thought that, in spite of everything he had done and had observed since the beginning of the investigation that morning, he had not yet come any closer to catching Senator Magni's killer, not by an inch. . .

Unless. . . Unless he owed a debt of gratitude to the great Gualtiero Gerolamo Pietrosanto, who had instantly noticed the disappearance of an erotic volume, published in Venice in 1531, and stolen from the bookstore of Via Corridoni on the night between March 20th and 21st, 1926.

And that morning the sun, entering Aries, had marked the beginning of spring!

Chapter 11

At 10 pm, in the large square of Porta Ticinese, the Darsena, the once-bustling docks of Milan, look a metallic grey. The water is nearly motionless and behind the bulkhead grids, the mud grows thick and rises to the surface.

In his office, De Vincenzi looked at the clock and returned the volume he had been reading to its drawer.

They would come soon.

The bleak room was lit only by a weak lamp, which formed a circle of light on the desk and a short section of the brick floor. Everything else was in shadow. Within that circle, on the desk, there were some white sheets of paper, the shining surgical instruments, and two misshapen lead bullets. The sound of voices came from Sani's office.

"Let them in," De Vincenzi commanded.

Two people entered.

"Close the door, please."

Sani closed it.

"Have a seat."

There were only two chairs, in front of the desk, inside the circle of light. Dr. Verga and Pat Drury sat down.

The inspector mumbled:

"I'm sorry," and lowered the green lampshade on his side.

The light spilled toward the center of the room and illuminated the two young people.

Pat Drury closed her eyes and grimaced with her lips too red. The pale and contracted face of the doctor remained motionless.

"We came," Pat said. "Maybe you didn't think we would. . ."

"On the contrary, I was sure of it. I had no fear you would run."

"What, then, were you fearing?"

The inspector shrugged. The young woman clenched her lips in disdain.

"You misjudge him! I don't and that's why I love him."

"Indeed."

He touched the instruments. He took a bullet between the thumb and index finger of his right hand and rolled it mechanically. The doctor stared at the instruments.

The silence that followed was too long for everyone. Even De Vincenzi couldn't bear it. He was prepared for the interrogation, but now believed that such a theatrical setting, which he himself had unconsciously created, would not bear fruit. The scene must appear contrived and he didn't want that. His two suspects would now be on their guard, and he was hoping, instead, for at least a flash of sincerity from them. At that moment, however, inside that room, if their nerve broke, only a desperate collapse, a spasmodic outburst of tears or, perhaps, shouting were possible. And if they held their nerve, because they were prepared or aware of the upcoming danger, there was nothing to hope for.

He roused himself. The other two had a start.

"Let's just talk like good friends," he said, and picking up the phone receiver and laying it on his desk he added, "So no one will disturb us."

"Edoardo has something to say. But you have to believe him."

The girl was talking softly, with her strange accent that gave a certain harshness to the words, as if they were crushed by her teeth. But she had lost all her sarcasm and her eyes were not speckled with gold anymore.

"I'll believe him," said De Vincenzi.

The doctor was silent, still staring at the surgical instruments as if hypnotized. The inspector put them aside.

"What do you have to tell me?"

"Yes," said the young man, and stopped.

"Where were you last night from eleven on?"

"Why from eleven?"

"I thought so. It isn't true that you accompanied Miss Drury to her house, am I right?"

"I couldn't leave him alone!" the girl said, and De Vincenzi nodded.

"When we left the restaurant..." Dr. Verga finally began, ". . .we were both very upset. The scene with the professor had been more violent than I had foreseen. I had gone down there with the intention of talking to him firmly, but calmly. What he was doing was not worthy of either of us because the professor knew I truly loved Pat. For him, however, she was just a whim. His masculinity was at stake, and nothing else. For the first time a woman resisted him. But then, when I found myself in front of him. . . and I saw him smile sarcastically... and he tried to grab Pat, to keep her away from me. . . I lost control of myself and struck him! I would have killed him in that moment, if I'd had a weapon. But I had left my revolver at home, because reason had prevailed. So when we got out of there, we were both in shock. We walked a bit along the deserted streets, without talking. Pat was holding my arm and kept close to me. We arrived at the Como highway and would have continued, if the police had not stopped us—we were lost in our thoughts and totally unaware of our surroundings. I was afraid for Pat, more than myself. The professor was not a forgiving person. Or rather, he would have forgiven us if he had achieved his purpose. And this..."

The young man clenched his fists, his eyes glaring. The girl put a hand on his knee and immediately withdrew it.

"I know, my dear!" he murmured, then turned to the inspector. "The intervention of the highway patrol officers broke our reverie and brought us back to the present. Pat even managed to laugh. 'How about finding somewhere for dinner. I didn't get much to eat at the

Sempioncino and I'm famished!'

We took a taxi and went to the Savini restaurant. We wanted to have some people around us, a place that could distract us. After dinner, we were more calm. We left and walked through the Galleria. Pat told me, 'Don't worry, he'll understand that he was wrong. What happened is very unpleasant, but it will encourage him to leave me alone. Tomorrow, if he is a man of spirit, he will pretend that nothing happened.'

I was not so optimistic. I had realized that by striking him I had done something irreparable. He would have kicked me out, ruined me. Apart from being his assistant, I also work as an intern at the hospital, and he could have had me dismissed. Pat knew it, and even if she tried to reassure me, she was worried too. 'How about apologizing to him?' she suggested, and I heard her voice trembling, due to her great concern. 'I'm ready to,' I said instantly. 'But tomorrow morning it will be too late.' So, she suggested that I should wait for the professor in front of his house. It was about midnight and he was never home before one or two. I agreed. I was not ashamed to talk to him man to man, sincerely, with respect, albeit firmly. I would have tried to make him understand that Pat is my whole life. . ."

He paused for a moment. De Vincenzi stared at him. That love confessed so quietly, with such simplicity, moved him. Love was still one of the few religions he believed in.

"And then?" he asked, to overcome his own emotion.

"I wanted to go by myself. Pat insisted on coming with me. 'He must not see you!' I told her. 'In front of you, he will never confess his mistake.' 'We'll stay on the other side of the avenue. When we see him coming, I'll hide behind a tree and you'll approach him. I'm too anxious to know the outcome, to let you go by yourself,' she told me. I wasn't able to say no. We went to Viale Bianca Maria and waited for him. Time passed slowly. We could hear the chimes of the clock of the church on Via Conservatorio. We had not yet seen him at three o'clock. . . Not even at four. . . It was five when we decided to leave, thinking that he wouldn't go back home for the night. I accompanied Pat to Via Boccaccio, promising her I would go to bed. Instead, I could not. The café of the North Railway Station was open. . . I went in and stayed

123

until it was time for me to go to the hospital. That's it!"

"Are you sure you didn't see the professor?"

The doctor hesitated. He looked at his companion. The American woman responded:

"At around one-thirty, we saw two men coming from Via Corridoni. One of them seemed to be the professor. Edoardo said to me, 'How can I approach him, if he's not alone?' But then, suddenly, after walking a few steps on the avenue, the two men turned around and went back along Via Corridoni. So we thought we had been mistaken."

De Vincenzi had a frisson of excitement. His hands shook slightly.

"Concentrate, Miss Pat! Thinking back now, after twenty-four hours, does it seem to you that one of those two men was, indeed, the professor?"

"I don't know! If I have to trust my impression of last night, I would say yes. But why would he ever come all the way to his home, and then go back?"

"And what about the other man, the one accompanying him... what was his appearance?"

"Shorter. . .with a long coat and a floppy hat. . . But again, we saw them only for a few seconds at a distance of at least a hundred yards and the lighting was poor."

"Did he look like a person known to you?"

"Known? What do you mean? No. . . he didn't look like someone I knew. But almost certainly the other one was not the senator and you shouldn't give importance to it. We just told you because you asked."

"Of course."

But from that moment, De Vincenzi was confident that Edoardo and Pat had seen Senator Magni with his murderer at about one-thirty the previous morning. His confidence, however, was absolutely instinctive, and for no reason justified; what kind of weight could it be given?

At that moment, the door opened and Sani ducked his head in.

"Somebody has been calling you on the phone for ten minutes, at least. An important communication. The operator says that your telephone doesn't work."

"And she is right!" De Vincenzi answered laughing, and then he grabbed the handset.

"Hello! Yes. . . The receiver was off. . . No. I took it off . . .Whatever. It doesn't matter. . . Tell me!"

Then he stopped to listen. The doctor and Pat saw that he bit his lip, holding back an exclamation. He became very pale. He clutched the handset so strongly that his knuckles were white.

"All right," he finally said. "Leave a guard on the spot and alert the firefighters. At dawn, they will have to drag the Darsena and look for the girl's purse. There's nothing else to do. Don't say anything to the press tonight."

He hung up and called, in a metallic voice:

"Sani!"

The deputy inspector stuck his head in again.

"Call all the police stations again; they should all look for that Santini. . . do you remember?"

"Yes," said Sani. "The brother."

"Yes. They have to find him at all costs. You go too, right away. I'll stay here."

"I'm leaving now," said Sani as he rushed out the door.

De Vincenzi looked at the two young people.

"Norina's body was found in the water at the docks of Porta Ticinese!"

"She drowned!" exclaimed the girl in horror as Dr. Verga jumped to

125

his feet.

"Strangled," De Vincenzi said slowly.

They were silent. Unconsciously, Pat reached for Dr. Verga and took his arm.

"Good night!" De Vincenzi said softly. "You may go."

They left.

The inspector, once alone, passed a hand over his forehead. This murder upset him, not only for the appalling brutality with which it had been committed and the young age of the victim, but also because his whole theory—if one could define it so—had just been dismantled.

Who did it? The same man who had killed Professor Magni with two shots from a revolver? And why? Perhaps to get rid of a dangerous witness?

He had been so stupid not to question the maid immediately! He could have slapped himself! He wanted to give her time to calm down, without upsetting her even more with an interrogation, and ended up leaving her to her own terror, alone and helpless at the mercy of the murderer! And now they were looking for her brother.

He pulled out the sailor's photograph from the drawer and stared at it for a long time. Could he be the author of the two murders? A criminal, an outlaw? Shady and corrupt in both body and soul? But why would he do it? Was this a squalid story of blackmail and murder? Was it a vulgar crime, a crime of delinquency?

He got up and started pacing around the room. He was moving feverishly, his brain about to explode from the contradictions.

In his mind's eye, he could see the naked body of the girl, pale and muddy, on the marble table in the autopsy room.

Her killer had strangled her and then thrown her into the water. Though the square was deserted, the splash had been heard. The policeman on duty at the beginning of Corso San Gottardo had approached the water, more for curiosity than anything else, and he had seen the body half submerged, as her skirt was stuck on the bulkheads, on top of the grids. . . The body had been fished out of the water using hooks. . .

Poor girl!

She was beautiful. They were all beautiful women around the corpse of that man who had been killed among the books! Because De Vincenzi now knew that the senator *had been killed inside the bookstore.* Right in the place where he had been found.

He had already guessed it when he had noticed something odd about that strip dragged over the dust; but that afternoon he had found proof, because he had discovered the second bullet in the spine of a book, on a shelf of the third room in the back of the shop, right in front of the corpse.

Could the murder be that sailor? A crime of delinquency?

He stopped. He shook his head violently. It couldn't be. The porter had the key to the shop. . . He pictured the man sitting at the cobbler's bench while holding the shiny shoe knife in his hand.

He could hear him say with his little sickly voice: *"At the bar in Via Cesare Battisti. . . there are witnesses. . . I have an alibi!"*

And he must have had a real alibi!

Slowly, he returned to his desk and sat down.

He searched his pockets and pulled out the newspaper clipping with the portrait of Senator Magni. 'One of the brightest science luminaries' the caption said. And that poor girl had cut it out and kept it in a drawer in her room, among the letters from her parents!

He put his hand back into his jacket pocket and felt a card. He had forgotten about that. Suddenly, his face lit up. It was the inventory card that Pietrosanto had given to him. *"La Zaffetta - Venetia, 1531."*

"No!"

He almost screamed with joy.

127

It couldn't have been a crime of delinquency, a vulgar crime!

A very rare erotic work had been stolen!

He was not wrong!

The phone rang.

"Hello! Yes, hello for God's sake!"

"The Inspector from Via Meda is on the phone," the operator said.

"Let me talk to him. . . Hello! Yes. It's me."

"We arrested Pietro Santini in his home at Ponte Vetero."

"What time did he go back home, according to him?"

"At nine o'clock. He is under house arrest and had to be home at that time. If you can believe him."

"Good. Bring him to the San Fedele police station, right away."

He hung up.

Was Norina's brother really home at nine o'clock? He wished he had at least one reliable witness.

Chapter 12

As he got out of the taxi in front of the police station, the young man went into convulsions.

"Damn him!" the escorting sergeant murmured, "not that old trick." "Come on, guys, grab him by his arms and legs!" shouted the sergeant wearily.

The two officers grabbed the flailing man, who, despite his apparent convulsions, was kicking out with startling accuracy. The sergeant took one in the stomach and cursed, while reflecting that it could have been much worse.

Two *carabinieri* and some regular police officers came out of the station to assist, resulting in a remarkable cluster of convulsed and swearing bodies surrounding the "seizure victim." He was foaming at the mouth and rolling his eyes. He was quite good at it.

Finally, having restrained him with his own belt, they managed to immobilize him and bring him inside. But he continued to howl like a dog at the moon. It was a long, whiny howl, a howl which echoed through the entrance corridor and into the courtyard, disturbing the pigeons. They threw him on the floor of Sani's office, which was empty. De Vincenzi appeared at the door of his office.

"The usual fake attack. . ." he said, and shook his head.

It was exactly the person described in his file: a person under supervision, familiar with all kind of subterfuge and tricks!

"Take that jug of water, there in the corner."

An officer grabbed it from the washbasin and threw the contents in the man's face. He roared. But he stopped grimacing and gnashing his teeth. Through his open shirt, the water had run down his chest to his belly. It was flowing down his hair. Laying on the floor, the young man clutched his chest.

His whining got weaker and weaker. The comedy was about to end.

"Make him sit up!"

The sergeant, who was still feeling the effects of his previous encounter, got in one of his own and kicked him.

"What a beast! They are all like this! And what do they gain from it, in the end?"

The officers grabbed him and lifted him onto the chair.

The man opened his eyes, looked around and murmured:

"Who are you? Where am I?"

"At the Vatican!" an officer teased him.

"Remove the belt," De Vincenzi ordered.

Once he was free, the inspector approached him.

"How are you doing now?" he asked without roughness.

The man didn't understand why the inspector would treat him differently from the others. He looked puzzled and didn't answer.

All around him, the officers grinned sarcastically.

"You all go," De Vincenzi said coldly. "Leave him here. I'll take care of him."

"He's not to be trusted, inspector!" the sergeant intervened. "He's a recidivist capable of anything. He was in prison."

"I know. But he won't do anything here. Go back to your station. It will be enough for one guard to remain on the porch."

And then he nodded to one member of the squad.

They all went out.

The inspector closed the door behind them and returned to the man, who, fearing a trap, had contracted his face and kept his squinted eyes on the ground as in the photograph. De Vincenzi looked at him. He resembled his sister, they had the same features, even the same color eyes. Only, in him you could see the signs of gluttony and vice.

"Can you walk?"

He didn't get a reply and put his hand on Santini's shoulder.

"Get up and come over in the other room. I need to talk to you."

The young man got up and walked toward the door, which was open in front of him.

"Sit down."

And he sat in the spotlight of the lamp, where Miss Drury had been sitting shortly before, with her too red lips, her light body and legs wrapped in silk stockings.

"I have to give you some bad news. . . I have to do it, even if you've just come out of a seizure. How long have you been suffering from epilepsy?"

He spoke to him with great empathy and caring. He knew very well that Santini had put up an act, but to what purpose should he remind him of it? He had judged him at first glance and realized that he wouldn't obtain anything from him by threatening him. And then there was that corpse on the marble table of the Monumentale cemetery, which had its own importance. If he did strangle her, only by showing him trust and making him believe he was not a suspect could De Vincenzi hope to take him by surprise and snatch from him a revealing gesture or word. And if he didn't kill her—and De Vincenzi was ready to believe it—why should he be cruel, why should he trample on the fraternal feelings that the man might still nurture?

The man raised his eyes and looked at the inspector for a moment. Immediately, his gaze fled across the floor. He kept silent.

"You have a sister?"

He winced.

"What does it have to do with me?"

"Do you love her?"

131

"Is it to ask me this that you came to drag me from my bed while I was sleeping?"

"If she had a misfortune, would you care?"

"What are you talking about?"

Now, he tried to look the inspector in the face. He was frowning, and his eyes had become hard.

"When did you last see her?"

"It must be three or four days."

De Vincenzi scrutinized him.

"Did you go to Senator Magni's house to visit her?"

"A couple of times only. She could not get time off. I needed to talk to her. . ."

"Or was it rather she, who wanted to talk to you?"

"How do you know that?"

"Because two days ago. . . on Sunday. . . she asked for permission from her mistress to come to see you."

"It's not true. I didn't see her on Sunday."

"Are you sure?"

"I slept all day, Sunday. My landlady could tell you. No one came to visit me."

"Your sister told her mistress that she had to meet you. . . to say goodbye to you, because you had to leave."

"It's all nonsense! Where do you imagine I could go?"

"For what purpose would she lie?"

"Ask her!"

"Do you really want me to ask her?"

"Do as you wish!"

He wanted to look calm but he couldn't.

"Oh! Come on, I don't have anything to do with the story of the senator, and I even advised Norina to leave that house! I am what I am. . . but she's a good girl and I don't want to see her sell herself. Because that's how it always ends!"

"What do you mean?"

"Oh! You understand me! But he is a gentleman and of course you're ready to blame that poor stupid fool for what happened to him. What happened, then? Was she kicked out?"

"She ran away."

The young man shrugged.

"And you caught her! Send her back home. Our mother lives in Livorno. They'll starve together! Where is she? Did you put her in jail? She didn't do anything wrong!"

He seemed sincere. Only if he had been an extraordinary actor he could have pretended with such spontaneity, knowing that his sister had been strangled and thrown into the muddy water of the docks! De Vincenzi was increasingly convinced that he had nothing to do with Norina's death. What about the professor's? It was not very likely, thinking about it. Why would he have taken him into that bookstore? Ah! Sure, the people living in that apartment building were a bad lot. You could count on their *omertà,* their code of silence.

"What did you do, Santini, on the night between the 20th and the 21st? Between Monday and Tuesday?"

The young man grimaced.

"Last night?"

"Yes, try to remember."

133

"At home. . . in my bed, as always. I sleep at all hours!"

He seemed to be having fun.

"Do you have witnesses?"

"The police came at ten to check on me. . . they found me. I can show you the signature on my booklet. Ask the patrol."

"And after ten o'clock?"

"I rolled over and started snoring. . ."

"Do you sleep alone?"

"Is this why you're asking me so many questions?"

"I'm doing it for you. Can't you see I'm trying to help you?"

Santini shrugged.

"Last night, I was alone!"

"Too bad! Last night Senator Magni was killed."

"Ah!"

He was surprised, more than shocked.

"No kidding! And who's the murderer?"

"You!"

"Bull! I'm not involved in this! I never fired any gun, or shot anyone. You can accuse me of stealing. But I'm not going to get thirty years! Look elsewhere, inspector. You can't put this one on me!"

"We'll see. And what did you do this morning?"

"Do you want my alibi? I have it for the entire day. Go ask the Patron. I've been with him all day for business."

"And who is your Patron?"

"13, Via della Madonnina. Go there. Restelli, of *Fiori Chiari*. . . He's a

134

merchant."

"Ah," said the inspector, who knew him as a receiver of stolen goods. "His testimony isn't the most reliable!"

"I know! He will probably be afraid to say that he kept me in his shop to help him out. But it's the truth."

"And did you see your sister today?"

"No, but I was told that she came to look for me at home. I wasn't there."

"Do you have witnesses to this, at least?"

"Yes, I do! The porter of the house is one of your informants. You know him well."

"What time did she come?"

"It must have been about six, I think. . ."

De Vincenzi paused.

The young man was trying to dry himself, rubbing his shirt. De Vincenzi's questions didn't seem to interest him. Every now and then he glanced at the inspector and smirked.

"Now Norina will live in peace, if that bastard Magni is dead!"

"What?" De Vincenzi almost snapped, for that phrase had been said in such a tone that there was no doubt: he genuinely believed his sister was still alive.

"I said that my sister will finally stop thinking about the senator! He had his fun with her and Norina had fallen for it. She's a romantic, stupid fool!"

"She's not romantic anymore," De Vincenzi said slowly.

The man raised his head, surprised above all by the tone of those words.

"What? Why?"

"Because she was killed too!"

"No! By. . ."

And he cursed bitterly.

He stood up, clenching his fists.

"Is it true? Is it true what you just said? Because if you're doing this to try and trap me. . . I don't even know to what end, anyway! But if you're lying to me, if this is some sort of dirty trick ..."

"I'm not lying. Someone strangled your sister last night and then she was thrown into the water near the docks at Porta Ticinese!"

The man became very pale. All the veins in his neck swelled. He was panting. He seemed to want to throw himself at the inspector. There was in him the impetus of a furious rage. His cloudy eyes were seeing red.

"If you tell me who killed her," he yelled; but suddenly, he seemed to sag. It was as if for the first time in his life he had been taken by a great, irresistible emotion. His eyes filled with tears. A broken sob came out of his throat. He sat down and hid his face in his hands. He cried. Then he murmured:

"Poor creature! Poor girl. . ."

De Vincenzi had to turn his head and then go to the back of the room. Such authentic pain in such a depraved soul was profoundly moving for him.

Could he be pretending? Only his long-standing familiarity with criminals suggested to him that, yes, he could be pretending and, if so, he would act exactly like that. But he wasn't pretending. He wasn't pretending for the sole reason that he had not killed her and didn't even know she had been killed.

Another lead to be discarded. Another person who came in and out of the drama. He felt far from the truth, farther than ever! If only he had questioned the girl when she was alive!

He went to Sani's office, leaving the desperate man alone in order not to hear him cry. Those spasms of grief caused him physical pain.

He kept thinking about the woman's white, muddy corpse, and her blond, soft hair. . .

He remembered another woman. The obese, flabby one, predicting death. What if around us there really was another world we don't know anything about? Do the dead come back? Do they speak? Then, Norina could have talked. She loved the senator, she loved him too! "Poor creature! Poor girl…" He walked down the porch and called the officer who was pacing and smoking.

"Come here!"

"Yes sir," and he immediately put out the cigar, snubbing it out against the wall.

De Vincenzi went back inside with him.

He pointed at the young man, who was still bent over in the chair with his head in his hands.

"Take him away. Put him in a cell. It's useless for him to go back home tonight. Make sure he's alone and treat him well! He isn't guilty of anything."

The agent approached the man and tapped him on the shoulder:

"Let's go. Come with me!"

Santini got up. He continued to keep his hands on his cheeks. He looked like an automaton.

When he got up, he put a finger between his teeth and bit it angrily.

"Damn life!"

Then he followed the officer, no longer looking at anyone else.

De Vincenzi heard them moving away, as their footsteps echoed in the porch.

The pendulum clock in Sani's room chimed two o'clock.

He sat down, feeling a sudden sense of exhaustion. What else could he do for the night? He could no longer string two thoughts together. All the people involved in his investigation were innocent. Even the scoundrels were clean! Yet, now there were two corpses. One for each night. Both of them on the marble of the hospital morgue.

He got up. He would go home to sleep. He needed some rest. With a sense of infinite pleasure, he thought of the fresh comfort of his sheets.

He switched off the lamp on the table without thinking that the ceiling light was also off so he ended up in the dark. He saw the illuminated door frame, and the room of the deputy inspector.

He headed there almost at a run, because that darkness seemed to him full of palpitating shadows that were almost real. *A world that we know nothing about. . .*

When he reached the other office, he almost screamed. A man appeared in front of him. He was short, smiling, rosy, and clean.

"Oh, my God! What are you doing here?!"

"I'm sorry," Dr. Marini said smiling. "It was impossible for me to come earlier. The sick. . . the flu. . . the measles."

"And you're coming at this time?"

"I was told you are here all night."

"I had invited you to come in the afternoon," the inspector interrupted him coldly, back in control of himself.

"Indeed! But the flu. . . measles. . ."

"And do you work every night?"

"Sometimes."

"Well, walk home with me, if you'd like. We'll talk."

"With pleasure. Walking through the deserted streets at night is one of my favorite pastimes. My brain works best at night."

De Vincenzi left first and the doctor followed him. The inspector saw the doctor's shadow projecting on the courtyard stones, illuminated by the full moon, It was short and almost round. Marini himself was short and, with his open overcoat, he even had a stocky appearance.

Chapter 13

They entered the Galleria Vittorio Emanuele, crossed the Piazza del Duomo, turned around the Basilica and continued toward Piazza Fontana.

It wasn't the most direct way to De Vincenzi's house, but he was no longer sleepy, and now he no longer dreamed of the fresh comfort of his sheets.

He kept on walking and the doctor walked beside him. They were silent.

In front of the Law Courts, a woman approached them and looked at them shamelessly, winking. Then she moved away, singing *Io Son Pacifico* by Vittorio De Sica.

The café on the corner was open.

"Shall we drink something?"

De Vincenzi was surprised.

"Sure. Let's go in."

They sat at a table at the back. The room was deserted. The waiter was resting against a wall. He yawned, approached these customers he didn't want and cleaned the marble table with a rag that he had extracted from a spherical, shiny, nickel rag holder.

"What would you like?"

"A coffee," said De Vincenzi, and the doctor shot him a disapproving look.

"A coffee at this time of night! I'll have a double anisette, in a big glass, and a siphon of soda water. . ."

He just sprayed the liquor with soda water and then began to savor it slowly.

"There's nothing better to quench your thirst. I'm always thirsty at this time. You know, bad digestion."

But De Vincenzi didn't speak, it seemed as if he kept that obstinate silence on purpose. He was staring at the doctor, smiling calmly. *"He has a real magnetic attraction,"* Chirico had said and he wanted to see it for himself.

"Don't you ever sleep, inspector? I believe that yesterday morning you were at work at nine o'clock... and an officer, whom I asked a little while ago, told me you normally stay in the office all night."

"Uhm!" De Vincenzi said, drinking his coffee. "I'm not there tonight, for example."

"That's true. . ."

"What about you?"

"Oh, me! I'm a night-owl by nature. I do it to take care of myself. If I slept a lot, I would gain even more weight. And I don't want to get fat. It's a sign of old age!"

"The same age?"

"Pardon me?"

"Are you the same age as your friend, the senator?"

"No! You see what I mean? I am three years younger, yet Ugo looked much younger than me. The same for everything. He always had an advantage over people around him!"

"He didn't have the last advantage, though."

"Who knows? To die in that way could also be an advantage. You find yourself in the other world without realizing it. Do you think he suffered? The shot must have been like a bang on his head. And then nothing. I wouldn't mind going like he did!"

He made a grimace, as if he despised himself.

"But I won't die like that. Who's going to kill me?"

And he drank his anisette all in one go.

"Waiter, one more double anisette please, in the same type of glass."

Then he looked at De Vincenzi.

"Who knows what you think of me now! Don't pay attention to what I'm doing. Ugo's death shocked me a bit. I loved him. After all, we had been friends for almost thirty years. We met in boarding-school, I was ten years old. Now I'm forty. And we have always kept in touch. He graduated from university; I did too. He got married, I got married too. .. So..."

He was tapping on the table with his index finger in a strangely regular rhythm as if he were beating out the letters of some odd alphabet. "But they have no meaning," De Vincenzi thought to himself, though following them with great attention.

"Is that how you hypnotize people, beating that way?"

"Who told you that I hypnotize?" he asked, his voice slightly altered.

"Nobody. But I thought that more or less any doctor can practice hypnosis nowadays."

"True. It's a great treatment. I don't abuse it, though. It makes the patients tired, and I always try to spare them the effort."

De Vincenzi detected something odd in the doctor's words. Perhaps the alcohol made his voice hoarse.

"Have you practiced spiritism for a long time?"

"It's exciting!" the doctor exclaimed, without answering the question.

Then there was silence. Both of them followed their own thoughts, but voiced them only occasionally. It was as if someone were keeping his hand on the button of a radio, turning it on and off, at intervals. Most of the music was playing within their minds.

"What are we? Where do we come from? Where are we going? Is death the annihilation of our being or the dawn of a new life, completely different from the one we live down here?"

"So," said De Vincenzi, "you talk to the spirits!"

"Exactly, spiritism is based on the belief that spirits exist. But spirits are nothing other than men's souls. . . Ever since man came into existence, spirits exist."

"And they come back to earth! So, do you believe that a victim could go find his killer?"

"Waiter, one more double anisette!"

His eyes were shining. His finger kept on beating on the marble. De Vincenzi grabbed it and held it tight for a few seconds.

"Forgive me! But I am very nervous tonight. . . I'm tired. But you didn't answer my question!"

"I was thinking. There is an important book by Allan Kardec, which could hold an answer for you. In it, he says, 'According to spiritism, Heaven and Hell, and divine justice...' But you don't really think that spirits appear in the form of ghosts haunting their killers? Such spirits must be called, they need to materialize, they must be made present. And why would a murderer try such an experiment?"

"Indeed!"

The radio button was turned off. The music of their thoughts grew silent, trapped in their minds.

"Where were you two nights ago, doctor? The night Magni was killed?"

"Strange!"

"What?"

"That you didn't ask me this question before. I asked myself the same question right away. Where was I the night between Monday and Tuesday? For a night-owl like me. . . the most amazing thing, by pure coincidence, is that I stayed home. My wife wasn't feeling well. Nothing serious. She has little health problems related to her anemia. I adore my wife. So I stayed home with her all night."

He paused, then took his wallet out of his pocket, took out a business card and placed it on the table, giving it a push with his finger so that the inspector could reach it.

"I haven't given you my address yet."

De Vincenzi didn't touch the card.

"I don't care! Why should I come to your house?"

But he had read the address: Corso Plebisciti 17.

"As you wish! But if you need a doctor, I am at your service."

And with the card, the doctor made a little origami goose. His plump fingers moved quickly and skillfully. The little goose raised its tail and wings on the marble table. He looked at it, smiling. He reached for his drink, but the glass was empty.

Immediately, De Vincenzi called, "Waiter! How much is it?"

"Let's go out!" he added to his companion.

"I was about to tell you the same."

The doctor was still thirsty, so he drank a glass of water, now that there was no more alcohol.

When they arrived in Piazza Beccaria, they encountered the first street sweepers at work.

They went up Via Cavallotti; at the corner of Via Cesare Battisti, the doctor stopped.

"Where are we going?"

"To look at the bookstore from the outside."

"It's too late!" Marini mumbled.

The store was closed, of course.

They stopped. The doctor laughed.

"It belongs to Chirico. A strange guy!"

"Do you know him?"

"He's the secretary of the Circle of Psychic Studies. . ."

"Were you a customer of the store?"

"I went there sometimes. I like books, but I don't understand those maniacs who fill their houses with books, without even reading them! I usually read them and then get rid of them."

"All of them?"

"Almost."

"Which books do you prefer?"

"I don't have any preferences! I read to learn. In every book, even the worst one, there is something to learn, which is useful in life."

De Vincenzi shook the door of the apartment building, which immediately opened.

"This door is always open!"

"In poor peoples' buildings, it happens. They don't fear thieves."

The inspector thought to himself, "What if I went to wake up the porter and her husband?"

But why? They would curse him! And what could he hope to discover from them?

He had kicked open the door of the building, and looked into the entrance hall, lit by a reddish bulb.

"What do you want to do?"

"The killer came out from here."

"How do you know that?"

"Instead, to enter the shop he had used the outside door, lifting the rolling shutter. He was with Magni, then. And Magni, of course, was alive, and didn't know he was going to die shortly after."

"But. . . in that case, did they have the key?"

"Not necessarily. Those locks can be opened with the simplest of tools."

"By someone who knows how to use them, though!"

"Maybe!"

The inspector hurried away from the house.

"Now, I'm going to bed. It's now three-thirty in the morning and I want to sleep for at least six hours."

"Do you want to go together by taxi?"

"Not necessary. You live far from me."

There were two taxis at the beginning of Via Verziere. De Vincenzi put his hand on the nearest taxi's door handle.

"Thanks for your company."

"What about your inquiries?" the doctor asked suddenly. "Will you find the killer?"

"Do you know that last night Norina was strangled?"

"What?!"

He seemed upset.

"Poor girl! But why?"

The inspector sat inside the car. The door was still open.

From the back of his seat he laughed nervously.

"If I knew who killed her, I would know the name of the person who murdered the senator!"

146

The doctor, brightly lit by the street lamp, had taken off his hat and run his hand through his thick hair. He had a very high forehead. Without his hat, his round face gained nobility, became more spiritual, intelligent.

"What a terrible disgrace!"

And he stepped forward to close the cab's door.

De Vincenzi stuck his head out.

"Dr. Marini!"

"Yes?"

"If I asked you to let me attend a spiritist session, would you consent?"

"Oh! What an idea!"

"I've been meaning to do it for a long time!"

"But you are skeptical. Skeptics disturb all phenomena. They attract the mocking spirits. Nothing good can come out of it!"

"Who told you I'm skeptical? As a matter of fact, I firmly believe that the dead do come back!"

"Hmm! We'll talk about it. . . But not for the moment. I will not be able to set foot so soon in Via Broletto, at the Circle. I always went there with Ugo. Going back there now would be painful."

"Good night!" said the inspector and gave the driver his home address.

The doctor stood in the middle of the square and looked at the taxi moving away.

Chapter 14

Three days passed.

De Vincenzi had spent them reading books about spiritism. Now, the drawer of his desk at the police station contained works by Kardec, Léon Denis and Delanne. He had read two works by Delanne: *Les Fantômes des Vivants* and *Les Apparitions des Morts*; and then he had read them over again from the beginning.

He was silent, deep in concentration. He had passed all pending cases to the deputy inspector.

"Take care of them," he told him with a bitter smile. "It doesn't matter, anyway!"

Sani looked at him with affection. He knew De Vincenzi's moments of interior struggle were decisive for an investigation. The flash of clarity that would shed light on a case seemed to need a certain number of hours, or a certain number of days to incubate and germinate.

But it was a painful labor for De Vincenzi. They were days of discouragement, when he dreamt of his windy and beautiful village of Ossola. And so he would write, *"Dearest Mother, I wish I were there with you!"* There, at the foot of the Alps, in the house with its barnyard and hens, the dog, the faithful maid. . .

On the morning of the first day, he had released Pietro Santini, who had run to the Monumentale cemetery to see his sister's body, which had been dissected by the forensic experts for the autopsy. Then he had locked himself up at home and the parole patrol had found him there no matter when they checked.

The result of the autopsy was strangulation, death by suffocation before being immersed in water. Apart from the bruises on her neck— the murderer's fingers had tightened around it so strongly, with so much anger, that the jugular had been torn—the state of her lungs would have revealed it, as they contained no water. And the doctors had found abundant traces of alcohol in the girl's system.

"I expected it," De Vincenzi told the doctor, who had briefed him. "And there is hyperemia in the cerebral membrane, isn't there?"

"I see that you're familiar with medicine!" exclaimed the doctor.

"Not really," the inspector said. "But I imagined that the girl had been drinking before being killed, for the simple reason that her murderer is the same as the professor's."

"But... do you know who the killer is?"

"Me? I have no idea."

He lied. He did have a suspicion. But it was one of those suspicions that make one smile when they are voiced. And he was careful not to reveal it to anybody. He kept it quiet, locked in his office at the San Fedele police station.

He had not returned to Via Corridoni, nor to Viale Bianca Maria. Nobody had seen him there, nor did he summon anyone to the station. Not little Mr. Chirico, who lived these days with the anxiety of seeing one or even two police officers appear in his store or home. Nor Miss Drury and her boyfriend. Or the pale senator's widow. Not even the medium, who certainly would have arrived accompanied by her daughter.

Pietrosanto, in the bookstore, was waiting for him. The gentle compiler of that endless book catalog would gladly converse with such a kind and intuitive inspector.

"I'm sure he'll find the killer!" he said to his employer, but the latter, after scratching his head, had shaken it emphatically.

Gualmo nevertheless repeated it and kept on doing so with all the customers visiting the store, who had become so numerous and frequent that some of them came to the store up to three times a day, looking, supposedly, for books. What attracted them was, of course, morbid curiosity for that strange and obscure crime. And they found a thousand excuses to go to the back of the shop to look at the place where the corpse had been found.

The newspapers continued to write about it. Yet the girl's death was

149

what captured their imagination the most. It had been a brutal and dreadful murder. They pictured the killer's hands around the thin, white neck of that woman, a beautiful woman! If she had been ugly, her death wouldn't have been so glamorous.

De Vincenzi wasn't searching, nor investigating, not even moving. He had had a long conversation with the instructing magistrate in charge of prosecuting the case, after which the magistrate had left, shaking his head and saying "I'll give you the eight days you say you need. But if you don't bring me the killer on the eighth, I'll take care of it myself and I assure you that I'll be quick about it!"

"Of course," the inspector thought. "He'll do it quickly, indeed. Two arrest warrants and he will be done with it! Poor Pat! Poor Edoardo!"

Dr. Marini had never returned to San Fedele. The flu. . . the measles. . .

He had phoned twice and both times De Vincenzi had answered:

"There is nothing new! But aside from the crime, Doctor, tell me, when will you let me attend a spiritist session? You know, I'm no longer a profane, now. I keep reading books about spiritism, day and night. . ."

Marini had laughed at him. Worse, he told all and sundry about De Vincenzi's request and his sudden interest in the spirit world. "Who is looking after the security of our citizens? The very best of our police force has started to study spiritist texts instead of hunting down killers! Maybe he thinks he can just ask the victims who killed them instead of going to all the trouble of doing an actual investigation. I don't know if he's lazy or just crazy, but he's certainly unreliable!"

And the Superintendent, though not coming to such a severe conclusion, began to think that De Vincenzi was, indeed, a little crazy.

He had asked him to account for his actions and the inspector, after having endured his dressing down, merely replied:

"Superintendent, maybe I will discover the murderer and arrest him; but it will take me eight days. If you give me free rein for eight days, on the eighth day I will either bring you the killer of the senator and the girl or I will bring you my resignation."

150

"Some choice!" the Superintendent had thought. "Your resignation means nothing to me as I will probably have to hand in mine as well."

Then he had granted him his eight days; but he had also hastened to send Rome a detailed report of everything, asking for instructions.

Eight days.

Three days had already passed.

The third day offered a little, unexpected twist. A farce within the tragedy. But that grotesque interlude shook De Vincenzi from his apathy.

In the morning, the Superintendent asked Sani to go to his office and the deputy inspector immediately sent Cruni to wake up the inspector. His maid, the ever-loyal Antonietta, started to complain about his rude habit of dragging her master from his bed, but De Vincenzi cut her off:

"Bring me a coffee and run a bath for me."

On the way to the Superintendent's office, he asked Cruni no questions and it was the sergeant himself, who, after a long silence, could no longer keep the news from him:

"Do you know, sir? It seems that the police station of Via Meda has found a good lead."

"On what?" De Vincenzi asked.

"On the killer."

"Good."

A good lead! As if the killer had left a lead!

A rag had been passed on the dust, leaving a trace that was meant to deceive the police. And a book had been stolen. . .

In the Superintendent's office, he found, in fact, the inspector of the Via Meda police station. He was a robust and big-bellied man, boasting the big moustache typically donned by a marshal of the Carabinieri. *Cavaliere* Roberti—that was his name—was a good man, despite his flamboyant appearance, but he had an irrepressible urge to stand out and get one over on his colleagues at headquarters.

His mustache was more menacing than usual and his gaze was glaring. His black pupils looked like two pieces of coal.

"Ah! De Vincenzi. . . This time it looks like we have him! Listen to what Roberti has to say."

"Good morning," De Vincenzi warmly greeted his colleague. "So you're helping us, huh?! Thanks. We can do with a hand. . . What did you find out?"

Roberti blushed slightly.

"Actually, *I* haven't found anything! But one of our informers seems to know quite a lot. He claims he's heard a complete confession by the author of the double murder himself."

"Ah! An informer! De Vincenzi murmured. "And the author of the *double* murder would be. . .?"

"A previous offender of about sixty years of age but still strong and robust. He lives in the farms and the countryside around Milan, he's a thief and a robber. . ."

"So, he would have acted on behalf of someone else?"

"Of course," said Roberti, but his brief hesitation gave De Vincenzi the impression that he had not thought about that particular.

"On behalf of whom?" asked the Superintendent, carefully observing his two subordinates.

The embarrassment of the inspector of Via Meda was obvious.

"We will know who it is when we arrest him."

"And what about this informer of yours?"

"He's downstairs. . . if you want to see him. . ."

The Superintendent thought for a moment. That morning, he was more elegant than usual, but the look in his eyes was quick and penetrating.

He frowned.

De Vincenzi observed him and smiled to himself, for he realized that the Superintendent had two opposing feelings: the desire to immediately acknowledge the reliability of that deposition and the fear of compromising his authority if that testimony turned out to be useless and perhaps even absurd.

His fear won.

"It doesn't matter. . . I have entrusted Inspector De Vincenzi with the investigation of this crime. Turn over the informer to him and let him deal with it."

He accompanied them to the door.

Roberti went out first.

The Superintendent held De Vincenzi back for a moment, grasping his arm:

"Listen. . ." he said, staring into his eyes.

"I understand," said the inspector.

"I do want you to understand. If the information is good, don't ignore it. . . for your personal belief that it doesn't fit with the *psychological framework* you have in mind. Psychology be damned! Arrest that person. Do you understand me?"

"I'll do as you ask!" De Vincenzi said, joining his colleague on the staircase.

"Listen, Roberti. . . This informer of yours. . . why is he talking?"

"What do you mean?" the good man asked nervously, as he was beginning to feel uncomfortable with his discovery.

"I think it's clear what I mean. How did you convince him? Offering him money? Is it fear? Is he out on parole? In short, what binds him to the police?"

"He's out on parole," said the inspector, pausing and curling his moustache nervously.

They had stopped on the landing. An agent with a bundle of documents in his hands ran in front of them. Trying to salute, he dropped his documents, so De Vincenzi bent to pick them up.

"Oh. . . Thank you, sir! I'm sorry. . . I'm sorry. . ." he apologized, then breathlessly resumed his mad dash.

As De Vincenzi rose to his feet, Roberti looked at him with embarrassment.

"I must tell you. . . This man isn't really our informant. He's mostly one of Harrington's men, you know? The private detective in Via Dante. . ."

"Ah!" said De Vincenzi with such irony that Roberti blushed again.

"Don't you think that Harrington is an honest man?"

"Of course. . . An honest man, who is paid by his clients not to be so honest. . . I would like to know who is paying him this time."

Roberti let out a sigh.

"Why do you care? The essential thing is that this informant tells us the truth! It doesn't matter why he wants to tell it."

"Of course!"

They had arrived in the yard. Roberti waved at a man who was leaning against a column.

The man threw away the cigarette he was smoking and followed them inside the police station.

De Vincenzi, passing through the first room, quickly whispered to Sani:

"The guy who's following us, hold him here, in your office," and then he went into his office with Roberti.

"Do you want to be alone while you interrogate him?" Roberti asked.

"If you don't mind. Forgive me, Roberti! I have my methods. They are worth what they are worth; but in the end, they are all I have, and I use them. Moreover, this damned case keeps me awake at night. I've got an idea, which I'm afraid even of confessing to myself. I've been chewing on it for three days now, unable to decide whether to verify my suspicions or discard them as something crazy. Believe me, this is one of those knotty cases, in which taking a false step means going back to the beginning."

"Of course. . . of course. . ." stammered Roberti, made dizzy by all those difficult concepts.

He was not exactly an intellectual, Roberti. Nor was he driven by his own subtlety, or even by intuition. He was schematic and approximate.

"I'll go, then. You'll let me know. And if I can help you in arresting the killer, please count on me. I just want to be useful, that's all."

Now he was offering his help, fearing that he could appear offended or envious. He really wasn't envious, but he didn't understand why an informer's piece of information shouldn't be taken seriously. If informants didn't exist, how could a police station function? That's what he was thinking, and it wasn't his fault if he continued to use the old methods from the times of the King's guards.

De Vincenzi cordially shook his hand. "Thank you, I hope you understand! Your assistance is always valuable."

As Roberti left, De Vincenzi said, "So, please send him in on your way out," and went to the corner where the window was, turning his back to the light. He wanted to closely observe this new character in the drama as he came in.

He was a character, indeed. The first thing that caught one's attention was the color of his face. He was not pale, nor red, nor livid, nor cyanotic, nor dark-skinned, nor mulatto, nor was his face of any common or natural color, albeit rare and unusual. His face was ash-grey. Not even that. It would be more correct to say that his face had

155

been cut and molded in clay as it was mellow, wrinkled and porous like clay. It was upsetting.

His eyes looked lifeless between his semi-closed eyelids and beneath his low forehead. His jaw was weak, the chin barely visible, his thin lips increased the impression of a human being morally spineless, devious, and slimy. His head lay on heavy shoulders falling onto a small, scrawny body.

He entered the room, holding his hat with one hand behind his back, as if hiding it, and with the other hand he was touching the pendants hanging from the copper chain on his waistcoat.

As a greeting, he bowed his head to his chest and waited.

"What do you do?"

He opened his eyes, which appeared lifeless, opaquely inexpressive.

"What do you mean?"

"I mean, what do you do for a living?"

"I'm custodian of the Church of Maria Consolata. . . at Porta Nuova. . ."

"You are sacristan, in short?"

"I serve the parish priest there, and the faithful."

"And you are a police informant when you're not working?"

"Who told you? That's not how things are."

"Let's hear, then."

"All right."

But he remained silent.

"Take that chair behind you. . . Yes, that one. . . and sit down. . . Well. . . Now, tell me how things really are, then." De Vincenzi instructed.

156

The man sat down and put his hands on his knees, holding the hat with his fingers. But he had such a habit of putting his hands on his chest and rubbing them one against the other, while speaking, that the hat fell the moment he spoke. He glanced at it but didn't pick it up.

"I'm custodian of the Church of Maria Consolata because Harrington wanted me to take that job. . . He needed a man of his in that place. . . Perhaps, he thought that everyone would trust me."

"And he also thought that you could have brought him some new customers, taking advantage of the familiarity that the devotees—especially the female ones—would have with you."

"I don't know... "

"And moreover, you would have been useful by informing him about both marriages and adultery."

"I don't know... ".

"Well, I do. Go ahead."

"So, actually, I'm one of Mr. Harrington's agency informants. . . and not an "informer" for the police station."

"Good. So, you are paid to do what you're doing now."

"What are you talking about?"

"Where did you find Senator Magni's killer?"

"In a tavern."

"Which one?"

"I'll show it to you. . . it's far away. . . near Taliedo. . . It's a country tavern. . ."

"Keep talking. . ."

"I swear to Christ that this is the truth!"

"Leave Christ in peace. I haven't accused you of lying, yet."

"It was by chance. . . I heard about an almost new hat and a woman's overcoat they wanted to sell. . . 'Who has them?' I asked. I knew that they had been stolen. But the young man who offered them didn't tell me anything. It was only when I had him drinking that he hinted at the Worm."

"And this Worm is. . .?"

"I don't know his real name; but he is known at the Carrobbio and in the Porta Ticinese district. . . He's old but he's terrible. . . Even young people are afraid of him. . . I have been looking for him, and last night I finally found him. . . He took me to a farmhouse in the area of Monza. . . It's the farmhouse of a baker, who gives him shelter in the barn, because he does some work for him. . . Under the hay. . . they were hidden. . . The Worm showed me a woman's coat and a floppy, almost new felt hat. . . In the inside, there were still two letters in gold: U and M. . . I don't know why. . . But looking at the old man's eyes, when he touched those objects, I had a sudden insight. . . The newspapers talked a lot about Norina Santini's overcoat and bag, which weren't found at the docks of Porta Ticinese, or elsewhere. . . I thought that it could be her overcoat. . . I suddenly asked the Worm: 'And where did you put the bag?' He was upset and looked at me with bloody eyes. 'Are you a spy?' he asked me fiercely. I laughed. I invented a story of crimes and convictions. And then I told him, 'Let's go drink. Breathing in all this hay has made me thirsty.' He came along. I made him drink as much as I could. Finally, he spoke. It was he who killed the senator and the girl. He also showed me the revolver with which he shot him, and as for the girl. . . I assure you, just looking at the hands of that old man, I shiver!"

De Vincenzi had listened to him, without interrupting him.

"Of course you can describe to me the physical characteristics of this Worm, right?"

The other one began to talk with his monotonous voice, as if he were repeating a lesson.

"An old man, but still strong. . . He's got a sly and repugnant look. Small, very lively eyes underneath his reddened eyelids."

"Hold on," De Vincenzi said, and went to the door.

"Sani," he said. "Call Cruni and you both come join us here."

The sacristan sitting on the chair had turned to watch the inspector. He seemed worried.

When he saw him coming back, he went on:

"His hair is gray. . ."

"Hold on, I told you!"

De Vincenzi was usually very kind with everyone, but with him he was unusually rough, almost as if he were disgusted by him.

Sani and Cruni entered.

"Sani, please, write down what this man is going to say. And you, Cruni, listen to him carefully."

The deputy inspector sat at De Vincenzi's desk and readied himself, with a pen in his hand.

"Go ahead, repeat; but first give your personal details."

The man got up. He picked up his hat and approached the desk.

"Angelo Panzeri. . . son of Antonio. . . from Intra. . . born in 1880. . . But, inspector, I swear to Christ that I have told the truth."

"Like I said, let's leave Christ out of it for the moment. Please, repeat it all from the beginning, your story. . ."

The sacristan began the story again, using almost the same words as the first time. He sounded like a phonograph. And every now and then he looked at De Vincenzi, and his lifeless eyes seemed to light up with malice, as if he thought, "If you hope that I will contradict myself, you're wrong!"

But that was exactly what De Vincenzi didn't hope for.

When he finished, the inspector took the last sheet written by Sani and placed it in front of the man, then handed him a pen.

"Please sign. It's your deposition."

The sacristan hesitated, then he grabbed the pen and signed.

"All right. . . Cruni, take him the guardroom. . . Then come back to me immediately."

"Are you holding me here?" the man groaned.

"No!" De Vincenzi replied, making an effort to smile. "Why would I? But I need you and I have to put you somewhere. . ."

He went out slowly, looking around.

"Do you believe him?" Sani asked, when he had gone.

"Part of what he says is the truth. And this is the terrible thing, because all the rest of his lies are based precisely on that truth."

He picked up the phone.

"Call Harrington's Private Detective Agency and tell him I want to talk to him right away."

Cruni came back into the room.

"Cruni, go look for the Worm. By tonight, you must have found and taken him at all costs."

"There will be at least ten Worms among the previous offenders in Milan. . ."

"You have a description of this particular one. We need to find him."

"I'll do my best, sir," and Cruni left, shaking his head.

With his simple common sense, incapable of tortuous subtleties, the sergeant didn't even believe that the man described by the sacristan existed.

De Vincenzi started pacing the room.

Sani got up.

"I'll leave you alone," he said when he was at the door.

The inspector smiled.

"Thank you. But now I no longer need loneliness. The decisive phase has begun. . ."

"So, you think we'll take in the Worm?"

"Of course we will!"

"Did he murder the senator and the maid?"

"That's another story!"

And De Vincenzi laughed, as he hadn't laughed since that morning when he was delivered the bundle with the surgical instruments and the corpse of Senator Magni had been found, lying among the books and the dust of the bookstore in Via Corridoni.

Chapter 15

As De Vincenzi had expected, it was long after dark, about midnight, when Cruni finally returned bringing the Worm with him.

He had arrested him at Cascina Maria, a farm just outside of Monza, where he found him asleep. It was a good thing that Cruni didn't go there alone, because, even then, the old man had put up fierce resistance, kicking, hitting, and biting like a Molossian dog.

The Worm was dragged from the car, handcuffed and wrapped in a cloak that made him look like a highway bandit, with a workman's cap shoved so far onto his head that you could barely see his eyes. They almost had to carry him to the squad's offices, for in order to defend themselves, Cruni and the two officers accompanying him had been forced to hit him so hard that the Worm could hardly stand, let alone walk.

He fell on the chair and remained there, gazing at his captors like a chained animal. De Vincenzi shuddered. He had never seen so much hate in a man's eyes.

"Take his hat off," he told Cruni.

The portrait painted by the sacristan was fairly accurate. He was an ugly specimen of the human race. His gray hair was ruffled over his head, his mustache was gray and drooping, his nose was crushed on one side, and his mouth was toothless and crooked.

"What's your name?" asked the inspector.

He answered with a grunt.

"Take his fingerprints."

Sani and Cruni took them, without removing his handcuffs.

"Go wake up the archivist. I want to know his name before we leave here tonight."

Cruni, who was limping a little because he had been kicked by the old man, took the sheet of paper with the man's ten blue fingerprints—they had used the ink used for the official stamps for this purpose—and left.

De Vincenzi was looking at the man and wondered what grotesque and horrible circumstances had gotten him involved in a story that clearly didn't have anything to do with him.

He had never thought that the old man had really murdered the senator and Norina, and now that he saw him, his conviction grew stronger. For no reason in the world, would the senator have consorted with such a person, much less enter a bookstore with him in the middle of the night. And the Senator certainly would not have turned his back on him and let him shoot him in the head!

Moreover, why would such an obviously alcoholic—and probably illiterate—beast have pilfered a rare book from the 16th century?

But if he was not the killer, it might still be true that he had found the senator's hat and the girl's overcoat.

"Did you find anything in the hay?" he asked the two officers who had accompanied Cruni.

"The sergeant searched the area," one of them answered, "but there was nothing. . ."

"Go get Panzeri from the guardroom."

The agent left.

On the chair, the old man began to close his eyes, as if he wanted to sleep.

"You won't be able to make him talk, not even flogging him," said Sani.

"I think so too!" De Vincenzi exclaimed. "But even if he spoke, he couldn't tell us much!"

The sacristan came in, with his absurdly gray face and those swampy eyes.

"It's him," he said immediately, as soon as he saw the old man.

"I know. Who else could he be?"

The Worm opened his eyes. He looked at the informer with a sudden flash of recognition. Then he started gnashing his teeth and squirming furiously on the chair.

"Villain! Spy!" he roared.

The sacristan backed away, frightened, raising his hands as if to protect himself.

"Don't be afraid. He's handcuffed. Repeat in front of him what you said to me!"

The man repeated the story for the third time, again using the same exact words. The Worm seemed not to be listening to him.

De Vincenzi approached him and shook him.

"Have you heard? He accused you of murdering Senator Magni and Norina Santini!"

"He's a villain!" said the old man.

"But is it true?"

"He's a villain!"

"So, you're confessing it?"

For the third time, he repeated: "He's a villain!"

Cruni entered with the prisoner's rap sheet and handed it to De Vincenzi. "Here you are, sir."

It was massive. De Vincenzi flipped through it quickly.

"Well, you've been a busy boy! Your name is Francesco Ravizzani. You started your career in 1890 with an arrest for rape and from that day on you have been arrested and convicted countless times: ten convictions for rape, about forty for theft, assault, sedition. . ."

He raised his head and stared at the old man.

"But in sixty years, you have never killed anybody. Why did you do it this time?"

No reply. The man glanced at the sacristan, who was trembling.

Cruni approached De Vincenzi and said, lowering his voice, "Harrington is here, he asked if he could attend the interview."

"What are you waiting for?" De Vincenzi asked, and ordered the officers to put the old man in a cell. "Alone, of course. He mustn't see anyone."

"May I go?" asked Harrington's man, when the sergeant and the prisoner had left the room.

"Of course not! Where do you want to go now? The sergeant will give you a blanket and you can have a nice sleep."

The man's tremor became more pronounced.

"So, do you believe that I. . .?"

"I don't believe anything! By the way, no hat or overcoat were found."

"He must have burnt them."

"Sure. Goodnight!"

The inconceivable gray color of that face seemed to increase. The sacristan took a few steps toward the door, then came back. De Vincenzi pretended to ignore him; he sat at the desk, and only his hands were visible in the light of the lamp, sorting some sheets of paper. The rest of his body was in the dark. Sani was standing next to the desk, vaguely visible as a menacing black shadow. All the light was projected in the middle of the room, and in that bright circle, the sacristan seemed to be caught by a net of rays.

He was blinking.

"Because, if you mean to blame it on me. . ."

"You are responsible for what you have written and signed."

"I didn't get a penny to lie."

"You will prove this."

"At six o'clock there's the first mass. . .The parish priest will look for me. . ."

"Aren't you here doing a good deed?"

"I have to pour the wine in the ampoule and open the church."

He was stammering. If De Vincenzi had given him another push, he would have fallen. But De Vincenzi didn't want to.

"Did you know that Harrington is here?"

Instantly, the man stiffened.

"So, do you really want me to go sleep in a jail cell?"

"I told you."

"Ok, goodnight."

He left.

De Vincenzi went to the door.

"Harrington, come in."

The detective quickly moved away from his man, who had stopped to talk with him, and went toward the inspector. In the meantime, the courtyard door closed behind the sacristan.

Harrington was wearing all his jewelry, worse than a courtesan. He blinked in the light of the lamp. The diamond on his tie and those on his fingers gave red flashes of light. He was short, with a malicious face that telegraphed his great unease.

"I sent for you at eleven this morning and you show up at midnight!"

"I am extremely busy, *Cavaliere*! I barely have time to breathe!

166

Moreover, I had sent Panzeri to you. He knows this matter better than I do! He did a good job, didn't he?"

"Sit down, Harrington. I think our interview will be quite long."

The man blinked again and shielded his eyes with his jeweled hand.

"This is like a car's headlight, inspector!"

"When you sit down, it won't bother you anymore."

The detective grimaced, not at all persuaded, and sat down.

"Who asked you to find the senator's killer?"

"No one, *Cavaliere*."

"Not a good start, Harrington!"

"Maybe not. It's the truth, however. What do you think? That for me it's not a matter of honor to be of some service to the police department, even without turning a profit?"

"Hmm. And you are convinced that human wreckage, that Worm, who lives in the shadows of the night, stealing a few chickens or whatever he happens to find in barnyards and farmhouses, was able to kill Senator Magni in the back rooms of an antique bookstore?"

"He probably killed him somewhere else and then carried him there! You must know the apartment building in Via Corridoni. . ."

"I know it. But the senator was killed inside the bookstore, not outside."

"How do you know that?"

"I know. Moreover, where is the revolver? You found the killer. . ."

"It wasn't me who found him, *Cavaliere!*" the detective protested suddenly. "Let me make this point clear. Panzeri came to me and said: 'I know the killer of Via Corridoni and the Darsena docks.' And I immediately alerted Inspector Roberti."

"Why did you go to him?"

"Because the Worm always wanders the areas of Carrobbio and Ticinese, and I wanted him to be arrested by the local police, before calling headquarters."

"Ah! How helpful. You wanted to prepare everything for me, did you?"

"What's wrong with that? It proves my scruples."

"Yeah. Now, let me resume. How would you explain that no hat, no overcoat and no revolver have been found?"

Harrington shook his hand in the air and his diamond shone in the light.

"They were hidden, or destroyed. He probably got scared after talking with Panzeri."

"An inveterate thief like Ravizzani doesn't destroy stolen goods, even if they are worth very little And as for the revolver. . ."

"You'll see, the revolver will be found, *Cavaliere!*"

De Vincenzi frowned.

"Listen to me, Harrington!" he said slowly. "If you "find" the gun for me as well, I will put you in jail and leave you there for a long while."

The detective turned pale. He looked at the inspector with terror in his eyes.

"What do you mean, *Cavaliere?*"

"Exactly what I said."

"But. . . but how do you suppose that I. . .?" he sputtered indignantly.

De Vincenzi smiled affably.

"Come on. Harrington, tell me. For whom are you risking jail?"

"Jail? What are you talking about, *Cavaliere*? You offend me. Twenty years of honored service! Not a single incident. How can they complain, at this police station, about me and my agency? Just three days ago, I gave five hundred lire to charity!"

"When?"

"Three days ago. Do you want to see the receipt?"

"I believe you, Harrington. You are a noble philanthropist! But you still haven't told me. *Who asked you to find the killer three days ago?*"

"No one, for God's sake!"

"For God's sake? Why don't you say, 'Give me a break!', Harrington? All American detectives say 'Give me a break!'"

Harrington's face turned red. He was about to explode with indignation.

"Oh! How can you joke at a time like this! It's not professional!"

"Who said I'm not taking you seriously, Harrington? After all, your real name is Caputo, and if you chose Harrington, why wouldn't you want to appear even more American? 'Give me a break!' was just a suggestion!"

The detective stood up. He was livid. His lips were trembling.

He tried to project an aura of outraged indignation, but mostly, he just looked lost.

"Tomorrow, I'll go to the Superintendent! You're not treating me, a gentleman, properly. A gentleman who has done all he could to serve you, for the sole purpose of justice! It isn't right!"

"Calm down, Harrington! If you tell me who you are working for, I promise you won't get in trouble."

"I told the truth, *Cavaliere*! Why don't you believe me?"

De Vincenzi realized that he wouldn't have revealed the name even if he had been tortured, because that person had obviously paid him to be quiet. He probably asked for a considerable amount of money. And that secret, in his hands, was like gold, no question about it.

"All right. But if you make me put an innocent man in prison. . . if you have gathered this evidence against the Worm on purpose. . . you shall have to deal with me, Caputo, and I guarantee you that I'm not as nice as I look."

Harrington knew the inspector was not joking.

"I'm amazed!" he murmured. "The facts will prove me right. I never had the slightest doubt about Panzeri's truthfulness. He's a God-fearing man."

"We'll see. Perhaps I was wrong. Let us hope so, at least I hope so for you. And for the moment, I have nothing more to tell you. Goodbye!"

"Goodnight!" Harrington replied, remaining for a moment in the circle of light.

Then he turned and walked slowly toward the door.

"Harrington. . ." the inspector called in a soft voice.

"Yes?"

He stopped.

"Harrington, remember my advice. . . Don't come up with the gun."

Harrington shrugged and left.

De Vincenzi smiled. He felt more relieved now. He had recovered his manic fervor, the fervor he felt when approaching the truth. After three days of terrible indecision, he now knew he was on the right track. He smiled again. Which track? He didn't know anything yet! Not a name. Not one good clue. But it was exactly that absolute lack of clues what convinced him that he would find the criminal. The killer would be revealed through his own subtlety. The very fact of having staged all that comedy regarding the Worm was proof of it.

He got up, turned on the main light at the center of the ceiling and switched off the lamp that he used like a projector.

Sani appeared on the threshold.

"Well?"

"Things started to move."

"I know."

"Why?"

"Because you're back to normal!"

"I've had three bad days, Sani!"

"I noticed!"

"And I'll still have some awful ones, I can feel it!"

"It doesn't matter. You will succeed this time as well."

"I hope so!"

"I'm sure of it. Are you leaving?"

"Yes, I'm going to bed. Tomorrow, the day will begin early."

"Do you want me to come here early as well?"

"Yes, please. Thank you!"

He went out quickly, and when he was in the courtyard, illuminated by the brightness of the moon, he lit a cigarette.

Vincenzi smoked once a month, only on special occasions.

Chapter 16

The Superintendent walked nervously back and forth in his office. As the room was narrow and long, he had ample space for his agitated pacing.

The inspector stood against the closed door and watched his boss with quiet serenity.

De Vincenzi looked younger and fresher than usual. Spring, which had conspired to make the last mornings of March more playful and luminous than usual, dominated Piazza San Fedele which was laid out in all its splendor below the Superintendent's office balcony. Certainly, the changing of the season must be responsible for the inspector's flourishing appearance, for that look of resplendent joy that even the Superintendent's worried agitation could not dampen. What other explanation could there possibly be?

The rapid pacing had been going on for a few minutes. Now, the Superintendent suddenly stopped in the middle of the room, facing De Vincenzi. His small, penetrating eyes seemed to pierce the young man's impassive face.

"So, you would like to release Ravizzani, send him back to his farms and his thefts, just because you didn't find the hat and the overcoat! What about Panzeri's formal accusation? And the fact that the old man doesn't even deny having committed the crimes? And what about his *earlier crimes,* don't they count for anything?" The Superintendent paused, mastering his wrath.

"Do you know, De Vincenzi, how many dangerous suspects you've released into Milan's streets even in just the last four days? Let's count them, shall we? Dr. Verga... Miss Drury..."

"Oh, that woman!" De Vincenzi smiled.

"*That woman* indeed! That American woman is very clever, capable of deceiving any man. She's capable of killing not just one, but ten men like Senator Magni! And what about the maid's brother? And the porter of the apartment building in Via Corridoni and his wife? Don't you think they are enough? Not to mention that my list is probably incomplete. You disregard evidence. . . appearances. . . *earlier crimes.* You disregard motives. You observe people, question them, examine them, judge them with your *psychological method* and then set them free, having decided that they *cannot* be guilty, because they lack the moral, intellectual, temperamental, or emotional capacity to commit a murder, *this murder.* And now you want to release even this confirmed criminal, because he *doesn't have the moral capacity?* Where will we end up, De Vincenzi? Your obsession with the *psychology of murder* is madness!"

The inspector smiled. It was a good smile, full of affectionate respect, and it managed to somehow assuage his superior's anger.

"Do you know where we'll end up? Let me tell you: In a madhouse!"

And he smiled, too. He peered at the carnation in the buttonhole of his suit, and gave it a tap with his finger, to put it in place. He loved De Vincenzi. This didn't stop him, however, from thinking that the situation they were facing was very serious. He couldn't give him free rein to do anything he wanted. It was necessary, not just to encourage him, but, for his own good, to keep him on the path of pragmatism and common sense.

"You believe that what I'm telling you is all nonsense, don't you?"

"Not in the least, Superintendent!"

"I see! However, you will, of course, keep on doing exactly as you please. Oh, hell. You may be right, after all. But if you get it wrong this time, De Vincenzi, I won't forgive you! There will be consequences and they'll be out of my hands."

"I know! That's why I wouldn't arrest Ravizzani. . ."

He paused. He had just had an idea. What an idiot he had been, not to think of it before!

"Actually, sir, maybe you're right. Let me go call the judge and get the warrant signed. I'll send the Worm to the San Vittore prison before noon."

The Superintendent stared at him with immense suspicion. "What are you plotting, De Vincenzi?"

The inspector no longer smiled but was frowning intently.

"It's a horrible double crime, Superintendent. Especially the strangulation of the girl."

He lifted his head.

"Now, I'll tell you what I really think about all this. Of course, I don't believe that Ravizzani killed them, just as they were not killed by Dr. Verga, Miss Drury or the others that you mentioned. There is someone in the shadows, someone who has committed the two crimes and who has been able to make those shadows so thick that it's now very difficult to recognize him. Who is he? I don't know. I can suspect at least two people; but it's an extremely imaginative, even fantastic suspicion. But *there is someone*. And, of course, he is very much interested in sending someone else to prison. Indeed, he has done all he could to this purpose. So, if we pretend that we have fallen into his trap, if we put Ravizzani in prison at San Vittore, maybe we can convince the true killer to lower his guard. Who knows, then, what will happen?"

The Superintendent had listened carefully to him. After a pause, he shrugged.

"It may be that things are just as you suppose. Anyway, a few days in prison won't work any injustice on that old thief. . . in fact, I'm sure he deserves much worse!"

"As for that, I have no doubt!" said the inspector.

"So. . ." concluded the other.

De Vincenzi opened the door to leave but the Superintendent held his gaze.

"You asked me for eight days, and this is already the fourth."

"I told you, sir, on the eighth day I will come to give you my resignation."

"Nice consolation! All right, go!"

And he began pacing the room again.

De Vincenzi returned to his office, where Sani and Cruni were waiting for him.

He hurried through the first room, saying:

"Cruni, Sani, with me!"

The two men rushed to follow him. He had already picked up the phone receiver.

"Get me the instructing magistrate who's taking care of Magni's case. Do you know who he is? Good. Tell him this is an urgent matter."

Sani and Cruni looked at each other. What if, instead of sleeping that night, he had found the killer? De Vincenzi saw them and let them know he hadn't, energetically shaking his head. Then, putting his hand on the receiver, he said,

"I didn't find anything at all! But wait. You'll see!"

He took his hand off the receiver and spoke into it:

"Good morning, sir. No, no. . . The eight days haven't passed yet. . . Don't worry! However, today I need an arrest warrant for Francesco Ravizzani. He's out on parole, a recidivist. . . he was convicted about forty times. . . Of course, for the crime in Via Corridoni. . . Who? Him? Oh no! He's more innocent for those crimes than I am for original sin! I can't explain more by phone, but please trust me! The Superintendent gave me the OK. Well, you can say that he's accused of possession of objects belonging to two murdered people and, therefore, that he's the alleged killer. You'll see, in a couple of days you will have to release him. That's all! Thank you."

He hung up and looked at his loyal colleagues.

"Did you understand?"

"I understood," said Sani "that you're putting the Worm in prison knowing he is innocent."

"Yes. It's necessary. Cruni, go immediately to the public prosecutor, get the mandate and then come back here to take Ravizzani to San Vittore. But when you leave, take four officers with you and make sure you make a big scene, with handcuffs, police van and everything else. Let the journalists see everything. And if they ask you something, as they will, let them know, in the greatest confidence, that the prisoner is the alleged murderer of Magni. The more people know about it, the better."

"I understand, sir," said Cruni as he hurried off.

"And now it's your turn, Sani. You have to go to Harrington."

"To his agency!"

"Yes. Go to his agency, and treat him with the utmost respect. Tell him that last night I was tired and nervous. Tell him whatever you want, that my job wore me out, that I'm going crazy. It doesn't matter. In short, make him believe that we have fallen for his deception and that the judge sent Ravizzani to San Vittore as the perpetrator of the double killing."

"Do you believe that Harrington. . .?"

"Harrington knows nothing. It's imperative that his client believes that the investigation has come to an end, or is about to. Do you understand?"

"I get it. But who is his client?"

"Heh! If we knew that. . . What are you doing here?"

At the door, a guard had appeared.

"There is a lady who wants to speak to you, sir."

"What does she look like? Is she young? Blonde?"

"No, sir. She's middle-aged and brunette. Very beautiful, her face is white as a sheet. . . She appears to be in mourning."

De Vincenzi looked surprised.

"Let her in immediately."

The guard disappeared.

"It's the senator's widow! Why did she come all the way here?"

Sani went out to meet the visitor, let her into the inspector's room and closed the door behind her.

De Vincenzi stood waiting for her respectfully.

Mrs. Magni had raised the heavy widow's veil covering her beautiful face and slowly advanced, with a small smile on her red lips. She always looked like a great, matronly and aristocratic woman; but something in her, especially in her eyes, betrayed her anguish.

"I came here so that you wouldn't have to come to the house. . ."

De Vincenzi offered her a chair. She sat down. She laid her veil over her shoulders and leaned against the back of the chair in tired abandonment. But she immediately recovered and straightened up.

"I would have come to you again already, Madam, if I hadn't been afraid of upsetting you by my presence. Moreover, I couldn't, unfortunately, tell you anything new about the death of your poor husband."

"Still nothing?" she murmured in a sad, disappointed tone. "I thought so."

"And yet, we will find the killer, Madam!"

De Vincenzi sat at his desk and, though he pretended to be dealing with the documents in front of him, never took his eyes off her face.

"You're skeptical about the efficiency of police work."

"Oh no. I'm sure you do what you can. But the death of that poor girl. . . that horrible and monstrous crime… it almost killed me. I'm terrified myself! Who can be so cruel? A poor, innocent child! Why? Why?" she choked, biting back tears.

"Yes, it was horrible! But we will take revenge for your husband and

Norina! Do you have any idea why your maid might have been killed?"

"Me? How can I? I don't have the foggiest idea."

"We could assume," the inspector said with indifference, "that the poor senator was killed because he was keeping a secret, and had told Norina about it."

"But… what are you saying? He wouldn't tell a maid!"

There was so much disdain in her words that De Vincenzi understood that only her pride in her social position could have given that woman the strength to pretend for so long that she was happily married.

"What you are suggesting is insane!"

"I admit it. In fact, I never gave any weight to such a hypothesis. The reasons for killing your husband are different! Ah! If you could help us, telling us what the senator's habits were, the people he went around with, the relationships he had. . ."

Pulling back her head, she said with an icy voice and a glaring gaze:

"I ignored it! I've always ignored it!"

"Of course."

The inspector was playing with an ivory paper knife all stained with ink. He had now assumed the air of a good boy, mortified and almost anxious.

"This morning, the judge signed an arrest warrant."

The lady turned, breathing fast, her chest rising and falling under her crêpe, thin dress.

"Who? Who did they arrest?"

"A bad man, Madam. A man capable of anything. There is a witness who claims that he confessed to the two crimes. And it looks like he was seen hiding your husband's hat and the girl's overcoat."

"But then. . . who is this person? Why?"

"I told you, he's a common criminal. A thief. Until now he had never murdered. Nonetheless, he is quite capable of it."

"But my husband wasn't robbed!"

"Indeed!"

The lady went back to her detached apathy. Only for a moment she had seemed revived. It was clear that she didn't believe—no more than De Vincenzi did—that her husband had been killed in that way, by a common criminal.

"And I must confess, too, that it was not the police who found this man. . ."

"Who, then?"

"Now your skepticism about our efficiency will increase, Madam," he continued with a smile. "It was a private detective, his name is Harrington."

"Oh."

She had lowered her eyes. She seemed embarrassed.

"Do you know him?"

"He has an agency in Via Dante."

"Precisely!"

There was silence.

"Did you have a chance to meet him? He isn't a bad man; moreover, he is very competent. Of course, it only works if he is paid and I wonder who paid him this time. He didn't want to tell me."

The lady blushed slightly. A slight rose-colored shadow appeared on her ivory cheeks.

"I went to him. I was told he is a very competent man. I asked him to find my husband's killer and, because I was afraid that this might upset the Superintendent—and you—I told him not to reveal my name."

"I see!"

This time De Vincenzi had to make a great effort not to show the deep surprise caused by Mrs. Magni's revelation. So much for that idea! His hypothesis had just collapsed like a house of cards.

"No need to apologize. It was very understandable, Madam. We couldn't be and we are not annoyed by your actions!"

He was sincere, though, perhaps, he was protesting too much.

"And who suggested that you contact Harrington?"

"I don't remember! And in any case, it wasn't a real suggestion. We were talking and I was told that Harrington had found the criminal who had committed a theft in a jewelry. . ."

"In Via Santa Margherita?"

"Precisely! And he had found and recovered the stolen goods."

"In fact!"

"So, later, I thought about it and I decided to call him."

"Sure. And you really don't remember who told you about Harrington?"

"No. Let me think about it. . . What can I say, so many people came to see me in the last few days… I could have done without all the company! No, I really can't remember. Is it important?"

"No. Not important at all!" De Vincenzi said quickly, even if it was of the utmost importance to him.

"And this man… this man that you arrested, did he confess? If it really was him, he must have been sent by someone."

"A criminal for hire. Yes. If it was him, he's just a hired killer."

The woman stood up.

"Poor Ugo!" she murmured.

Then she shook her head as if to shake off a nightmare.

De Vincenzi approached her. She gave him her hand and the inspector bent to kiss it. 'He has a gentleman's habits,' his colleagues used to say, teasing him behind his back.

"Don't tell Harrington that I mentioned him. I shouldn't have insisted that he kept this secret."

"Certainly. And forgive me, Madam, if I'm being pushy. . . could you tell me how much money you gave to Harrington for his investigation? Forgive me, but we always ask about this because we try to keep an eye on private detective agencies."

"Not much, especially if it really brought results. Two thousand lire."

"A fair amount. Thank you."

He accompanied her to the door, escorted her through Sani's office and from there to the porch. He bowed and watched her walking cross the sunny courtyard.

He walked back slowly, ignoring Sani, who followed him with a look full of questions. He returned to his room and closed the door.

So, Harrington would have put at risk his position, possibly having his license revoked—or worse—for two thousand lire?

Absurd! Yet, that woman wasn't a liar. And even if she were, there was no reason why she would.

Everything was up in the air again!

He had hoped that, as soon as he found out who had paid Harrington, he would know who had committed both crimes. Instead. . . nothing.

He went back to the door.

"Sani!" he called.

"This situation is inconceivable, my friend! I won't go through all the details, because then you'd be driven as crazy as I am, and we can't have that! I want you, at least, to be in your right mind. Listen. First of all, go to Harrington, as I told you. Then, I need Magni's driver to come here to my office, today in the afternoon. Obviously, I should send an officer to summon him, but I don't want to. I don't want his mistress or anyone else in the house to know that I asked to see him. Do you understand?"

"Easy enough!"

"That's why I'm sending you. Try to talk to him outside the house. Tell him what you think will be appropriate, as soon as you understand what makes him tick. You'll probably need to scare him or perhaps to flatter his vanity."

"I'll take care of it."

"Good. Ask him at what time he can come here without having his mistress or anyone else notice."

"All right."

"I'm not finished! Send an officer to ask Dr. Verga to come to my office this evening at ten o'clock. He should be asked with the utmost caution as well. Do you understand?"

"Yes. I'll ask him myself."

"Thank you, that's exactly what I hoped for."

"See you later, sir." said Sani.

De Vincenzi began to pace about the room.

He was about to put on his overcoat and pick up his hat when Cruni came in. The poor sergeant's face was very gloomy, as if he had been to a funeral.

"Well? What happened to you? Did you take him to the prison?"

"Oh yes! I brought him there. But we made a huge blunder, sir!"

"What do you mean?"

"When I handed Ravizzani to the prison director, he looked at him and then exclaimed: 'What's your problem? You can't stay away from us for more than three days? Your cot is still warm and now you're going inside again?' Then he turned to me, 'What did he do this time? The usual petty theft, isn't it?' 'Oh, no,' I told him, '. . . this time it's a serious matter. He murdered Senator Magni and Norina Santini. Look at the mandate.' The director started to read it, as if he didn't believe his eyes. 'But. . . when was the senator murdered?' he asked me. 'On the night between the 20th and the 21st.' Then the director passed his hands through his hair: 'What have you done?' 'What do you mean?' 'Well, you're getting sloppy. This man has a pretty good alibi.' 'How so?' "He was right here, in prison, until the morning of the 22nd. Here's the register. See for yourself!'"

Cruni had told his story all in one breath, in a dramatic tone.

De Vincenzi burst into laughter. "Excellent! This is a good one!"

"You're laughing?!"

"If I don't laugh now, when do you want me to laugh?!" He put his hat on.

"Come on, don't think about it. Everything's alright. A couple of days in jail won't harm the Worm! All is well, trust me!"

And he laughed again. He thought of the look on the Superintendent's face, when he informed him.

When he reached the door, he turned around.

"Is Panzeri still in jail?"

"Yes, inspector."

"Good. He will go to San Vittore in Ravizzani's place."

He went out, smiling. Life was good.

Chapter 17

When he was at the corner of Via Cappellari, De Vincenzi stopped to wait for the tram which would take him to the Sorbelli house with its spiritually-sensitive mother and overly-sensitive daughter.

For three days he could not decide whether he should go visit the medium. He had thought to have her come to his office, but it would have been useless. Both the woman and her daughter would certainly have come. They would both have displayed their repertoire of grandiose and sophisticated phrases and their exuberant vocabulary. In short, they would have gone through the whole pantomime, and nothing would have changed.

Also, he wanted to experience the environment in which they lived, to sample the atmosphere.

Going there at midday could be the right moment.

He got off the tram at the corner of Via Cosimo del Fante and immediately found the house, which was the third one toward Corso Italia.

It was one of those buildings from the beginning of the twentieth century, when—very briefly, thank God—the terrible Liberty style dominated with its curves and monstrous flourishes. The building still had a pretentious appearance, but had prematurely faded and crumbled. Inside, the entryway was too narrow, and the porter's glass door opened right onto the first steps of the staircase.

"The Sorbelli ladies?"

A noise of pans and the scuff of slippers, and then the woman appeared. Like the house, she looked prematurely faded, even though she could not yet have been forty.

"Third floor, first door. Are you looking for the daughter?"

"For both."

"There is only the mother. Her daughter is at school until twelve-thirty. Are you from City Hall?"

De Vincenzi closed the door and walked up the stairs. But the custodian ran after him.

"Wait! If you're going up for a consultation, you'd better come back after lunch. There are already people up there, and it's late."

The inspector turned around and descended the few steps he had taken.

"What kind of consultation?"

The woman seemed embarrassed.

"I don't know. . . I thought. . . But. . . anyway, who are you?"

"It doesn't matter who I am. Tell me about these consultations."

"Why? Go ask Mrs. Sorbelli, if you want to know!"

She disappeared through the door, which she closed firmly behind her. De Vincenzi had the urge to follow her. But he didn't. After all, it was better not to make her suspicious by asking specific questions. It was easy for him to imagine what "consultations" were. The medium, with her distinguished air of an impoverished noble woman, perhaps was also a fortune teller or something similar. He was pleased with the discovery, if that was the case. What he had to ask for would now be easier to obtain.

On the stairs he met two elegant ladies coming down. He had to lean against the wall, to let them pass. They stared at him as they passed. A scent of perfume enveloped him. It was the scent of people who had money to waste having their fortunes told using cards or coffee grounds. When they had reached the lower landing and had disappeared, he heard them laugh.

On the third floor, he immediately saw the brass plate with the name written in italics, in black letters, no capitals: *"wanda sorbelli."*

"Clever!" thought De Vincenzi as he reached for the bell.

But before he could ring, the door opened.

"It's too late!" Mrs. Sorbelli began to say, but she recognized him and smiled, feigning cheerfulness.

"Oh! Inspector! Please come in to our humble abode."

Her tone had immediately become sophisticated and slightly pretentious, but she had turned pale and was panting slightly. She moved aside to let him in.

The foyer was like that of any bourgeois house.

"This way, sir."

She had regained her distinction and that great lady's air, which had puzzled De Vincenzi from the first.

There were three doors. She opened the one in front of them. A dining room with light, honey-colored wood furniture, thick with inlay. In the middle of the table, a crystal vase with some withered carnations.

The inspector looked around quickly. On the sideboard he saw a plate of meat, apparently from the day before, and bread still wrapped from the baker's. Certainly, it was not the consultation room and the woman clearly preferred to show him something other than cards and coffee grounds.

"Please sit down."

She took the meat dish and made it disappear into the sideboard. She threw the bread into a drawer.

Then she went to sit by the other corner of the table, at his side, and turned the chair so she could see his face.

"Tell me what I can do to help you. I'm sorry my daughter is out. But if you'd like to wait, she'll be back soon. She finishes her lessons at twelve-thirty, and it only takes her a few minutes to arrive home."

De Vincenzi was silent. He was embarrassed and would have preferred that the porter had not spoken to him about consultations. On his way there, on the tram, he had decided how to proceed.

He thought he had known where to start but now he wasn't sure any longer. The woman's split personality was upsetting him. How could someone with her musical, vibrant voice and her sophisticated, genteel air *tell fortunes?*

Mrs. Sorbelli, faced with his long silence, began to look at him with an air of puzzlement. Suddenly, a shadow of fright passed over her face.

"Is there something new? Tell me! I read in the newspapers that the maid was killed too!"

She was almost shouting.

"So! You are here for this!"

"Eh? For this what?" De Vincenzi asked.

"Because you believe I know more than I said in your office."

Though taken off guard, De Vincenzi was never one to miss his cue. "Do you really know more?"

"Of course not! How could I? When I saw you at the door, I didn't recognize that you were a police inspector. Let me explain. . . I called you "inspector," but it didn't occur to me that this might be an official visit. It seems odd, but in my mind, you were an ordinary visitor, even a friend."

"In other words, a customer," De Vincenzi insinuated. He had begun to regain his composure.

She grew silent, stricken and pretended not to understand.

"A customer?" she asked, stiffening.

"Forget I said anything."

"I don't think so! You clearly have something in mind. You are referring to some concrete suspicion. Why do you want to play cat and mouse? You have been silent and staring ever since you entered. Enough. Out with it! Do you think I'm hiding some great secret?"

"Not really a great secret, perhaps. . ."

"But. . . Come on! Tell me!"

"A small, tiny secret."

"Ah."

They observed each other warily. Stalemate. Neither of them wanted to speak first. She was afraid to say too much. He was afraid she would say too little. The inspector was hoping that the woman would betray herself. After all, he was walking in the dark, driven only by his own intuition.

"Could you tell me why you honored me with your visit?"

Her golden voice had become cold, almost imperious. De Vincenzi placed his hand on the table with his palm facing upward.

"Do you want to read my life?"

It was a matter of an instant. Her flaccid, pale face crumbled. Her eyes became imploring. Two tears flowed down her cheeks.

"You know?" she murmured. "That's why you came! I beg you, don't ruin me. Or rather, do what you must, but don't let my daughter know about it! If I didn't get a license, if I didn't register with the police, it wasn't to hide. After all, I sincerely believe in palmistry as in all the magical arts. What I say and do is something I am compelled to do. I'm moved by a superior force. I swear to you! But I didn't want my Tina to know about it! You heard how she got angry at me for attending the spiritist sessions! No! Don't tell her! I would die, you have to believe me, I would die of shame!"

She sobbed, as white as a sheet. "Dear God, she's probably got some heart condition, too!" thought De Vincenzi, who began to fear he'd soon have yet another unconscious woman on his hands.

"No! I won't tell her! It doesn't matter. Calm yourself!"

He looked around franticly.

Sure enough, the woman seemed about to faint. She raised her hand and gestured at the closet. The inspector rushed over and opened all the doors before he finally found some water and made her drink. She kept crying.

"I will never tell your daughter," De Vincenzi said earnestly. "Please. Calm down."

Finally the woman calmed, convinced by his firm tone.

"It's passed," she murmured in a soft voice. "I'm much better now."

A very sensitive temperament! Anyone who wanted to use hypnosis or magnetism on her, could make her do anything, reflected De Vincenzi. She wouldn't even know what she had done.

De Vincenzi's brain began to work feverishly.

Did they use the power of suggestion to make her predict Magni's death? In that case, they were trying to make the senator worry, perhaps to induce him to do something which would make the murder's work that much easier.

"Will you really keep this secret from my daughter?"

"Of course."

"Thank you!"

"But I have something to ask you in return."

The woman's eyes became hard.

"Yes. I'm ready for anything to avoid causing pain to Tina. She doesn't know that her salary and my pension aren't enough, that they don't suffice! My poor husband used to gamble, he left many debts. I chose to pay them without letting Tina know, because I want her to have a good memory of her father. Do you understand? I started almost as a joke, with friends. Then I got paid for it. My clients come only in the hours when my daughter is at school. I warned the porter not to let anybody come here when Tina is at home."

That was the reason why the porter had asked him if he was going for a consultation. It had to be the truth, indeed, it was certainly the truth.

"But you'll keep this quiet. You won't tell anyone, will you?"

De Vincenzi shook his head.

"And will you let me continue?"

"Until others find out. I have no interest in your fortune telling. Consider me completely unaware of it."

"Oh! Thank you! Thank you!" she exulted. But again, her eyes hardened.

"So, what do you want from me? What can I do for you? Is it perhaps. . .?"

The inspector nodded, gravely.

"But I don't know anything!"

"It doesn't matter. But if I ask you to attend a spiritist session for me, with some of my friends, will you do it?"

She looked upset.

"I don't understand!"

Perhaps she feared a trap.

"Do you want to test me?"

"Not in the least. I don't doubt you."

He got up. The woman grabbed his hand.

"Remember, you promised me!"

She was pitiful. She had lost all her pride. For a moment, De Vincenzi had the fear that she would kiss his hand. Quickly, he withdrew it.

"Don't worry! I'm a gentleman."

He never used that phrase, which he abhorred, because men who made such claims usually were not gentlemen. But he felt that, with this woman, dramatic words, as well as theatrical gestures, were required.

The bell rang. Two or three consecutive rings.

"It's my daughter! What will you tell her, to explain your presence?"

She stood up, eagerly awaiting the answer before going to open the door.

"I'll interview your daughter, too. Our investigation is ongoing. Your daughter can't possibly be surprised."

"True!"

But she didn't seem completely persuaded. She crossed the foyer unsteadily.

"Tina, the inspector is here. He wants to ask us some more questions."

"Has he already talked to you?"

"We have exchanged a few words. He just arrived."

"Good morning, inspector. Still inquiring about spiritism?"

She was even smaller, more insignificant, and more evanescent than the first time De Vincenzi had seen her. Perhaps because of her gray dress, with the white collar, her short skirt that showed thin and bony legs, black socks and low-heeled and square tipped shoes. Underneath her small, dark hat, her dull face seemed to be flat and blank.

The inspector bowed, looking at her.

"Correct!"

A flash of anger suddenly passed over the girl's face.

"Was my mother taken ill?" she asked, pointing at the carafe of water and the glass on the table. She stared at De Vincenzi in reproach. "What did you do to her?"

"I'm fine, Tina. And the inspector was very kind."

"What do you want from me?"

She was not aggressive. Only bitterly resigned.

She suddenly realized she was still carrying a book and some report cards in her black-gloved hands, so she placed them on the table. De Vincenzi coughed.

"I would like you to try and remember who came here, last Saturday, to invite your mother to the Circle in Via Broletto."

The girl looked at her mother, who was standing in the doorway.

"Didn't you tell him?"

"He didn't ask me."

"Apparently, he wanted to ask me," she said, always with that tone of calm resignation. "It was Mr. Chirico. He came on Friday night, just before dinner."

"What did he say?"

"I don't know. I certainly don't remember his exact words!"

"Did he insist? Did he seem to attach particular importance to that session?"

"No more than the other times. He was always insistent, especially when I was present, because he knew I didn't like that kind of thing."

"And did your mother go to Via Broletto alone?"

"I couldn't go with her. On Saturday afternoons there is always educational cinema and I have to take the children."

"When your mother came back from the sitting, did she tell you anything special about it?"

"Poor Mom!" But in her compassion there was a bit of blame, almost contempt. "When she comes back from one of those sessions, she can barely eat before going to sleep. She went to bed right away that night, she was so exhausted. I brought her something to eat in bed."

"And the next day, when she felt strong again, did she mention the prophecy she had made during her trance?"

"No. I heard it for the first time when you did, in your office. But I wouldn't have been shocked if she had told me. I don't believe in spiritism."

"Not even that your mother has the gifts of a medium?"

"It doesn't matter. We are in the field of hypnosis and suggestion, in my opinion. My mother is very impressionable, like a child."

She always had that air of compassion without indulgence. It was easy to imagine that she was the mistress of the house. And she was probably quite strict in imposing her own will.

"Thanks, Miss. That's all."

He bowed again. Her mother was waiting for him in the foyer.

At the door of the dining room, the girl called him back.

"Inspector!"

"Yes?"

"In case this might be of interest to you, I will never allow my mother to go to the Circle in Via Broletto again."

"I think you are right to do that, Miss, since you genuinely believe that your mother's health suffers from these visits."

The mother opened the door and, as he left, whispered:

"You can count on me! But you must keep your promise!"

"I'll let you know. Thank you."

And he went quickly down the stairs. While passing, he saw the porter spying on him with disapproval from behind the glass door.

He went out into the street, lost in thought. The swirl of impressions he had received during his visit were slowly slotting themselves into place. He couldn't say why, but he knew he was approaching the center of the mystery. What threads connected this mother and daughter and the senator's death? One thing was for sure, it had nothing to do with money. There was something more mysterious, more ethereal, that tied them together. Something that even the people connected by these threads didn't fully understand.

As he walked, the trams passed in front of him, without stopping; they were crowded, crammed with people: employees, sales clerks, typists.

He walked down Corso Italia slowly. At home, his maid Antonietta was waiting to serve him lunch. As usual, it would be cold before he got there. He would call to let her know that he wouldn't be home after all. But when he found a phone near a tobacconist, he called the San Fedele police station instead of his house. He asked for Sani.

"Any news?"

"I did as you asked. At 2 p.m., the driver will be here."

"Thank you. Anything else?"

"Dr. Verga hasn't gone to Viale Bianca Maria in three days."

"And the nurse. . . the American lady?"

"She did go. She's the one who's taking care of the surgery. Of course, the patients are almost all gone, now that the professor is dead."

"Send Cruni to Verga's home in Via Leopardi. Have him bring the doctor to me, at the police station, this afternoon."

"All right."

"Thank you. Ah! Please, phone my house. Tell Antonietta I'm not going home for lunch. I'm afraid to call myself. She'll shout at me."

"Sure. I'll call immediately. I'll apologize for you and tell her that you're having lunch with the Superintendent."

"Do as you like. But she's heard the Superintendent excuse before. Ciao!"

He left the tobacconist and went through Piazza Missori to Via Carlo Alberto.

Crossing Piazza del Duomo, he realized that it was one o'clock. He normally had modest habits; however, almost without realizing it, he turned into the Galleria Vittorio Emanuele and entered Café Biffi, one of the most expensive restaurants in Milan. He sat in the last room, where there were fewer people. He ordered what the waiter suggested.

"Wine?"

"Mineral water."

The waiter left.

"Are you a teetotaler, Inspector? A little alcohol is good for your health!"

He turned. At the table next to him was Dr. Marini, who smiled at him with exuberant cheerfulness and expansive friendliness.

"I'm a doctor. Trust me!" said Marini as he saluted De Vincenzi with his beer mug.

"Do you always have lunch here?"

"Me? No. But I sent my wife to the countryside. She's in poor health. So, if I don't want to starve, I eat wherever I happen to find myself at the moment. Today, it's here."

"Ah! Is your wife sick?"

"Not seriously. Women's problems. A change of scenery usually does the trick."

"You have no children, do you?"

"No."

The waiter served De Vincenzi.

"Virgilio, the gentleman is a friend of mine. Take that away, and bring him the plate of the day, instead. Take my advise, Inspector! When you come here, always order the plate of the day."

Virgilio, surprised, watched De Vincenzi, uncertain of what to do. The inspector took the plate out of his hands and put it in front of him. "Next time. I'm in a hurry today."

Marini shook his head. Then, as if he had a sudden idea, he leaned toward De Vincenzi and asked, lowering his voice:

"Any new developments?"

"Maybe."

"Is it true there was an arrest?"

"It's true."

"So you have a good lead on the killer, then?"

"I hope so."

De Vincenzi was laconic, but not rude. In fact, he seemed open to being indiscreet.

The doctor turned to his fruit salad and chased the last piece at the bottom of the cup with his spoon. He drank the remaining maraschino, wiped his mouth and got up.

"May I?" he asked, grabbing an empty chair at De Vincenzi's table.

"Yes, please."

"You know, I'm usually not a curious person. But the fear that Ugo wouldn't be avenged has been torturing me!"

"And the other one?" De Vincenzi asked, looking at him.

"The other one?"

"The maid, Norina."

"Yes, of course. A horrible thing! But Ugo was my friend. We loved each other."

"Did you know that the autopsy found the girl was pregnant when she died?"

"Oh!"

He had turned pale. For a few moments, he didn't speak.

De Vincenzi ate, surreptitiously watching him.

Lunch was over and the room had emptied. The waiter changed the plate and put the fruit basket on the table.

"Would you like coffee?"

"Yes."

"Spirits?"

"No."

The cigar seller passed and offered them a copy of the afternoon edition of the *Corriere della Sera*.

Finally, they were alone.

"It's monstrous!" the doctor murmured.

"What? The fact that she was pregnant or that the murderer strangled her and threw her into the water at the docks?"

"But then. . ." he stopped.

"But then what?"

"She, like the others, was in love with him too!"

"Apparently."

"Are you sure it wasn't a suicide? That would explain everything!"

"Except for the fact that strangling yourself is a neat trick, yes."

There was another silence.

"And the person you arrested. . .?"

"An old thief, who apparently betrayed himself, trying to sell the hat of the dead man and the coat of the girl. . ."

"Idiot."

"Indeed."

"And how did you find him?"

"Ah," De Vincenzi said, smiling. "I can't take the credit for that. Nor the police. One of Harrington's men found him."

"The private detective?"

"Yes."

"The one who found the jewel thieves of Via Santa Margherita?"

"Right!" the inspector said, bending over to pick up a napkin that had fallen. The napkin seemed difficult to locate as De Vincenzi remained with his face hidden under the table for quite some time.

When he got up, he drank his coffee quickly and called the waiter to pay the bill.

"If you allow me, I'll pay your bill with mine. The other night you paid for both, at the coffee shop."

"It isn't the same thing. But thank you!"

They went out together. The Galleria was full of bustling people. Only at the center were there the usual group of people, chatting quietly. The tables at the *Biffi* and *Savini* restaurants were emptying.

De Vincenzi turned into the Manzoni passageway and headed toward Piazza della Scala at the end of the Galleria. The doctor walked beside him.

"Do you think it's all over?"

"All over?"

"I mean, you caught the killer. . ."

"Yeah."

"Did he confess?"

"He doesn't talk, not even to deny his involvement."

"But he must be a hired killer, no?"

"Naturally."

"And the instigator?"

De Vincenzi stopped in the middle of the square, in front of the Da Vinci monument.

"What would be your hypothesis, doctor, as a friend of the deceased?"

"I told you already that I wouldn't know who could have hated him enough to want to kill him. Jealousy? Envy? It's not enough to hire a killer!"

"True. Someone like that would act impulsively. So. . .?"

"I don't know. I'm lost. You ask for a hypothesis? There could be many. For example, a woman seeking revenge."

"Here, too, we are talking of passions."

"You're right!"

He started, then stared at De Vincenzi.

"What if it was that maid's brother? The newspapers said he was a previous offender. Someone like that would know how to contract out a murder."

"And he would have his sister killed after avenging her?"

"The girl could have discovered something and threatened to talk. A woman in love is always dangerous."

"Your hypothesis is subtle," De Vincenzi said gravely as he began walking in the direction of the police station. "I'll think about it. You see, you were, indeed, able to help me! Too bad you disappeared for so many days."

"Ah!" the doctor said, widening his arms. "If you knew. . . I didn't have a moment's peace."

"But your night walks, you still have time for them, don't you?"

"Yes, but you spend your nights closed up in the police station! You work. I didn't dare to disturb you."

"Come when you like. It will always be a pleasure. Also, I haven't abandoned the idea of the spiritic sitting. You know that I am converting to your beliefs? *There is a whole world around us that we know nothing about!*"

"Oh!" exclaimed the doctor. "Those who are satisfied only with what they have, are satisfied with very little!"

"Well, why don't you help me, too, not to be satisfied with what I have?"

Marini was silent, his gaze was fixed.

His usually rosy face had whitened. His lower lip trembled slightly.

De Vincenzi waited.

Finally, Dr. Marini spoke. His voice was hard, metallic, though low and almost choked. It almost sounded as if he were talking to himself.

"It has been ten years since I became involved in spiritism, deeply convinced that there is another invisible world and that it's possible for men to communicate with it. Believing in spiritism means believing in the survival of the soul after the body, in its individuality after death and hence in its immortality. *Those who leave us can come back.* Since then, I have had no other converts to my faith but one. It was Magni. Today, Ugo is dead. . . Murdered. And I won't risk the same experience with someone else!"

De Vincenzi laughed.

"You can't believe that the senator died because he dedicated himself to spiritism!"

"No. But I'm superstitious. Things that appear to others as absurd, comical or grotesque often mean something different to me. But that's me. Just ignore what I said."

He offered his hand to the inspector.

"And now I go to see my patients, who have no interest in understanding the afterlife and rely on my efforts to keep it that way."

His usual joviality had returned.

"Goodbye. I will surely come see you one of these nights. But we won't talk about spiritism. One shouldn't speak of it lightly, and to speak of it seriously, one must be in a state of grace. Trust me!"

He moved away quickly and disappeared down Via Agnello.

De Vincenzi entered the San Fedele police station, repeating to himself the words that the doctor had uttered in a moment of almost hallucinatory meditation, *Those who leave us can come back.*

Sani approached him, saying, "Cruni is here with that Pietro Santini. He came in voluntarily and he wants to talk to you."

"Let him in," said the inspector, entering his office and hanging his overcoat and hat on the stand in the corner.

Chapter 18

As he waited for Norina's brother, De Vincenzi glanced at the closet in which the four surgical instruments and the white coat were locked—the cotton of the latter was too common to belong to Professor Magni. *"The Professor's lab coats are made of pure linen. Using precious materials in his surgical instruments was one of his conceits."*

That remained a mystery. *"Please deliver to the police station."*

Who owned those tools and that coat? And why did he send them to him?

"Come in!"

The young man entered with his characteristic stride, walking as if he were on a fashion catwalk. He was no longer the wild young man he had been when they had brought him in, tied up with his own belt. He wore the uniform of his debaucherous calling: his trousers were too wide, the jacket tight at the waist, a gray silk shirt with pink and white wide striped tie.

His elusive glance met for an instant with that of De Vincenzi, who was staring at him.

"Did you want to talk to me?" asked De Vincenzi.

"Yes. About *her*."

"Sit down."

He sat, pulling his trousers at the knees.

"Well? What's up? Have you discovered something useful?"

"I don't know, they said that you have arrested an old man, that he was found with Magni's hat and Norina's coat."

"So?"

"I don't know about the hat. . . But the coat. . . I gave it to the Worm myself so that he could sell it."

He spoke in a low, raspy voice, with a sing-song rhythm betraying his Tuscan origins and made all the more noticeable by his obvious agitation.

"Explain."

"Norina came to look for me at my home on Tuesday afternoon, around six o'clock. I told you, when you asked me about that night. Surely you remember!"

"Go on."

"I wasn't there. I was in my patron's shop. You must have verified my alibi, since you didn't arrest me. So, Norina spoke to the porter. She told her that she would come back later, later that night, before she locked up, and she left her coat there, because she was hot—that's what the porter told me—and she still had to run several errands around town."

"And you. . .?"

"I had been very upset for two days. The porter had given me the coat, but I had ignored it. I had left it in my bedroom. . . Eventually, I realized that my girlfriend had commandeered it and was flaunting it to her friends. I tore it off her. Seeing her wear it made me sick to my stomach. I just couldn't bear it so I gave it to the Worm and told him to sell it."

"Anything else?"

"No."

"Why did you come to tell me?"

"Because it was not the old man who strangled her. And I want you to find who killed her."

"All right. If you don't know anything else, you can leave."

The man got up and went out slowly.

So that was how he got it! Panzeri had actually seen the coat in the hands of the Worm and, starting from that clue, he had invented the story of the hat and everything else. It was clear; but it didn't explain much. That the Worm was innocent, he already knew.

Sani came to tell him that the senator's driver had arrived.

"It's two o'clock."

"All right. Let him in."

A young man came in, the same one who had opened the door to him at Magni's house the second time the inspector had been there. But, without his bottle green uniform, he exuded a studied and pretentious elegance, something between a barber's apprentice out for a night on the town and a manual worker in his Sunday best.

"I came without anyone knowing," he said, nonchalantly advancing toward the inspector's desk, "just as you asked."

"Sit down."

He sat down.

"Did you always drive when the senator went out by car?"

"All the time. The master knew how to drive, but he only did it rarely and only in the countryside. And even then, I would accompany him."

"So you can tell me where he's been?"

The young man smiled.

"I've been in the senator's house for three years. How can I remember all the places we went to?"

"Don't be silly! I didn't ask you for all the places. I'll ask you precise questions."

De Vincenzi's voice sounded harsh. The driver became serious and nodded.

"I'll tell you what I can."

"No one asks you for more. And you are obliged to do so."

He wanted him to understand that there was no complicity between them. The fatuous smile with which he had said he had come without anyone knowing had annoyed De Vincenzi. It was presumptuous, as if the young man were trying to be too familiar with him.

The target of his displeasure began to feel uncomfortable and squirmed in his chair.

"Senator Magni used to go out almost every night. Did he always use the car?"

"Sometimes, not always."

"And where did he go?"

"If he used the car, he went to the theater or to some restaurant, either in our area or on the outskirts of town."

"To the Sempioncino restaurant?"

"Almost never. He preferred to go somewhere in Monza. Sometimes farther."

"By himself?"

The young man hesitated. He had been paid for his silence. But now his employer was dead . . .

"This is an official inquiry. You are required to answer my questions. And there are two corpses to be reckoned with."

"When he went to restaurants or hotels, he was never alone."

"Always with the same lady?"

"*Rarely* with the same lady."

"So one-night stands?"

"Yes. . . it seems to me. . . but not the kind of women you might be thinking of."

"Don't try to guess what I'm thinking. Tell me what you know."

"I told you. Not prostitutes."

"All right. So, you said that he had different companions. But was there a favorite? Perhaps his real lover?"

"Not in the evening."

"When?"

"In the afternoon. From three to six. Some days, he asked me to take him to the hospital first, but he would only stay for a few minutes before leaving again."

"Where did you take him?"

"He had a small apartment."

"Give me the address."

"Close to the park. . . on Via Abbondio San Giorgio."

"Number?"

"18, on the ground floor."

"And in that particular apartment, always the same. . . lady?"

"Yes. At least, recently. Earlier, many."

"Three months? Four months?"

"Maybe six months. It started in October, I believe."

"How can you be sure it was always her?"

"I had to take her back home. Of course, she got out of the car some distance from her house."

"Where?"

"Where she lived exactly, I don't know. She got out in Piazzale Tonoli and I saw her taking Viale Dei Mille."

De Vincenzi was startled. A strange tension had taken hold of him, as if he could sense his quarry just in front of him. To hide his agitation, he became rude. He was sorry he had to investigate the intimate life of a dead man like this. But there was nothing for it. It had to be done.

"Do you know who she was?"

"No!" replied the young man, too hastily, and the inspector didn't insist, although he was sure he was lying.

"It doesn't matter. And when the senator went to these appointments, did he take precautions? For example, did he ever seem afraid of being followed?"

"I don't think so. Only, he ordered me to take the *tangenziale*, the ring road, when I went to Piazzale Tonoli from Via Abbondio San Giorgio. An endless trip."

"And how did the Senator get home?"

"Sometimes he walked, or took a taxi. Other times, I went back to pick him up with the car."

"The keys to the apartment?"

"The porter. Neither he nor the lady had keys."

"And before. . . before six months ago, was the lady always the same?"

"For a while. Then she changed. He also had two in the same period. Of course, on different days."

Those details made De Vincenzi more and more uncomfortable, almost ashamed.

He cut the interview short.

"Nothing else. You may go."

The driver, surprised by the sudden dismissal, stood up.

"If you need me. . ."

"I doubt it. Out."

The young man left quickly, unsettled by the sudden change in the inspector's behavior.

De Vincenzi was pensive. What an awful, repugnant comedy was life! He, was, in the end, both a romantic and a puritan. A wife's betrayal hurt him, just as if he had been betrayed himself. If he were sitting on a jury, he would absolve all husbands of crimes of passion. Except in this case, he thought immediately, because there was also the corpse of that poor girl. There could be no forgiveness for that. It was just too monstrous.

He got up and put on his overcoat and hat.

On his way out the door, he glanced out his window and stopped. He looked at the tree that was sprouting its new spring leaves, in the courtyard, beyond the dirty railing. He longed for the countryside. So much purity! His mind held a strange mix of discordant, even opposing, feelings. On one hand, his spirit wanted to immerse itself into that life, yet at the same time, he rejected the confinement of its simplicity. No one who had seen him act, had heard him speak, with his sharp, mathematical precision, and his biting, implacable logic, would have suspected that his soul was that of a child and a poet.

A noise next door made him start, as if he had been caught doing something wrong. He left hurriedly.

"I'll be back in an hour. Maybe earlier."

"What if Dr. Verga arrives?" Sani shouted at his back.

"Don't let him leave."

In the square, in the spring sun, the pigeons were sunning themselves on the monument to Manzoni.

De Vincenzi got into a cab and gave the address of Via Abbondio San Giorgio, 18. Without thinking, he lowered his voice to talk to the driver. It seemed to him that everyone would soon understand why he was going there. For him it was as if he was about to betray a personal secret, more than a professional one.

If it is true that *"those who leave us come back,"* he thought morosely, I'll find his spirit there, trying to stop me from entering the apartment!

Why was he seeing the excessively red lips and the white face of the widow in her mourning clothes, with her chest rising and falling under her crêpe dress?

And why did he hear the voice of Chirico, that bilious and withered little man, the owner of the blood-stained bookstore, intoning, *"There is a whole world around us that we know nothing about"*?

Then, Pat's strangely voluptuous body came to his mind, as he had seen her leaning on the marble table of Magni's surgery, with her head tilted back ever so slightly and an ambiguous smile on her supple lips hiding her healthy, pearly teeth.

And then Norina's naked body, still throbbing, though inanimate, with her throat marked by her killer's strangling hands.

A parade of ghosts, both of the living and the dead.

Fioretta Vaghi, with her anonymous call and her sobbing concern for the lover that had spurned her was the first piece of the puzzle. The medium, who worked as a fortune teller to pay the debts of her gambling husband. The diminutive teacher who, under her appearance of cynical resignation, hid an iron will. Dr. Marini, who believed in the afterlife, to the point of affirming that the dead return. . .

Shadows or creatures made of flesh and blood?

Fruits of his imagination or real people?

In his mind, he could see a picture of all of these people surrounding the dead senator, present, but strangely out of focus, viewed through the hazy filter of a crime committed with both cautious subtlety and wild imagination.

The taxi stopped in front of a black marble atrium, on a street with a row of tall, white, new buildings on one side, and a green slope and a meadow closed by a yellow wood fence on the other.

The sun was shining, not yet hot, but sharp, like the beam of an X-ray machine.

De Vincenzi came out of his reverie; it took him a few moments before he remembered why he had come. He paid the driver who was smirking as if he knew that he had accompanied him to a garçonnière. In embarrassment, the inspector gave him such a generous tip that he turned the car around whistling a popular cabaret song with an unprintable refrain.

He found the porter in a small room with big windows, which looked like a living room. The building was luxurious, and the woman matched her surroundings. She wore a silk dress and sat idle with her legs crossed and well visible. She had a ferret-like face, with slightly bent ears and irregular features.

She smiled at De Vincenzi as he came in.

"Can I help you?"

"Which apartment is being rented by Senator Magni?"

"Excuse me?" she challenged as she stood up.

"I'd like to visit it. I'm a police inspector."

The woman picked up a register from the table and opened it, instantly compliant.

"It's this one," she pointed.

"I need to see inside."

He didn't even look at the register. "I'll take the keys."

She took them from the wall. They were a bunch of small, English-style keys.

"Should I accompany you?"

"Of course."

A few steps. A door polished like a mirror.

"I'll go in first, to open the windows."

"It doesn't matter. Turn on the lights."

As he entered he was blanketed by a heavy, complex odor. He detected cigarette smoke, cologne water, and other, sweeter, scents that he couldn't identify.

In the antechamber there was a chest, a sofa, and a coffee table. On the ground was a large terracotta jar, used as an umbrella stand. The apartment looked uninhabited. Even the two oil paintings hanging on the walls were impersonal, almost as if they had been manufactured.

There were three doors opening in directly in front of the entrance door and on either side. The porter opened the first. "The bathroom," she announced pointlessly.

White and turquoise, all porcelain tiles. A large, straight-sided mirror faced the rectangular tub. A large number of taps, handles, arms, and nickel-plated hooks.

Here, again, the feeling of something new, uninhabited, like the washbasin of a luxury restaurant, even though a glass shelf carried perfectly-aligned bottles of cologne, lotion, aromatic vinegar, and against the white and light blue of the wall hung a large fleshy sponge and a garnet-colored bathrobe.

De Vincenzi took everything in at a glance.

"Let's continue."

The second door was that of the drawing-room. When the woman switched on the lamp, a yellow light spread like gold over a large black velvet sofa, a low armchair, and a small table. It looked like a theater set. All around the walls, yellow silk curtains hung from the ceiling. At the window, a heavy velvet curtain darkened the room. In a corner, a small rosewood bar held colored liquor bottles that seemed to glow in the dim light. On the shelf, alongside two crystal glasses, a silver shaker gleamed.

Everything was as intimate as a tomb.

Nothing in the room held the slightest personal touch. There wasn't even a bit of disorder, which would have revealed the presence of a living human being. The velvet of the couch was tight, smooth.

"Let's see the rest!"

The porter's voice became ambiguous, almost suggestive: "This is the bedroom."

Here, reflected light spread over a white stucco ceiling, with a rosette in the middle. On the walls, light blue curtains; at the window, another blue velvet curtain but darker and thicker. The bed was huge, low, with an old cashmere shawl as a blanket. Next to it, on both sides of the bed, two tables. Against a wall, a large cheval-glass, with two tall columns supporting it.

At the foot of the bed there was a massive candlestick like something in a church. It contained a large candle with an electric bulb instead of a wick.

De Vincenzi took a few steps inside the room, while in him the sense of discomfort almost became anguish, it was so acute. Then he hurried to examine another small table in a corner, which had been hidden by the bed. He had seen, in a large silver frame, the face of a woman.

He knew immediately. It was *her*.

It was a disappointment. This one was beautiful enough, but as almost all women are beautiful. He observed the picture, picking up the frame and examining it closely. The woman's short hair was curly and voluminous, framing her face. Her small nose finely drawn but without character. Her lips were smiling, showing her small teeth. The pronounced chin slightly stretched her oval face. Her cheekbones were a little high, and the only notable feature in an otherwise common face. The eyes, too, were smiling under the thin arch of eyebrows that were well-shaped, plucked and drawn.

De Vincenzi could feel the porter's lewd stare on his back. He replaced the portrait and asked in an unsteady voice, "Is this her?"

"Yes, sir," the woman acknowledged shamelessly.

"Are there any other rooms?"

"No," and she seemed to be about to add that no other rooms were necessary.

"Did the furniture belong to the professor?"

"Certainly. He took care of everything, four years ago, when he set up the apartment. . ."

De Vincenzi thought that all that velvet and silk, all the furniture, the bar and the silver frame were now a part of Magni's widow's inheritance.

On the landing, he nodded goodbye to the porter, who walked behind him, and went out quickly, almost fleeing. He had the impression of emerging from a tomb.

Chapter 19

From the moment he returned from his visit to the building which held the sad remnants of the many affairs of Senator Magni, De Vincenzi engaged in the strangest and seemingly most irrational behavior yet seen in his already-unusual career as an inspector.

Even Sani, who had blind faith in him, had to wonder if his superior was cracking under the strain. Everyone in the department felt the pressure of the Magni case but it was only De Vincenzi who would have to answer to the Superintendent.

It was almost as if the unidentifiable sweet odors in Magni's private apartment were some sort of hallucinogenic drug that had caused De Vincenzi to become untethered from reality. That might be the simplest explanation for his otherwise-inexplicable actions.

Back in San Fedele, when Sani announced the arrival of Dr. Verga, the inspector refused to see him, even though he himself had sent Cruni to pick him up at home.

"He's really sick. Cruni had to drag him out of his bed to come here. . ."

"Send him back to bed. It will do him good!"

Sani looked at him, surprised, but said nothing.

"He's just tired," he thought. "When this case is over, I'll insist that he takes a few days off."

But De Vincenzi didn't appear to be tired at all, at least physically, and they heard him pacing in his office, which he had locked, until about six o'clock in the afternoon.

At six o'clock, he opened the door with a big smile on his face. But his eyes was feverish and his smile was more a nervous rictus than a sign of happiness.

He went to Sani's desk and stared at him. "You see!" he said slowly, after a few moments of silence. "Everything would be clear if not for those surgical instruments and that lab coat. They are what makes every theory collapse! I can't make them fit with the rest, as hard as I try."

Sani realized how much that problem was disturbing him and didn't dare smile.

"They must have belonged to the professor," he said, reaching for the simplest hypothesis.

"No! One doesn't go to the Sempioncino restaurant with four surgical instruments and a lab coat in one's pockets."

"Then they must have been with the killer."

"His property?"

"Maybe. Which would help us find him."

"It still doesn't fit! Can you believe that a man, diabolically clever like the one who killed Senator Magni, would purposefully provide a critical clue that could help identify him unless he was forced to do so by circumstances? Even if he wanted to defy man and destiny, he wouldn't push the envelope to that point! He would do something more subtle, more in character."

"Are you sure that bundle and note are connected to the murder?"

"No! I'm not sure. And that's exactly what's driving me crazy! How can you believe that finding that bundle at that very moment is pure chance? In that case, you should also believe in an intelligent force that uses the impossible to bring us into the light of understanding. . ."

He laughed and added:

"And so far, there is no light at all."

"There is the handwriting of the note."

"Yes, but it doesn't help. *It isn't the handwriting of the murderer.*"

"So you know who he is?"

"Who?"

"The murderer."

"No!"

"But you must have a well-founded suspicion?"

De Vincenzi shrugged.

"What does that matter? You know I never chase after suspicions! And so much less now. If I told you that I'm sure that the handwriting on the note isn't that of the murderer, without being able to explain why, but only because my intuition tells me so, you'd have me taken away in a straight jacket. . ."

He turned and went back to his office. Shortly after, he returned with his overcoat and hat.

"Are you leaving?"

"Yes. Tell the Superintendent. I'll be gone for several hours. Maybe all night. And in that case, I won't be back here until tomorrow at noon. Maybe even later. . . It depends on the journey I have to make."

"Going far?"

"I don't know, yet. And to find out, I'll have to run the risk of ruining everything."

Sani looked at him and couldn't completely hide his concern.

"You're more puzzling than the crime itself!"

"Yes, of course. When you play with puzzles all the time, they become a part of you. You make connections inside your head that make perfect sense to you but that no one else can see. And this puzzle is still missing some pieces. I don't know what they are, but I can see, inside my head, where they are."

He paused for a moment. "The most horrible action is still the most plausible! If you take a good look into the waters of the docks, you'll see the killer's face reflected in them. Goodbye!" intoned De Vincenzi as if he were some sort of modern-day sibyl.

He rushed out, leaving Sani gaping in his wake.

It was still daylight. The streets were busy. One could barely walk in the Galleria Vittorio Emanuele and along the porches. Once the inspector reached Piazza della Scala, he changed his mind and turned around and, passing by the police station again, took Via San Paolo, crossed Corso Vittorio Emanuele II, and arriving in Piazza Beccaria, took Via Felice Cavallotti.

Soon, he was entering the bookstore on Via Corridoni, hands in his pockets and wearing the innocent expression of a book-lover.

Gualtiero Gerolamo looked at him with surprise and a flash of anguish passed through his mild, moist eyes. Chirico jumped out from behind the counter to greet him, taking off his hat and scratching his head.

"Inspector. . ."

There were a couple of customers browsing the shelves. One of them, fat and bearded, with a large gold chain on his belly, had a small monograph in his hands on which he discoursed in a Bolognese accent while everyone ignored him. He paused to look at the newly-arrived De Vincenzi from over his eyeglasses.

De Vincenzi greeted the bookstore owner with a nod and smiled at Pietrosanto's anxious look. He approached the counter and picked up a few books, one after the other, reading the titles, turning them over in his hands, observing them closely. It almost looked as if he were about to ask for their price.

"Any news, inspector?"

Chirico had spoken to him in a low voice, but immediately everyone held their breath waiting for his answer. Even the two customers knew or understood who he was and they were not deceived by his casual browsing.

"Any news?" he repeated, as if he didn't understand the question. "Ah! Yes. . . Perhaps. . . *It's all over.*"

"Excuse me?!"

Even Gualmo, no longer able to restrain himself, leaned forward to listen, his eyes wide and staring.

The bearded man put down the monograph and took off his glasses.

"Exactly! Someone has been arrested. You'll hear all about it soon enough."

"But who is the killer? And why did he come to my store, of all places?"

"How did he come in?" asked Pietrosanto, still fixating on this enigma. "And did you find the stolen book?"

De Vincenzi suppressed a gasp and silently cursed himself.

Yes! There was the stolen book. *"La Zaffetta - Venetia 1531"*. He had almost forgotten it and had certainly not fully considered it when piecing together the puzzle. Yet it was a fundamental piece, a necessary piece. Now that he had smelled the perfume of the apartment in Via Abbondio San Giorgio, that book, published for revenge against a courtesan, took on a definite and precise meaning. He could almost see it there, on the shelf above the body, as if someone had switched on the light in those gloomy rooms at the back of the shop where the Senator had met his undignified end.

"The book! Yes! We will find that as well. Let me see the exact place from which it was stolen."

He headed down the hallway, preceded by Gualmo and followed by Chirico.

The two customers watched all this with rapt attention. They would have followed along, if only the shop owner hadn't closed the door behind him.

Chirico had closed the door automatically; but as soon as he reached Pietrosanto, who was telling the inspector where to find the "erotic" bookshelf, he grabbed him by one arm and pushed him towards the door.

"You! Back out front! Those two customers are alone. . ."

Pietrosanto, in his burning curiosity, was not pleased by this order. Yet there was nothing to be done. He knew his curiosity was as nothing compared to his boss's fear of theft.

De Vincenzi looked around. The corpse was no longer there, of course, but he could still see it in front of him, lying on the ground. Only now his face was no longer icy, motionless, but animated. He could see the corpse as though it were alive, entering the secret apartment, sitting on the black velvet sofa, approaching the rosewood bar with all the liquors. He could see it before his eyes, alive! And the woman in the portrait as well, though he had never met her, dead or alive.

What part did that woman have in the murder?

Maybe she wasn't a piece of the puzzle at all. Or maybe she was the center that connected all the other pieces. It had to be one of those.

But why was he also imagining the Widow Magni, in her mourning clothes, walking up Via Dante, to enter Harrington's agency?

"Have you held any other spiritist sessions these days?"

"No!" exclaimed the little man.

"Why not?"

"We don't hold sessions all the time, it depends on the members' wishes. The Circle is really more of a place to meet, discuss, read magazines and books, and so on."

"Or perhaps you are hiding the real reason from me?"

Chirico took off his hat, passed a hand over his short bristly hair, "Which reason would that be?"

"The medium's prophecy. . ."

"Yes, that was certainly very upsetting. . ."

"Do you know that I talked to Mrs. Sorbelli again?"

"Ah. You did?"

"She promised to hold a session for me. I'm interested in spiritism, now. . . Perhaps it's your fault, it was you who convinced me that *"There is a whole world around us that we know nothing about!"*

Chirico looked at him with distrust. He didn't think he was making fun of him; on the contrary, he felt that De Vincenzi was angling for something, that he had a well-defined plan, a goal to be achieved. But what did he want?

"She's a very sensitive lady. . . too sensitive, I'd say!"

"I want you to attend the session, too, Mr. Chirico. . ."

De Vincenzi put his hand on Chirico's shoulder. "Can we organize one in the headquarters of the Circle?"

"It depends on the President. . ."

"Or on the Secretary? That's you, I believe! The session *has to be* held there, Mr. Chirico. *It's essential."*

"When?" the little man murmured, now convinced that he wouldn't be able to refuse. Chirico was not a fool. He understood that De Vincenzi had come to the shop expressly to talk to him about this session he was planning. But what did he have in mind? What trap was he laying? Was it for him or for someone else?

"I'll let you know tomorrow. Maybe we should hold one tomorrow night. Yes, before Monday."

"Tomorrow is Sunday."

"Oh! Yes. That's right. I could call you at home. . . Or we can just schedule the session for Monday at nine. On Monday night it will be eight days since Senator Magni's murder."

Chirico shuddered and stared at the inspector in terror.

"What do you want to do?"

"Nothing!"

"Will Mrs. Sorbelli really come?"

"Of course!"

"I don't believe it!"

"Sure she will! You'll see. Do you really think that the dead can come back?"

Chirico went as white as a sheet and didn't answer.

De Vincenzi examined the place from where the book had been taken. If only he could have seen the hand that had taken it! But he *could* see that hand, white, tapered, vibrant, the hand of a surgeon. For he was convinced that the senator himself had removed that volume from the shelf. But where this conviction came from, he could not yet say.

They went back to the front of the store. The two customers were still there, waiting. Gualmo studied the inspector. Then he saw Chirico's pale face and his eyes widened even more.

"We will also invite Mr. Pietrosanto!" De Vincenzi said without smiling. "We are all set."

"Invite me? To what?"

"You'll know on Monday."

And he left the shop, repeating to Chirico, "We are all set, understood?"

The little man ran after him. Catching up with him on the sidewalk, he had to grab him by the flap of his overcoat to stop him and make him listen.

"Who else will attend the session?"

"I'll let you know on Monday. I'll take care of the invitations."

"Okay." whispered Chirico. He went back into the store moving as if he had a great weight on his shoulders, crushing him.

De Vincenzi caught a cab in Piazza del Verziere, just in the car park where, four days earlier, he had left Dr. Marini after their late-night stroll through the city.

"Corso Plebisciti," he told the driver, getting in.

He had given this address thoughtlessly, almost unconsciously. He knew he had a reason for going there, but he didn't know what it was. In any case, he couldn't do otherwise.

When they reached Corso Plebisciti, he had the car stop in front of number 17.

A huge building, similar to all the others preceding and following it. An entrance door with a few plants set against a white and vast courtyard, which opened on other façades of internal buildings, different in color and shape from the main one.

No one in the porter's lodge. In the middle of the courtyard, bending over a flower bed without flowers, removing the straw around a palm tree which April's imminence was releasing from its winter shelter, was a man with a black, glossy smock hanging almost all the way to his heels.

De Vincenzi's steps crunched over the gravel. The man straightened up and turned in his direction. He still had his hands full of long straw. He had two dark eyes in a tanned face, a face so gaunt that the fleshless outlines of his jaw and protruding nose were clearly visible.

"Can I help you?"

"I need a piece of information."

"Isn't my wife in the porter's lodge?"

"No, she isn't."

"She's probably cooking."

The porter threw the straw onto the naked and hard ground of the flowerbed, clapped his palms and rubbed them on the sides of his smock.

"What's it about?"

"Are you the porter?"

"Yes. But who are you?"

"If I ask you for a confidential piece of information, will you be able to keep it confidential?"

The man shrugged.

"I don't know anything about the tenants or their money. You're not allowed to look into anybody's pockets! I don't know anything about income and salaries. You won't get anything out of me."

De Vincenzi smiled. "I'm not a tax inspector!"

The man shrugged again.

"They're always pestering us. What do you want, then?"

"I need to find Dr. Marini's wife . . . she's now in the countryside. . . So I need her address there." The somewhat disdainful indifference of the porter became blatant scorn.

"Ask her husband!" he said, looking at the inspector with suspicion, his dark eyes full of malice.

But De Vincenzi didn't want to reveal his identity. With his cordial joviality, Dr. Marini had certainly gotten on the right side of his porters. Either this man or his wife would report his inquiries, something that the inspector wanted to avoid at all costs. It was better to pretend to be a lover, an idle Casanova chasing a woman.

"Well. . . As a matter of fact. . ." he said, smiling with a hint of complicity, "her husband is the last person I would want to ask."

He pulled a twenty-lire coin from his pocket and held it between his fingers. "No one will know that you told me."

The man looked at the coin and rubbed his palms again on his hips and chest to clean them.

"It's after seven. . . the time when the doctor comes back for dinner. . ."

"Who's in the house?"

"The cleaning lady. . . The maid has left with her mistress. . ."

He lowered his voice:

"They went to Pegli. . . Villa Doria. . ."

He held out his hand, stealthily, looking around.

The piece of silver disappeared into the waistcoat pocket under the polished smock.

De Vincenzi thanked him, left the building and walked slowly along Corso Plebisciti and then the tree-lined avenue of Corso Indipendenza.

Pegli, Villa Doria: on the Italian Riviera, then. He would take the 9 p.m. train to Genoa, where he would sleep. From there, Pegli was very easy to reach. He could be back in Milan the next day at 2 p.m., Sunday. He still had more than twenty-four hours to prepare for Monday's spiritic session.

This was all a bit desperate, and he didn't expect any great results. But there was nothing left to do. Evidence. Where could he find hard evidence? He had only worked on tentative clues. Nothing but *tentative psychological clues!* And the human soul had so many strange and winding tangents . . .

He was actually afraid to express in words, even to himself, the theory that was taking shape inside his brain. Somehow, he felt he knew the solution to the mystery. But he lacked too much data, too many links, to be able to arrive at a conclusion and act on it—or to explain it to anyone else.

Still, he *had* to act. The eight-day deadline imposed by the Superintendent and the instructing magistrate came up on Tuesday. Only forty-eight hours left. He couldn't hope that the criminal would somehow betray himself as so often happened with criminals. The author of these two murders demonstrated complete control and dominated the environment in which he moved with absolute confidence, the same way, perhaps, in which he had dominated his victim and left him to die in the bookstore.

De Vincenzi walked beneath the trees in the middle of a side boulevard, between two rows of benches occupied by mothers, housekeepers, wet nurses and housemaids, who were starting to leave for the evening. Around him swarmed running children, spurred on by the sound of their mothers' voices.

The day was dying in a lingering twilight as the sun sank in a diaphanous glow. In the distance, behind the city, above the halo of Saint Francis—the saint of Assisi, whose statue stands in Piazza Risorgimento, thin and stylized, hovering like a flight of swallows, all purity and, consuming passion—the last rays of the sun tinged the sky red.

De Vincenzi forgot himself, the horrible mystery with which he wrestled, and the suffering he had endured for the sake of his inquiry.

He became just a human creature in perfect communion with Nature, beneath those green trees, among those garrulous children, with his face turned to the reddening sky. He was alone, unique, far from all other beings and from the Earth itself. It was an incomparable feeling, as if he had been touched by the infinite. Or perhaps, he reflected, he had not been getting enough sleep.

The darkness and then the light of the lamps brought him back to reality. He took a tram to the *tangenziale* that took him, after a seemingly endless trip, to his home. He had decided to leave in the early hours of the morning. He knew there was a train at four. He would be in Genoa before eight and by eight-thirty he would be in Pegli.

The next morning, after spending four hours alone with his thoughts in a second-class compartment, he found himself in the Pegli train station, surrounded by flowers.

He had already seen the sea from the train's window, before arriving in Genoa. And, on the Riviera, he found the warm brightness of a blossoming spring.

But his throat became dry thinking of that imminent encounter with a woman he had never met, and yet knew, with her slightly high cheekbones that made her otherwise-expressionless face come alive. With her eyebrows, well-shaped, plucked and drawn. . . her airy, short hair. . . her smile of happiness over small, pearl-white teeth. . . Up until eight days ago, every Thursday afternoon that woman would enter the apartment in Via Abbondio San Giorgio and sit on a black velvet sofa.

What would he say to her?

And what if it wasn't her? What if Dr. Marini's wife wasn't the senator's lover? Because, in reality, he had no specific reason, no proof, to believe it was so. Now he wished he had spent that four hours on the train thinking of an alternative reason for his visit, just in case.

When the driver had told him of the mystery woman's habit of getting out of the car on Piazzale Tonoli and setting off in the direction of Viale dei Mille, he had had a sudden revelation. But what if his intuition were wrong? Viale dei Mille leads to Corso Plebisciti, but also elsewhere. . .

But it was too late, now. He was committed. "Where can I find Villa Doria?" he asked the only porter in the train station, who was watering the flower beds at the top of the stairs, in front of the station offices.

"You can't miss it. Just outside, turn right and then go straight. After the overpass at the end of the avenue, you'll find a large gate. That's Villa Doria.

"Thank you," said De Vincenzi, and he started walking.

"You need to enter the park, mind. The villa is inside. . . Ask the caretaker."

The park was huge. At the back, among the trees, was a large white building with green shutters. A princely villa. Was it possible that the doctor's wife lived there?

"Ah! That lady from Milan, who came two days ago with her maid! They have rented the inner pavilion. Go up the hill. Next to the main villa, you'll find a trail. And then you can't get lost, because the pavilion is halfway up and you will see it right away from below."

It was the old hunting lodge of the villa belonging to the Doria family. He found it easily, a two-story construction, painted in brick red, with a terrace garden in front.

As he climbed toward it, he could see it more and more clearly, without being noticed from above, because the path, all holes and landslides, went up between two hedges.

The windows were wide open and the sun flooded the house.

On the railing of a balcony, he saw the white sheets and the blankets of a bed that had just been unmade.

When he found himself below the terrace, he took a look at the garden through the iron bars surrounding it. He saw a woman in a blue robe, lying on a lounge chair facing the sea. It was a quick glimpse which he fixed in his memory: two bare feet moving in their slippers, and a mass of blond hair against the back of the chair.

He found himself on a landing from where he could see the side of the pavilion, with a small door accessible at the top of three steps, and to the left, in a corner, a gate to the flowery terrace.

He stopped, hesitating. Should he ring the bell or enter the gate, which was half open?

He decided to go through the gate and along the gravel driveway, between the main facade and a flowerbed of roses.

The woman was right at the edge of the garden terrace, in front of the railing, with her back to him. He saw again the great glow of her golden hair, shining in the sun.

In front of him, in the distance, beyond the town and the beach, was the sea.

He tried to make as much noise as possible, dragging his feet on the gravel.

"Who is it?" a sweet voice asked wearily, slightly anxiously. The woman, however, didn't turn around.

"Forgive me. . ." De Vincenzi said.

"Who is it?" she repeated.

"Mrs. Marini?"

"It's me. Please, come forward. . ."

She had turned around and looked at him indifferently.

He hadn't been mistaken! The woman in the portrait stood before him. More beautiful than in the picture, her gaze seemed slightly vague, almost lost. She must have been crying recently, because her eyes were still wet.

"How can I help you?"

De Vincenzi felt he would never dare tell that woman who he was and why he was there. The mere mention of his rank would have made her crumble. He was certain of it. He had to lie. A good story must be improvised in a matter of ten seconds. He had no other option, if his mission was to succeed.

"I'm sorry, Madam! I come from Milan. I have to talk to you. I'm. . . I was a friend of poor Senator Magni. . ."

The woman jumped to her feet. Her eyes became hard. A visible shiver went through her.

Her lips lost their color on her pale face and she moved them in an attempt to speak, but no sound came out.

"Don't worry, Madam. I'm a friend."

The woman sat down again, but no longer reclined, sitting perched on the edge, instead. Next to her lounge chair was a portable canvas seat and she wordlessly pointed it out to De Vincenzi, who sat down, murmuring "Thank you!"

There was a long silence.

The sea, in front of them, looked like an immense, shiny steel plate. Below them, stood a grove of large Mediterranean pine trees, which at the top of their tall trunks opened like an umbrella. Behind them, the villa was silent. Everything seemed engulfed in an almost magical immobility.

"Why did you come?" the woman finally said softly, without looking at him.

"Yes. . . why did I come? It's very hard for me to say. I was a friend of Magni. . . I was in school and then at university with him and your husband. Dr. Marini and I lost sight of each other. There was no real friendship between us. But with Ugo, it was different. Ugo trusted me and confided in me. He came to me every time he had some difficult or simply annoying case. He had no secrets with me."

The woman stared at him. She had recovered some of her strength. Her paleness was fading.

"What do you mean?"

"He showed me the apartment in Via Abbondio San Giorgio."

"Why are you coming to me?"

Her eyes were glaring.

"Because I felt it was my duty, a painful, bitter, but unavoidable duty. . ."

He hesitated.

"Go on!" she ordered.

"There's a portrait, in that apartment. If someone doesn't remove it immediately, it'll fall into the hands of his widow."

"Who cares?"

She said it abruptly, with deep sincerity. As if she didn't care for anything, any longer. Had she loved him so much, then? Was this her only affliction?

"Your husband, too, sooner or later, will see that portrait, even if the Senator's widow doesn't tell him about you herself. Given his friendship with the poor deceased, he will surely assist the widow in all that needs to be done after her husband's death. . ."

The woman didn't answer; but her face expressed deep indignation and almost sarcastic defiance.

"Is this all you have come to tell me?"

"What about you? I have come to tell you that I'm at your disposal! I thought you might need a reliable and devoted confidant."

"I told you, I don't care! Things have ended so tragically for me, that what may come next cannot touch me. I'm sorry you took the trouble to come all the way here."

"And if I told you I did it for another reason too?"

"What reason?" her voice again became hard, sharp.

"I want to ask you to join me in something that is, to me, a sacred debt to be fulfilled. Avenging Ugo!"

The woman stood up again, perhaps to hide her emotions. De Vincenzi did the same. She looked him in the eyes. If his words had upset her, she had now recovered.

"And how would you seek to avenge him?"

"Working with the authorities to find his killer."

"How could you do that? And how could I help you?"

"You, Madam, must know all about Ugo. Even more than I. Perhaps, you can provide an essential clue. He could. . . he must have confided in you. . . told you if he had enemies. . . if he was afraid of them. . . if he sensed any danger."

The woman shook her head.

"He didn't tell me any of this. I am certain he didn't know he was threatened."

"And you?"

"Me? What about me?"

"You never got the impression that he could be. . . that he was threatened?"

"This is ridiculous! If I had had such an impression, I would have warned him... I would have defended him!"

"And your husband?"

"What does my husband have to do with it?" the woman exclaimed, and once again her voice filled with scornful sarcasm.

"Your husband was a friend of the senator. He assiduously frequented his house. He could know something. He could have some hypotheses that he didn't share with others, but might have confided to you, his wife."

"No. He didn't. Besides, I have been ill for many days... I left him almost immediately, after the tragedy... to come here."

"I understand! Forgive me."

She bowed her head, as if to dismiss him. She had obviously stood up to make him understand that the interview had come to an end.

But he didn't move. He seemed pensive. He murmured:

"A weird... An inexplicable murder..."

He looked up at her. The woman kept silent.

"Not a murder of delinquency... They didn't steal anything... It was an act of vengeance, surely! And they struck him from the behind."

He paused. Her eyes remained inexpressive. "And why in a bookstore? Because, ultimately, they really did steal something. A book, from a shelf. A book, do you understand? One could imagine they killed for that book..."

Now, the woman looked at him intently, as if trying to understand. A question came to her lips, but remained there, unasked.

"And it was a book about obscene love... a slanderous pamphlet, *La Zaffetta*, attributed to Pietro Aretino..."

But Mrs. Marini had collapsed onto the gravel walkway.

Chapter 20

He picked up the unconscious woman and carried her inside.

Placing her on the couch, he shouted for the maid, who rushed in, flustered and frightened at the sight of a stranger looming over her unconscious mistress.

He poured some drops of cognac onto her lips; but her teeth were clenched like a vise and the liquid ran from the corners of her mouth onto her chin and chest. It wasn't just her jaw. She was as rigid as a corpse and, had she not been breathing, almost panting, one might have assumed she was dead.

He didn't know what to do. The maid, a curvaceous brunette—what was it about this case?— gaped at him suspiciously, completely at a loss to explain his presence and clearly thinking him a danger both to herself and her mistress. After a few moments of silence, the girl found her tongue.

"What did you do to her? Who are you?"

De Vincenzi ignored her questions.

"Go call a doctor, quickly. How long will it take you to go to the village and back?"

The girl at first, accustomed as she was to obey, started running for the door. But on the threshold, she stopped and turned to look at him, indecisive. Should she leave him, a stranger, alone with her mistress, inert and unconscious? And where had he come from? And why?

"I'm a friend of Dr. Alberto. Go. NOW!" he snapped, in a stern voice.

She went.

De Vincenzi looked at the woman lying on the sofa. Was she sick? Or was the shock too much for her?

But the shock of what? What was it about the title of that book that had made her collapse as if she had been clubbed over the head?

All hypotheses were possible.

He bent and gently touched her forehead. It was cold as ice.

When would that damn doctor arrive?

He began to look around. The room had only a few pieces of furniture, but each was beautiful. The room was divided into two parts by an arch, along which ran silvery and black snakeskin. In the fireplace, among the andirons, was a pile of fresh ashes. They must light the fire in the evening. It could become chilly by the sea after sunset.

At the moment, though, it was sunny and warm and the light spilled into the room. Outside, everything was a blaze of festive, bright colors. The flower beds were red, yellow, white, turquoise.

The woman, whose only sign of life remained her convulsive panting, had golden hair and a blue robe.

De Vincenzi looked back at her, and noticed that her robe was a little open, revealing the outline of a breast. He closed the robe gently on her chest. Then he regretted having done it, as if his solicitude was, somehow, an indictment of his professionalism.

He suddenly heard the sound of approaching voices, and stepped quickly away from the couch just as the doctor entered, followed by the maid. And even the doctor, after glancing at the unconscious woman, stared at the inspector suspiciously, wondering who he was.

He was a very skinny and bony man who had clearly been in the war because he had a long scar on his forehead and a lapel pin awarded to those who had been wounded in action.

He leaned over Mrs Marini, opened her lips and delicately lifted her eyelids. "I see," he said, standing up. "Hot water and alcohol. She needs an injection," he ordered the maid, who promptly disappeared.

De Vincenzi kept out of the way.

"Did she have some sort of emotional shock?" the doctor asked.

"I think so."

"Are you a relative?"

"A friend of her husband."

"Ah! Dr. Marini."

"Precisely."

"He should have told me that he was sending his sick wife here. As a colleague, you know. . ."

"Do you think it's serious?"

"No. But she'll probably suffer some fever, perhaps very strong. She'll need a few days to recover."

The maid came back with water and alcohol and the doctor pulled a small, shiny box out of his pocket. De Vincenzi though it best to make his escape before too many questions were asked.

"Well, doctor, I'd best be on my way. Goodbye."

"Oh. Well, would you please let her husband know what's happened here?" the doctor asked, looking at him with slight astonishment.

"Must I? If it was at all possible to spare him other worries. . ." De Vincenzi improvised franticly. "He has so many, at the moment."

"Uh, OK. I suppose it's not too serious, and the lady's young and healthy. But I . . ."

"Exactly! Best not to worry him. I won't tell him anything. Have a nice day!" And De Vincenzi shot out the open French doors, descending the path full of holes and landslides with long, hopping strides.

At the train station, he asked about trains for Milan. Why would he stay? Trying to extract Mrs. Marini's secret—whatever it was—was now impossible. Perhaps he should have hurried things along and carried out a real, formal interrogation. But he didn't want to. The outcome would have been uncertain, and he would have to give up the only hope he had to catch the culprit by surprise.

But who was the culprit? On the train, his brain continued to work without respite. He examined, one by one, each piece of the puzzle, laying them in front of him in his mind.

He moved them around, trying to match them. A game of patience that would have driven anyone else crazy. Yet, it was all about looking deeply into the human brain and heart, which, though they are tortuous, elusive and dishonest, even to themselves, are always clear and consistent on their most fundamental level.

But was that really all that was necessary? Did he really have all the pieces of the puzzle? Or was one—perhaps the most important one—missing?

Travelers went in and out of his compartment, some changed at the various stops, an old lady sat for the entire trip squarely in front of him. He didn't see any of them, even though he often stared at them, unblinking, completely absorbed in his thoughts.

He got off the train in Milan, feeling as if he had woken up from a long dream filled with ghosts, and went straight to the San Fedele police station. Back in his familiar environment, he began to regain his sense of serenity. And by the time he finally arrived at San Fedele, he was very serene indeed. He was certain that his trip had brought him that much closer to the truth.

Sani welcomed him with the silent joy that he always felt when he saw him, even after only a few hours of absence.

"What's new?" De Vincenzi asked, sitting at his desk.

"No important news, if you're asking about the senator's murder, as I imagine. The court has set the Worm free and put Panzeri, Harrington's man, in San Vittore prison in his place. . . The charges are false testimony and slander. If he's convicted, he'll only get what he deserves."

De Vincenzi became upset.

"They could have waited! I had only asked for eight days of patience, and the eighth is not until tomorrow!"

"It wasn't my idea! The judge did all this on his own! I only heard about it later."

"I believe it. It's not your fault. What else?"

"Nothing else. Dr. Verga is still sick in bed."

De Vincenzi nodded.

"Last night and early this morning, Miss Pat went to see him."

"Naturally."

"The widow continues to remain at home. She doesn't go out."

"This is also natural."

"About Fioretta Vaghi. . . the unhappy girl in love with Verga. . . there's nothing to report."

De Vincenzi, listening to his colleague's report, smiled.

"You smile?"

"At you. I'm impressed. You must have really exercised your memory, running through all the people involved in our little drama."

"Last night. . . you weren't here. I was bored. I compiled a list of everyone involved, including witnesses and suspects."

"Good job! Give it to me. I'll need it to write the invitations for tomorrow night."

"Invitations?" Sani asked, pulling a folded sheet of paper out of his pocket. "Are you preparing a receptions for the. . . actors?"

"Something like that. You'll see for yourself, because you and Cruni will be invited as well, though you won't be in the actual hall."

He accepted the sheet of paper from Sani and quickly scanned it. "Yes. It seems you haven't forgotten anyone... at least none of those you know."

He put the open sheet in front of him, on the desk.

"Today is Sunday. Nothing can be done. Tomorrow morning, then. So. You were saying? I believe you had arrived at Fioretta Vaghi?"

"Yes. Our previous offender. . . Santini, the brother of poor Norina. . . He was at home every time the police visited him. . . And he doesn't seem to have done anything even slightly suspicious."

"I don't think there is any doubt that his sister's death was a great blow for him!"

"Last night Dr. Marini went to visit Madam Magni. . . She didn't receive him."

"How do you know that?"

"The driver!" laughed Sani. "From the moment you questioned him, he got it into his head that he was our 'agent on the inside' and that he was indispensable to our investigation. So last night he came here and told me everything that happened that afternoon."

"Harrington?"

"He's under surveillance. Last night, Paoli had nothing important to report. He hasn't yet reported in today."

"Good. It seems you haven't forgotten anything. I, on the other hand, forgot someone and something. . ."

De Vincenzi rang for the precinct officer.

"Do you want me to leave you alone?" Sani asked.

"Oh no," said the inspector, turning to the officer who had appeared in the doorway. "Get me Sergeant Padovani, from the Public Morality Squad."

De Vincenzi explained, "I asked Padovani to handle a job on the very first day of the investigation. To be honest, I forgot all about it and I've just remembered him now."

He looked up at the sergeant, who entered with his springy and gliding step, looking more than ever like a male taxi dancer.

"Well, Sergeant! What did you do last Tuesday night?"

"I visited all the nightclubs, Sir. . . I didn't miss a single one!"

"And?"

"Nothing! No one saw Senator Magni on Monday night. In several places they told me they knew him. In the others, I showed them his photograph but no one could remember seeing him. Of course, he might have briefly entered some club but he certainly didn't stay."

"Well, that's that, then. Thank you, you can go."

Padovani bowed and left.

"Another waste of time!" De Vincenzi sighed, looking at Sani. "I have yet to collect a single piece of hard evidence that implicates anyone in this case! It could be anyone and no one! Even if I wanted to arrest someone, how could I convince a magistrate? And I've got one day left!"

"And that someone. . . a man or a woman?" asked Sani slyly, who knew De Vincenzi very well.

"Do you think it may have been a woman?"

"There are too many women in this case! That's hardly a coincidence."

"You are right, dear Sani! Yes! But not in the sense you may think. This isn't a crime that could have been committed by a woman. Remember Norina's death? No woman could have done that."

"I agree. But that doesn't change the fact that there are too many women.

"Yes. . ."

"Have you counted them? Go ahead."

"I have your list. Mrs. Magni. . . Miss Pat. . ." he said, counting on his fingers as he read off the names, "Fioretta Vaghi. . . Mrs. Sorbelli. . ."

"And her daughter."

"Those two count as one. The mother is important only because she's a medium. But in real life she counts for nothing without her daughter. So there are four, for now. . . And then there was poor Norina! And then another lady you don't know, whom I went to visit in Pegli! So! There are six women. . ."

"Six women around a corpse! It's like a Greek funeral. Except that Magni wasn't Greek and it's not 300 BC!"

"Six women. . . and one book!" De Vincenzi murmured. "A book with a woman's name as a title, as well!"

Sani looked at him speculatively. "And what are your conclusions?"

"None, dear Sani! I'm afraid to draw any conclusions. There are too many unknowns. Too many questions I can't answer!"

Sani looked at the inspector, silently. He didn't believe a word of it.

"So, instead of working on the case, you're inviting everyone to a. . . reception!"

"I'm going to see what happens when I gather them all around a table. And then, I'll ask the dead for some help, since the living aren't providing any."

His tone was light, but his voice crackled, and his eyes were piercing. Sani knew the signs. De Vincenzi was in the grip of strong emotions. Knowing what this case meant, Sani could only admire his iron self control. Still, why tempt fate?

"Well, there's nothing left to do here, boss. Go home. Get some rest. Don't wander around the city. It's Sunday and the streets are full of people on their day off, causing problems," he counseled.

"Would you mind if we keep talking, the two of us? I prefer not to think alone. It's less tiring, that way. . . Forgive me!"

He got up, went to pick up a bundle from the closet and put it on the table.

"In here are all the items found on the senator's corpse as well as all the other items which are relevant to the crime, or at least I think they are all relevant."

He opened the bundle and the surgical coat and instruments came out first.

"This, for example," and he lifted the white cotton coat, ". . . didn't belong to the professor. It's too common for him. That's what Pat said, and she isn't wrong. And the instruments weren't his either. He only used luxury surgical tools, scalpels with onyx handles. Still, I stubbornly continue to consider them closely linked to the crime. This is the piece of paper with the note left by whoever deposited these tools and coat on the steps of San Vito al Pasquirolo church. His words could be cynical, if they didn't reflect his urgent need to disassociate himself from these items. Two hypotheses: cynicism and urgency. Other reasons could be deceit, burglary, theft. None of them solve nor explain anything."

Sani listened carefully, staring at the four glittering surgical instruments. He pointed to the scalpel. "Those stains?"

"I didn't have them analyzed. Maybe it's blood. But if it is, indeed, real blood, this only makes the mystery even more obscure, and I don't really need any more complications! I prefer to postpone—till the major mystery is solved—the explanation of the minor mystery of these instruments and this coat. . . I'm not sure why, but I never believed that they would lead me to the culprit. Perhaps it's because they were intentionally sent to police headquarters."

He set aside the tools, wrapping them in the coat, and then he picked up the other objects, one after the other.

"The dead man's wallet. . ."

He continued the inventory.

"Three thousand lire. . . several business cards. . . an identity card. . . a Chamber of Commerce card. . . a permanent railroad pass. . . his

240

wife's photograph. . ."

He looked at Sani.

"Don't be surprised! All those who cheat on their wives keep their portrait in their wallet. . . There's nothing else in the wallet. And in his pockets were two handkerchiefs, a prescription pad, a pencil, a gold fountain pen, a pocket watch and chain, a small address book with his patients' addresses. I looked at it and didn't find anything useful. A golden cigarette holder with eleven Capstan cigarettes. Senator Magni smoked little or nothing, because tobacco is an anti-aphrodisiac. On his fingers, he wore his wedding ring and a diamond ring. Nothing else."

De Vincenzi turned toward the closet.

"There, in the closet, I left the clothes of Norina Santini. They are not useful. The purse of the deceased hasn't been found... Perhaps it contained something interesting. Along with her clothes I also put the newspaper cutout with the portrait of Senator Magni, which Norina kept in the dresser drawer. . . That's all."

"It's very little," Sani murmured.

"True. What isn't there is a great deal more. The hat. That wretched Harrington, he and his Worm, they only managed to misdirect us! If I had known where the hat was found, I would have been closer to solving the case. But there is another thing that, precisely because it is missing, is a critical clue. The erotic book. . . *La Zaffetta – Venetia - 1531!*"

"How can you believe that the killer. . ." De Vincenzi was smiling. Sani stopped.

"Go on!"

"An erotic book! Why would one steal it, after committing murder?"

"What if they killed *for* the book?"

"What do you mean?"

"Ah! No!" De Vincenzi exclaimed. "I can't explain it! *I feel that it is so.*

241

That it *must be so*. But don't ask me the reason. If I knew the reason, I wouldn't need to gather all the characters in our little drama in a room with the lights off."

He took the items scattered around the table and wrapped them again in the newspaper. He put them back in the closet and closed it. Turning to Sani, he said, "See? Having a good talk is useful! Just going through this inventory with you has made me recall, one by one, each day and each event in our investigation. I can see the facts, now. I am not wrong. I can't be wrong."

He grabbed his hat and replaced it on his head. "Let's get some air!"

As Sani moved to follow him, the slim figure of Pat Drury, the Senator's nurse, appeared on the threshold. "Good morning, inspector," said the girl.

De Vincenzi, hiding his surprise, smiled and offered her a chair, saying, "Your visit is most welcome, Miss Drury! Would you like to take a seat?"

Sani had disappeared into the room next door.

The girl sat down. She had a serious expression, her lips slightly clenched. Her eyes had lost their sometimes ironic, sometimes disdainful look. She didn't speak.

"Did you come to bring me news of your boyfriend?"

"He's better. He got up out of bed today. It was just a touch of flu."

"I'm glad."

He waited.

Suddenly, making an effort, the girl exclaimed:

"There is something that Edoardo. . . Dr. Verga kept from you when he told you about the night of Senator Magni's murder." Her voice, louder than necessary, betrayed her emotions.

"I know," De Vincenzi said.

242

She gasped.

"How do you know? *What do you know?*"

Slowly and distinctly, De Vincenzi said "That the two of you—while you were waiting for the senator in front of his house—saw Norina, the maid, come out of the door. . ."

Pat jumped to her feet.

"Who told you? Were you there? Where were you?"

"Me?" De Vincenzi smiled. "I was here, at the San Fedele police station! And as for who told me about it. . . nobody did. But the fact that Norina left the house that night can clearly be deduced from her death. Why would they kill her, if she hadn't left?"

The girl stared at him, deeply amazed and a little afraid.

"But you, Miss Drury, will surely give me some details which will be very valuable to me. One can't deduce everything! One needs to know. And you know something, because you saw. Tell me what you saw."

"Wonderful!" Patt murmured with admiration. Then she shook her head. "Like something from a book. What a wonderful American detective you would be!"

"Do you think so? I'd say no. I don't even smoke!" he said laughing. "Sit down and tell me about it, Miss. . . Pat. Can I call you that?"

"Naturally. I was fine with that the first time we talked. But at that time you did maintain a certain formality since you were half-convinced that I was the murderer!"

"I never thought anything like that! Not even that you were the killer's accomplice."

"Really? You had every right to suspect that! Anyway, I should first tell you that it was Edoardo who insisted that I come to see you. When we told you about what happened at the Sempioncino restaurant, he was silent about Norina out of respect for the girl and the deceased. . . I'm sure you understand. Later, when you told us of Norina's death, we

243

were both too shocked and upset to speak. Dr. Verga wanted to come here the next day and tell you everything, but he got sick. He would have told you yesterday, when you sent someone to bring him in to see you. But you refused to see him, so. . ."

"I see. And?"

"Well, it's simple. It was about one-thirty when Norina left the house. . ."

"Was it before you and the doctor saw—or believed you saw—the senator go home with another man, or after?"

"After. Immediately after."

"Of course."

"Pardon me?"

"The girl must have waited for the professor, looking out her window. She saw him approaching, but then leaving. She couldn't control her impatience, or maybe she had some other reason. . . In any case, she went down to the street in order to follow him, to catch up with him and speak with him as soon as he was alone."

"That's possible. Certainly, Norina left the professor's house shortly after one-thirty in the morning. We heard the bells, so we knew what time it was, and she didn't come back until about two. It was precisely because we had seen her come back after only half an hour, that Edoardo and I decided to remain waiting in the street until almost five o'clock, believing that Senator Magni must return soon."

"But, of course," continued De Vincenzi, taking up the story, "he didn't come back, because they had killed him! But Norina must have seen the man who accompanied the senator, and probably even where they went: the bookstore on Via Corridoni. Yes, all this was already clear in my mind, but I thank you and Dr. Verga for confirming it."

"May I leave, then?" asked the young woman who now, having done her duty, had recovered her self confidence.

"As you wish. . . I'll see you tomorrow night."

"You will?"

"Yes. I need you and Dr. Verga to be in Via Broletto, at the Circle of Psychic Studies, tomorrow night at nine. I would have told you tomorrow, but since you are here, I'm telling you now. Will you be there?"

"Certainly, if you wish. Didn't you ask us to be at the police's disposal? It is only our duty. Anyway, isn't that why my boyfriend's house is under surveillance?"

"Oh! Miss Drury!"

"Pat."

"Miss Pat! Thank you!"

"No. Thank you!"

And the American woman left, a slightly ironic smile dancing on her lips.

Chapter 21

Chirico was extremely nervous.

His normally pale face had become even paler. He could not have looked worse if they had told him that all his debtors had gone bankrupt.

All the excuses he could invent and objections he could raise that might have avoided the pending séance, he had invented and raised— even to the point of claiming that his wife was severely ill.

But it was all useless, even his wife. De Vincenzi had told him, "For a couple of hours, your wife can do without you. If you don't do as I have asked, however, your wife will do without you for quite a lot longer than that. I'll have an arrest warrant issued for you and, before evening, I will accompany you to San Vittore and find you a comfortable cell. So it's up to you. Choose wisely." Of course, Chirico had chosen the séance and now paced agitatedly up and down the vast reading room of the Circle of Psychic Studies, so pale that he appeared to be one of the summoned rather than one of the summoners.

It was eight-thirty and the room was empty. Chirico had organized things so that it would be so for the whole evening. It wasn't difficult. Only a few members typically lingered until late, and since he knew who they were, he was able to warn them off for the evening.

That evening, much to his wife's great wonder—she had recovered quite miraculously—he had been unable to swallow a spoonful of soup or a bite of meat and had rushed to Via Broletto shortly before eight, to begin his agitated rounds.

The Circle of Psychic Studies, although it had a secretary, had no staff. The cleaning of the four small rooms and the salon was done by the building's porter, who was also in charge of keeping the keys when the Circle was closed.

So Chirico had opened up the four rooms around the larger salon himself. There was the entrance foyer and three interior doors, one of which hid his office. He then turned on all the lights and began his uneasy wait.

Thanks to that damn corpse, his business, his books, and even himself had been cursed. The bookstore in Via Corridoni had become a focus of morbid interest, generating more curiosity than custom.

Was it possible that all that curiosity would be satisfied when the veil parted this evening? That when it did—as at the opening of the velvet curtain on a stage—the murderer would stand revealed to all?

Chirico believed in materialization, in transfiguration, in *ideoplastia*, which is the shaping of living matter through ideas. But they were all theoretical beliefs, a kind of spiritual creed. We believe in God, but if God were to materialize in front of us, the shock would cause an apoplectic stroke and kill us on the spot.

It was precisely such a deadly shock that Chirico feared for himself that evening. If Mrs. Sorbelli managed to bring back into the world of the living the visible spirit—the *ectoplasm*, he could even afford the luxury of using scientific terms for this—of the deceased Senator Magni, he doubted he would survive the experience.

He remembered a study by the illustrious Bozzano, whose words he had memorized, "The medium's subconscious is capable of fluidly creating or materializing animated and intelligent spirits of the dead unknown to him in life, but known by some of the attendants." And in this case, Sorbelli knew the spirit she was about to invoke perfectly well, both in life and in death!

Chirico was restless. When would it begin? He put down his hat and took off his coat which was too long for him. With just his jacket on, he looked even more scrawny, like the manager of a pawn shop in a Jewish ghetto in Rome or Venice.

Chirico continued his nervous pacing. This time, the situation in which he found himself was so much larger, so unfathomable, that he felt himself drowning.

He raised both hands to the ceiling and, on the way down, he rested one on his head to scratch it.

What was that damned inspector planning? Did he really intend to use this séance to catch Magni's killer, since apparently he was unable to find him by the usual, honestly rational means? If two or three people had apoplectic strokes and dropped dead tonight, how would De Vincenzi decide which one was the killer? Letting God sort out the innocent seemed, to him, hardly the correct conclusion to a formal police investigation.

And why was Fate targeting poor Chirico? It was one thing after another. He felt like he had been rolled downhill in a barrel and there was worse to come.

"May I come in?" asked a bleating voice, and the secretary of the Circle leaped to his feet.

Pietrosanto was at the door.

"Dear God! Is this the way to enter a room? Sneaking up on me like that?"

Gualmo had crossed the entrance hall with his silent rubber soles. How could he have done otherwise?

"But I haven't entered!"

Strictly speaking, this was true. Indeed, he was afraid to enter the salon, where he saw so many tables and chairs. He knew now that it was a séance and for him that meant tables and chairs rising up and careening around the room. It looked dangerous.

Gualmo, too, had suffered hours of frightened anxiety even though his desire to discover who had been able to bring a corpse through the closed doors of the bookstore was stronger than his fear of the unknown, a fear which he would be facing tonight.

"Come in and help me clear these out," ordered Chirico, pointing to a massive, four-legged table. "We'll only need one, the largest."

They cleared the space, pushing all the other tables and chairs along the walls. Chirico wanted to put the chosen table right in front of the open door of one of the three little rooms, the middle one, which only contained a bookcase and a chair. The bookcase had glass doors and

Gualmo saw the secretary lock them with a key, which was already in the lock, and then put the key in his pocket.

"It's here that materializations usually take place. . . The spirits appear in the frame of this door. . ."

Gualmo goggled. "But you. . . did you really see them?"

"Yes," said Chirico, with condescension. "Why do you think we are here? It may very well be that the spirit of Senator Magni comes back to tell us the name of his murderer."

Gualmo swallowed.

There was a sound of footsteps in the entrance hall. Both men turned around abruptly.

De Vincenzi, Sani, Cruni and two officers had arrived.

De Vincenzi, who had already visited the Circle's headquarters with Chirico that morning, went straight to the door of the small room to the right and looked inside. Then he turned to the squad.

"Here's where you'll stay. Bring your chairs."

Once they were all inside, the inspector locked half of the double door and, before pushing the other half closed, asked, "You know what you have to do?"

"Trust me!"

"Be patient, then, and not a sound."

He closed the door and looked around. De Vincenzi was pale, too, but when he saw Chirico's face, he had to laugh, "A bit agitated?"

"Uhm!" Chirico replied, looking at the clock. "It's almost nine. What time will everyone arrive?"

"Now."

"How many people?"

"When they're all here, count them."

He was nervous. Not because of the many risks he was taking. Failed career, resignation, humiliation, he didn't even think about it. But because, if this attempt were to fail, he would have definitive proof of his inability to dominate events and people by the force of his intellect and will. The certainty that all his methods were wrong. That his insistence on reading people's souls and looking for psychological clues, instead of tangible ones, was pure conceit and nothing else.

He didn't believe in spiritism, or at least he only believed in its power over the living.

But that the dead could come back, no. He didn't believe it possible. And they certainly didn't return to unmask a murderer. That was his job.

However, he knew that others believed it firmly and he counted on their belief.

For two hours, that afternoon, he had been alone with Mrs. Sorbelli at her home while her daughter was at school and she had not read anything for him, neither cards nor even coffee grounds. He had done most of the talking, and she had listened with staring eyes and trembling lips.

"This is what you want me to do? This? But. . . if I really fall into a trance, as always happens, how am I supposed to remember what you want me to say?"

De Vincenzi had reassured her over and over, almost hypnotically. If she thought intensely about what he said to her, if she imprinted his words deep in her memory, if she repeated them over and over, they would surface, even during a trance. And he had made her repeat those sentences, many times. Of course, he was mostly counting on her being extremely suggestible.

He had done what he could, but objectively, he knew he now had no further control over events and he wasn't sure of exactly what was about to happen. And yet, somehow, he was confident that he was right and that he hadn't erred in his observations or deductions. So much so that he didn't really believe it possible that events would unfold other than expected. And even if, somehow, some piece of the puzzle were missing, if one of the gears of the delicate machine he had built failed to engage, he was still certain that the truth would reveal itself like a flame in the darkness. It doesn't take much of a spark to set gasoline alight, he reflected, and he knew that, with this séance, he had created a most combustible situation indeed.

The next arrival was the thin, long, intense young man, Dr. Sigismondi. De Vincenzi had insisted he attend the meeting because he feared that, at some point, a doctor would be needed since the medium had a heart condition and all the women involved in this case seemed prone to fainting. He had his doubts about Chirico as well.

He came with his black bag under his arm and his sharpest expression on his face.

"Place that bag in a corner. . . we don't want everyone to see it until it's necessary. And sit down, please. Do you believe in spiritism?"

Sigismondi seemed willing to believe in it. And, in any case, he was certainly an expert on the subject. "A day will come, perhaps very soon, when all these things, which today seem paradoxical, will become accepted banalities. We are intellectually invalid and slow in accepting the evolution of science. Psychic research and the study of spiritual phenomenology belong to science and not to charlatans."

Chirico nodded his approval. Gualmo, listening attentively and anxiously, suddenly stuttered, *"The cradle has a yesterday and the grave a tomorrow."*

Everyone stared at him in surprise so he immediately apologized, "I read it in Victor Hugo."

The others didn't smile. This was not the time.

Now Mrs. Sorbelli entered, accompanied by a mostly-recovered Dr. Verga and Miss Pat.

The medium wore a black dress, closed up to the neck, and no hat. Her hair, still very black, was parted in the middle and pulled back on the sides. Her plump face, pale as it was, appeared refined, spiritualized.

Her eyes glittered like polished stones.

She advanced stiffly, and De Vincenzi immediately offered her a chair, bowing in front of her as if she were nobility.

Miss Pat had lost nothing of her boldness nor of her subtle, physically exciting charm that had men look at her with burning eyes and dry lips. De Vincenzi did not bow to her.

Standing next to her, Dr. Verga resembled someone in a romantic comedy posing for a close-up. They were the femme fatale and her romantic lead. But, after all, everyone in the room had assumed a theatrical and artificial appearance. Everyone, even De Vincenzi, who was wearing an impeccably cut, yet supremely boring, gray suit. Everyone, even Chirico, so miserable and sordid, and Gualmo, in his Sunday best.

The aura of unreality centered on that woman dressed in black silently sitting in the middle of the room, her bone-white face under the black curtains of her hair, her eyes staring into an unseen void. Everything and everyone in the room seemed to take on a measure of her eerie, inhuman rigidity, marionettes waiting for the show to begin.

Even Miss Pat, who might have been expected to be most resistant to the room's miasma, eventually lost her insouciance. Her smile became fixed, almost a rictus.

De Vincenzi watched the entrance, smiling mechanically. Even he had succumbed to the stillness. Only the slight, rapid movement of his thin nostrils showed his anxiety and anticipation.

Shaking himself mentally, he began to spin the smooth, gold ring which he wore on his right hand, pushing it with his thumb. It was a habit he had developed to calm himself in moments of agitation.

No one noticed. Everyone was too busy controlling their own emotions to note the signs of internal struggle in anyone else.

The widow of the late Senator Magni arrived wearing her mourning clothes. Everyone bowed, except for Mrs. Sorbelli, who remained separate, apart, in her preternatural stillness.

De Vincenzi went to greet her. "Please forgive me, Madam," he said in a low voice. "Maybe this is too hard a trial for you in your sorrow."

"If it's really as you explained in your letter. . . well, thank you for asking me to go through such a trial."

And she sat down.

Everyone else, apart from Mrs Sorbelli, was standing.

No one asked what they were waiting for, nor what part they had been assigned. That they were there for something very serious was now clear to everyone. And, so, the tension mounted. Suspicion reigned. Unseen and unacknowledged, two corpses were now present among them.

From the foyer came the sound of a man's voice and then another, answering. The latter was warm, exuberant, almost jovial.

De Vincenzi turned back to the front door as Dr. Marini and Pietro Santini appeared.

Santini entered looking shifty, as always. His jacket too tight, his trousers too large, he wore a devious expression. It was another spot of color. Another character on the scene.

Marini went straight to De Vincenzi. "I met this young man on the stairs," he said. "He was looking for the Circle. I told him to follow me. I hope I didn't do anything wrong, leading him here."

"No," replied De Vincenzi. "And thank you, Doctor, for not missing this appointment. As you see, I am persistent in my intentions. I had decided I wanted to participate in a séance and here we are."

Marini scanned the room. He saw Mrs. Magni and started. "But why is she here? Her, of all people? You did wrong, you did wrong, De Vincenzi!" he whispered hoarsely.

De Vincenzi shrugged. "She wanted to come!" he said.

"Ah, well!" sighed Marini. "I hope you aren't counting on me to put the medium to sleep."

"Look at her," said the inspector interrupting him loudly and nodding towards Mrs. Sorbelli, who still sat unmoving. "Would it take much? Don't you think you'd just need to turn off the lights for her to fall into a trance?"

Everyone's eyes snapped to the lit chandelier hanging motionless from the ceiling. "But surely you wouldn't do that!" protested Marini. "It would be foolhardy, with consequences you can't imagine. Don't joke with the other world. Don't joke with the dead, Inspector!"

De Vincenzi went to lock the front door and then, on his return, the other door opening on the hall.

Dr. Marini fumed silently, astonished that the others hadn't joined him in trying to convince the inspector of the danger of such an experiment.

"Among the flowers there is an aster, which is the symbol of Christ!"

A sepulchral voice that seemed to echo from another world. The medium spoke and all the lights were on.

The two women and seven men were startled. The widow shuddered in her mourning clothes.

De Vincenzi stared at the woman sitting in the middle of the room, who had spoken without moving her lips. Was she pretending or had she really fallen into a hypnotic trance? What else would she say? And from where had that phrase come? It was nothing De Vincenzi had taught her. He wondered if he had pushed this overly sensitive creature too far.

Someone grasped his arm. It was Marini. "Be careful! The lady is sick. I hope you know what you're doing. If anything happens, it will be on your head."

De Vincenzi ignored him. If he was right, he would be taking responsibility for quite a lot of things tonight.

Mrs. Sorbelli was now silent. Her hands lay on her knees, her body leaning slightly forward. Suddenly, she leaned her head back, her eyes staring into the light. Her hands shook as she lifted them up.

254

De Vincenzi braced himself. Events were now taking their course and nothing could stop them.

He felt a sudden cold on the nape of his neck. He had the strange sensation that he no longer had control, that he, too, was at the mercy of a force that was as powerful as it was occult. And De Vincenzi had arranged all this himself. Only God knew what the others must be feeling!

He went to the wall and flicked the switch. Blackness descended. Shouts of "No!" and a muted scream. Terror stalked the room.

In the darkness, came the anxious breathing of the participants and the wheezing of the medium.

"The blood-like and vivid rhododendrons. . . the clematis blue turquoise like a flame. . . loving bluebells. . . And then there is the sun loving bitterwort, and the wolfsbane with its crow feather. . .."

Words. And the voice spoke them all in the same way, without expression. Cold, like the edge of a blade.

Someone's teeth were chattering like fingernails on ivory keys.

Everyone strained into the dark, hoping to see. They were expecting a light, an evanescent and fluorescent body, some visible manifestation of the horror that gripped them.

De Vincenzi didn't understand where all this discussion of flowers was coming from. The woman seemed lost in an enchanted garden. None of the phrases he had taught her even remotely related to floriculture.

Was it all just a pretense? Was it some unconscious need of hers to talk for the sake of talking?

Or was it something more terrible?

De Vincenzi tried to remain detached, a spectator, to maintain what control he could. He concentrated on the two corpses, something solid, existing, material.

"The water's mirror is cold and still and there's a woman's face, staring at me. . ."

The voice sounded more emotional, now. The words were no longer running on the edge of a blade; instead, they had become like flexible steel, vibrating.

De Vincenzi felt his blood flowing again through his veins. That was more like it! This was, more or less, a sentence of his creation. Was this all an act, then? Had she prepared the entire scene and was merely playing a part? He had not imagined anything like this and he was almost ashamed of having been so thoroughly taken in.

But she was truly wonderful! It was all De Vincenzi could do not to break into applause.

Even the prophecy of Magni's death had been an invention!

A terrible, inhuman, tortured shout flashed through the dark like a living thing. Time stopped.

The shout was heard again. And in the darkness, the unmistakable sound of a fight, of two bodies desperately struggling.

De Vincenzi ran to the wall, franticly searching for the light switch. He found it and the room flooded with light.

Mrs. Sorbelli lay on the ground and, bending over her, a knee in her stomach, his hands inexorably tightening on her throat, was Dr. Marini.

De Vincenzi leaped towards him, but Pietro Santini was faster. He grabbed the doctor by his hair and bent him backwards, ripping him away from Mrs. Sorbelli's now-inert body with unexpected strength. He was about to pound Marini's head against the massive table when De Vincenzi intervened. "Let him go!" he shouted, stunning Santini with an uppercut to the jaw.

Santini, reeling, released his death grip on Marini's head.

The doctor collapsed backwards against one of the table legs and remained there, panting, wheezing, his eyes bloodshot, his mouth slobbering.

On the ground, the woman had lost consciousness. Everyone else merely stared with terrified incomprehension.

"Sani," De Vincenzi shouted.

The door of the small room burst open and four men rushed out.

"Search him!" the inspector ordered, pointing at Marini.

Sani and one of the officers wrestled Marini to his feet and patted him down, searching his pockets. From the right pocket of Marini's jacket, Sani pulled out a small black revolver.

"Give it to me!"

De Vincenzi put it in his pocket. Then he turned to look at Dr. Sigismondi, who was kneeling near Mrs. Sorbelli and listening to her heart.

The doctor stood up, ran to his medical bag and pulled out a vial.

"Water!" he commanded.

One of the officers rushed towards the door to the entrance foyer.

"No! There," Chirico wheezed, pointing to the third door.

Water procured, Sigismondi measured a few drops from the vial into the half-full glass and then poured the liquid into the lips of the unconscious woman.

"There's nothing else I can do," he said. "I don't have a syringe with me. I didn't expect this! If her heart holds out, it will be a miracle."

Despite the doctor's pessimism, Mrs. Sorbelli's breathing soon returned to normal.

"Get her out of here!" De Vincenzi told the officers, so they lifted her up and carried her to the small central room where the materialized spirits were supposed to appear.

Dr. Sigismondi followed them and they saw him taking the woman's wrist as she lay in the armchair where they had placed her.

"Cruni, take him, too!" De Vincenzi said, pointing at Santini.

The young man was mortally pale and kept staring at Marini with homicidal fury in his eyes.

"Put him back under house arrest."

Cruni grabbed the man by the arm, and Santini let himself be dragged away.

Then De Vincenzi turned to look at Mrs. Magni.

She stood ramrod straight, and stared at Dr. Marini with almost inhuman intensity. The truth—if indeed what transpired was the truth—had revealed itself to her so suddenly, so dramatically that, even now, she still could not fully understand its implications.

The inspector approached her, gently took her hand and led her toward the entrance foyer. Mrs. Magni came to herself with a start.

"I assume my presence is no longer required?" she asked.

"I don't believe so. Thank you."

When they passed in front of Dr. Verga, who in all the commotion, had grabbed Pat by her arm and was still holding onto her, De Vincenzi said to him:

"Would you please take the lady home, Doctor?"

Verga let go of Pat and bowed, but his eyes lingered apprehensively.

"I have my car in the street," said the widow. "We can take Miss Pat home first."

The three of them left, Mrs. Magni in front, Pat and Verga right behind her.

De Vincenzi, who had accompanied them to the doorway, returned to the room and surveyed the scene.

Only Chirico and Pietrosanto were still there, slouching on two chairs in a corner, inert and extinguished, like candles at the end of a Mass.

Hunched over as they were, the really did resembled blackened and spent candle wicks.

And then there were Sani and the two officers, watching and observing.

Sani stood by the table against which Dr. Marini still slouched. Though he had not moved, Marini's eyes were returning to normal, his lips drying.

When he saw De Vincenzi return, he began to speak.

"That woman is a charlatan!" he said, glancing at the room where Mrs. Sorbelli was being attended by Dr. Sigismondi. "She was about to spout another horrible, unholy lie just as she did when she predicted Magni's death! A man can only take so much. I lost my reason. Please forgive me."

And now we come to it, thought De Vincenzi. He said, his voice icy and hard, "While you where here this evening, they found a copy of *La Zaffetta* in your house."

The effect of De Vincenzi's words was remarkable. As he watched, Marini seemed to physically shrink. The doctor gave a faint groan, his round eyes pleading, "I had to kill him! You have to believe me! I had to!"

And De Vincenzi let out a sigh of relief and triumph, because no one had gone to Marini's house that night, and no one had found a copy of *La Zaffetta.*

Chapter 22

"Shall we talk now or tomorrow morning?"

"As you like! Better now. Let's get this over with. I first. . ."

"Whoa! Hold on! I need to have a magistrate present for this. Just sit down for a moment."

"No. First I want to talk with you! I need to make you understand."

"How can that help you?"

"I want to bare my soul to you, to make you see. Yes, yes! I know it will not save me. But tonight, after what happened, I need to explain! Tomorrow, I'll tell the others everything. I'll sign anything they want me to. But you, you have to know, to *understand*, the reasons I killed him."

"I know them already!"

"No! I tell you, you don't know them. You *can't* know them!"

He was back to normal, with only a little anxiousness betrayed by his slight panting, or perhaps that was due to the fit of madness he had suffered shortly before. Because he had suffered a fit of madness, of genuine temporary insanity. De Vincenzi could not doubt it: the look in his eyes and the whitish foam that still flecked the corners of his mouth were clear indications.

But now the fit was over and Marini was smiling sarcastically.

"You think I killed him because my wife was having an affair with him! That's what you think! But you're wrong! I'm telling you, you're wrong. If I had not hated, I wouldn't have killed him and I wouldn't have suffered the betrayal. I would have thrown my wife out six months ago, when it all started. I knew it immediately. I'm not blind. Not I! And I was suspicious anyway, because I knew he would try to take her away from me, too. Just like he had taken everything else! But my hate for him was so strong, had such deep roots, roots so deep that it was no longer possible to tear them out! Can't you see that you don't know anything, yet?"

He tried to stagger towards a chair and Sani pushed it toward him and held it. He sank down, now exhausted. His hands began to shake slightly.

De Vincenzi nodded to the officers who had remained in the middle of the room, ready to intervene, and the two of them retreated to the entrance foyer.

Sani, who had taken out a pad of paper and a pencil, looked questioningly at the inspector. De Vincenzi gave the slightest of nods so Sani sat down on the other side of the table, behind Dr. Marini's back, ready to write. Marini didn't even notice. He was looking at De Vincenzi, who remained standing with his hands in his pockets, a bit hunched over, his eyes tired. Now that the tension of the battle had broken, now that he knew he had won, a great sorrow filled with bitterness and discouragement had invaded him. That terrible drama of the last seven days crushed him with a sense of how mean and dangerous life was, how unnecessarily full of thorns and snares. And also a sense of dismay, an unshakeable feeling that all he had done was petty and pointless. What was the meaning of that room, with those men, with *that* man, who was a murderer? What was Earth? Just a planet. And many more stars with many more planets, bigger, far away, the universe an infinite kaleidoscope. And on Earth, in that tiny corner of the infinite universe, sat a man who at that moment believed that all the stars, all the planets, the entire universe were watching him, revolving around him and his agony, his tragedy! Perhaps they were.

"I told you I wanted to talk and now I realize that perhaps words will not be enough to explain why I had to kill him. Thirty years! Thirty years of hatred for hatred's sake! We were children, students at the same boarding-school. Our dormitory, where we spent most of our studying and free time, had a single window, which looked out onto the garden. The rest of the room was dark, sad. From that window the sun came in, trees could be seen. It wasn't just a window, it was a window opening onto the miracle of nature, onto freedom. We each had our own desk, with our books, with all our belongings. We thought of it as our shrine. Well, I had my desk right in front of that window, and it brought me joy. A few weeks earlier my mother had accompanied me to the boarding-school and had left me there. I was so homesick that I spent my nights sobbing. They gave me that desk and it was my lifeline, my one consolation.

"Then Magni arrived. He was already much as he was the day I killed him, tall, thin, very handsome. People, even the teachers, loved him on sight. He had a smile which immediately conquered everyone. Was it that smile? Was it because he had been accompanied by the rector himself to our dormitory, and delivered to the tutor with many whispered recommendations? Or was it me, my destiny, my curse? Whatever it was, the tutor ordered me to give up my place to the newcomer. From that moment on, I hated him. At night I had horrible nightmares and I always saw him dead, with my hands around his perfect neck. I was obsessed. I tried to escape it, I really tried. I even tried befriending him. They called us inseparable. But he had accepted my friendship as if it was owed to him, like a slave submits to his master. Every day that passed, he rubbed my nose in his superiority. He had everything and I had nothing. I lived in his light! I ate the leftovers of his meals! As we got older, as soon as I looked at a girl, he immediately tried to seduce her, to make her fall in love with him! All this just to keep me in my place. Hatred for hatred's sake! Can you understand?"

He stopped talking, slowly winding down.

In the silence, Sani's frantic scribbling filled the room.

The sound of Sigismondi tending to the unfortunate Mrs. Sorbelli broke the spell and De Vincenzi went to close the door, returning to stand in front of the sitting Dr. Marini.

Chirico and Pietrosanto remained sitting in their corner, ignored and motionless.

"Do you understand now? Do you at least begin to understand?"

"I knew," De Vincenzi said slowly, and Marini looked at him surprised.

"You knew? That's why you suspected me? That's why you prepared a trap for me? That's why you sent your colleagues to get that book from my house?"

"In part."

"Well, then I'm glad it was you!"

He was silent, again. Then he lifted his head and his eyes glittered.

"If it hadn't been you, no one would have found me out! Mine was a masterpiece! Do you want to know how I killed him? Of course you do! I must confess, I hadn't set my mind on that night. I was determined to kill him, yes, but I was waiting for the right opportunity. I wanted to kill him in such a way that I wouldn't be blamed for it! I was stalking him like a hunter. I knew he was my wife's lover. He had taken her away from me, too! I had expected it, anyway, and I had done nothing to prevent it. It would have been useless. And it wasn't even her fault! She only succumbed to a stronger power. She had to love him and betray me, because *my* destiny demanded it."

De Vincenzi remembered the apartment in Via Abbondio Sangiorgio, the portrait in the silver frame, the woman lying on the deck chair, against the sun and the sea, with her blue dressing gown, her golden hair and those bare feet in her slippers. . .

"That night," the doctor continued, in a triumphal voice, almost bragging, "he came looking for me. He knew that in the evenings I always went to a café in Porta Venezia and he came in at about ten o'clock. He seemed nervous. He was biting his lip the way he always did when something or someone opposed him. "Time for a walk!" he told me, giving me an order, as usual. We walked all over Milan. He was doing the talking, also as usual. He said he had had enough of women and that he was bored with it all. He talked to me about his wife. I spoke to him about my wife, on purpose. I was feeding my hatred. I was living off it. I needed it like a drug addict needs cocaine. Several times I touched the revolver I had in my pocket. I had a sudden urge to take him out to the countryside. Perhaps, I was already thinking of killing him. But he didn't want to go. We went into four or five bars, drinking without even sitting down. He was drinking whiskey and made me drink it too. It seemed to me that things became clearer and my brain started working better. It was after the fourth or fifth whiskey, that I decided to kill him that night. But how? Suddenly, I remembered I had in my pocket the keys to the bookstore on Via Corridoni."

Chirico and Pietrosanto suddenly came to life. From their corner, came the squeak of shifting chairs and exclamations of amazement and protest. Even De Vincenzi was startled.

Sani's pencil kept running on the paper, and the filled sheets were scattered on the table.

"Why did I have them? Again, it was destiny, I tell you! A couple of weeks earlier, I had gone into Chirico's shop to have a look at a book on occultism. I was carrying my bag, a newspaper, my gloves, and I don't know what else. I had left all that on Chirico's desk as I browsed, so as I was leaving, I went to pick everything up. There was a key-ring with two keys next to my gloves. I was distracted. . . you know how it happens. . . those keys looked like mine. . . I assumed I had put them down with my gloves and I picked them up and put them in my pocket without really thinking about it. A few days later, I realized I had them and I went crazy trying to remember where I might have gotten them. I finally did remember, and I meant to bring them back right away. But I didn't. I didn't find the time. I even, somehow, forgot to mention to Chirico that I had them. Or perhaps I didn't forget. Perhaps it was destiny, once again, stopping me. . .

"That night, when Magni told me that he wanted to go home and we started walking from the square of the Duomo, toward Porta Vittoria, passing by Via Corridoni, I remembered the keys. I immediately thought of killing him in the bookstore and then locking it up. It was perfect. No one would suspect me. I even had to suppress a burst of laughter imagining what would happen in the morning when they found the corpse.

"We were talking about spiritism. I told him that Chirico had a very rare and interesting book on that topic, and I suggested we go and get it right away. 'I have the keys,' I added. 'Chirico gave them to me so that I could borrow the book myself.'

"There was nothing strange about it. Chirico is the secretary of the Circle and Magni knew him very well and wouldn't question me. But he didn't want to go. He said he was tired. We continued all the way to

Viale Bianca Maria and I saw that my plan was derailing. But I knew another weakness of his, an aspect of his obsessive licentiousness. 'Do you know Chirico has a collection of pornography?' I said. That did it and he happily agreed to come with me. We retraced our steps. The street was deserted, we didn't see a soul all the way up Via Cesare Battisti.

"I unlocked the rolling shutter and, between the two of us, we managed to lift it. When we got in, I lowered it again. 'If they see the light,' I said, 'they might think we're thieves. How embarrassing would that be!' He laughed. 'Where are the erotic books?' he asked me. We had to look for them. When we finally did find them, he immediately picked up *La Zaffetta*. He browsed a few pages, his back to me and I heard him say, 'Ah, those were the days! They knew how to deal with women then, like the whores they are!' So I shot him. I couldn't help it. I still would have done it, perhaps, even if he had said nothing. But those words were like a lash on my back. I knew that, at that moment, he was talking about my wife."

Another silence.

Chirico leaned over to say something to Gualmo and received a puzzled look in return.

"Then you took a bag," said De Vincenzi, "that you found in a corner, and dragged it through the dust on the floor, to make it look as though the corpse had been brought in from the outside?"

De Vincenzi spoke slowly. After Marini's outpouring, he wanted to give Sani time to catch up. At this point, everything was so clear to him that he could have answered the questions himself. . . All except for one, one he was keeping for last.

"Ha! You figured that out as well? Yes. He had fallen in front of the door of the third room. I grabbed the book he had dropped and put it in my pocket. Why? I don't know! Maybe it was a trophy, something that would always remind me of what I had done that day. But whatever the reason, I wanted to keep it. I told you that I hated him and I was filled with my triumph! But I also felt somehow detached, like an observer, uninvolved, yet keenly aware of everything. I took great care to confuse things as much as possible, taking an almost artistic pride in my work. I marked the strip on the ground. I opened the door to the courtyard, and went out and made sure that the main door to the building was open. I could leave that way, I realized. Then I wouldn't need to raise the rolling shutter, which would be both difficult and noisy. I returned to grab Magni's hat and turn off all the lights. Then I closed the door behind me so that people would initially think it was locked. A nice piece of theater, wouldn't you say? Once outside, I checked to make sure the street was still deserted and locked the shutter so that everyone would conclude that Magni's corpse had been brought in from the courtyard."

"But after all this, you didn't realize one of the bullets had passed through Magni completely and was lodged in a book, in front of the corpse?"

"No, I didn't know that. How could I have? But I thought about the hat!"

It was a cry of victory.

"I held it tight against my chest, under my overcoat. I walked up to Via della Commenda and let it fall against the wall of the homeless shelter. I knew someone there would find it. . . with any luck someone with a record, which would have confused the trail even more."

Ah! So the Worm must really have found that hat, though De Vincenzi. If only Harrington hadn't muddied the waters. And then De Vincenzi thought of the widow who had gone to see Harrington, trying to help.

"Did your wife see the book you had brought home with you?"

"Yes. How do you know that? I had left it on the desk in my study. I slept a bit late the next morning and when I did get up, I found her turning it over in her hands. I snatched it away from her, saying that I had bought it for my researches. It was the only excuse I could think of off the top of my head!"

So that was why the woman had suddenly collapsed in front of him as soon as he had hinted at *La Zaffetta*. She knew!

And now they had reached The Question.

"And what about that girl? What about Norina?" he asked with a cold voice.

The man shuddered. His eyes filled with horror.

"Ah! No! Please don't ask! I'll proudly confess, give you the details of everything, but not that! Norina had seen us from the window. . . She followed us. . . She saw us entering the bookstore. . . The following night she came to look for me at home. Poor girl! Another one of his victims. She loved him, like all the rest. I felt lost. I didn't know what to do. . . I made her go out for a walk with me. . . I made her drink. . . Then. . . then. . . on the parapet of the dock. . . Oh, God!"

He covered his face with his hands.

De Vincenzi looked at Sani. Both of them were very pale. Sani returned to his work, then nodded. He had written everything down, even that.

But it was up to the inspector to insist, to have the details. Normally, he savored the solutions to his cases like a fine wine. This was like drinking poison.

"Did she suspect you?"

"No," murmured Marini. "She just wanted to know why I hadn't told you we were together. She didn't threaten to speak. She just wanted to know! But she would have spoken! No matter what I told her, she would told someone that I was with Magni that night. I had no choice. She had to be silenced."

"And you would have strangled Mrs. Sorbelli, too!"

"Oh! Her!"

And, taking his hands off his face, he glanced at the closed door. Again his eyes became bloodshot and a tremor coursed through his body. A sick man, thought De Vincenzi.

"Her!" he repeated.

"Were you the one who got her to predict his death?"

Marini appeared about to deny it but then surrendered.

"Yes. I wanted to frighten him. I knew he was superstitious and feared death."

"Did you get him interested in spiritism for the same reason?"

"Perhaps. Probably. Yes. In my hatred, I was always looking for some way to damage him, to give life to my revenge. Manipulating his fears using spiritism was easy."

"And Mrs. Sorbelli? Why did she participate in this charade?"

"I had influenced her. At first, I considered just paying her. But I quickly realized that was both dangerous and unnecessary. She's so suggestible, she could be influenced by the postman, and I, I'm quite a good hypnotist. She could no more resist my commands than she could remember them consciously afterward!"

"And what about tonight?"

"Tonight, I realized immediately that she was not fully conscious, and in that state, she would be able to repeat what I had told her. Not only that, she would have. For some reason, she was very focused on the two deaths."

De Vincenzi doubted this explanation. Oh, he was sure that Marini believed it now. But at the time, there had been nothing cold, nothing calculating, about Marini. It was something more basic, more primal. It had been fear: fear of the dead.

Marini began to have another fit. He stood up, glaring at De Vincenzi. He raised an accusing finger toward him. He quivered, foam again forming at the corners of his mouth. Sani got out of his chair. The two officers, still at their post by the door, started forward.

"You. . . It was you who influenced her. . . It was you who taught her what to say tonight!"

De Vincenzi looked at him sharply. "I'll ask the questions!" he told the doctor firmly. "You convinced Mrs. Magni to go to Harrington, hoping he would pin this crime on an innocent, didn't you?"

Marini didn't answer. He began to visibly collect himself. He lowered his hand, still panting.

"Answer me!"

"Yes. It was part of the plan I had in mind when I dropped off the hat."

"How much money did you give Harrington?"

Marini paused, "Ask him. None of this matters any longer!"

So his guess about Harrington was correct. "Is this the gun with which you killed the senator?" De Vincenzi asked, pulling the black revolver out of his pocket.

"Yes. I only have one."

"Fine. That's it then. It's over."

The other said, "I know it's over."

"Sani, it's time." De Vincenzi ordered.

Sani gathered his notes.

"Does he need to sign this?"

"Not now, tomorrow will be fine. Search him again and cuff him."

"Are you afraid that I'll try to poison myself?" Dr. Marini said in a sad voice, while the deputy inspector searched him. He was quiet now. Resigned. "You needn't worry. I'll let Justice take its course."

Sani placed the *manette a catenella* on his wrists and the lock snapped shut. The two officers grabbed him by the arms.

They started to leave, but De Vincenzi stopped them.

"Why did you put four surgical instruments and a lab coat on the steps of the San Vito church?"

Marini didn't understand. The inspector had to ask the question again.

"Four instruments and a coat? I don't know what you are talking about. I didn't put anything on the steps of San Vito."

It had to be true. There was no reason for him to lie.

"OK. Go ahead." said De Vincenzi, waiving his hand.

It was the doctor who stopped this time.

"Please! One request. My wife is in Pegli. . . at Villa Doria. . . Please, tell her what's happened."

De Vincenzi knew he wouldn't. It was the one thing he didn't have the courage to do. Poor Sani had an unpleasant trip ahead of him. He nodded evasively. "Take him to prison. I'll alert the Superintendent myself."

"Are you staying?" Sani asked eyeing him with apprehension. De Vincenzi looked terrible, very pale, his tired eyes surrounded by black circles.

"Yes," and he pointed to the room where Mrs. Sorbelli lay. "I'm worried about her."

Then he had a thought. The guards were already going down the stairs with the prisoner. He took Sani by the arm.

"Hang on! As soon as you leave him in San Fedele, go to his house, in Corso Plebisciti 17, and find the book, *La Zaffetta*. It's dated Venice, 1531. Find it at all costs."

"Sure. No problem. Don't worry."

It was all over. De Vincenzi remained in the center of the room, deflated, staring into the void.

He felt a hand on his arm. It was Chirico. His cheeks were flushed.

"My keys!" he said. "Can I have my keys back?"

Epilogue

It wasn't until the trial, when those four surgical instruments and that lab coat appeared among the crime scene evidence, together with the note containing the strange invitation to deliver them to the police station, that their place in the drama became clear. No one had been able to unravel the mystery of their connection to the double murder. . . because there wasn't one.

The popular press reported the trial widely and, the next day, a student came to the police station to claim them, a fourth year student of medicine. They had been "stolen" from him—a fellow student's joke—while he was at the university for a dissection class.

Dr. Marini was sentenced to life in prison. The judge refused to consider mental illness as an extenuating circumstance.

De Vincenzi left for Ossola that night, keeping the promise he had made to Sani to get some rest.

And he could relax, back in his little house with the vegetable garden, his mother, her maid and the dog. . .

On starry nights, he sat on the grass and looked at the sky. And he couldn't help but think,

"There is a whole world around us that we know nothing about!"

The End

The Publisher

No, this is not another chapter of *Death in a Bookstore*. Since you're a fan of Golden Age mysteries, we think you'll enjoy a taste from another of our international novels, *The Man in the Cellar* by Danish author Baron Palle Rosenkrantz. But first, a word from our sponsor, which is us!

Kazabo Publishing is a new idea in the literary world. Our motto is, "Every Book a Best Seller . . . Guaranteed!" And we mean it. Our mission is to find best-selling books from around the world that, for whatever reason, have not been published in English. Augusto De Angelis's novels are very popular in Europe but very few have been published in English. Why? We don't know. But we think you will agree that they should have been. And now they are.

We have found there are also many contemporary writers who are very popular in their own countries but who have not made it into English. We think this is a real shame so we are working to bring those books and those authors to you.

When you visit Kazabo.com (our website!), we hope you will always discover something new, either a book from a favorite author you didn't know existed or a completely new author with a fresh perspective from a country you admire. We promise you that everything you see with the Kazabo name – even authors you have never heard of – will be a best-seller; maybe in Italy, maybe in Japan, maybe in 1902, but a best seller. We hope you enjoy reading these literary gems as much as we enjoy finding them and bringing them to you.

But enough about us. Here is an excerpt from *The Man in the Cellar*.

Thanks for reading!

The Kazabo Team

Kazabo.com

The Man in the Cellar

By Palle Rosenkrantz

1.

Chapter One

"It is dirt cheap, sir, dirt cheap! Three and a half guineas per week for the whole fully furnished house, consisting of studio, two living rooms, a large dining room and three bedrooms—not counting the garden. Electric light in the whole house and gas in the kitchen. It is dirt cheap. And it is only by chance that I can give you the house so cheap."

Mr. Sydney Armstrong clicked his tongue and tapped a walking stick on his brown leather leggings. He was dressed sportily as usual, for sport was his main occupation. In addition, he worked to earn his living as an agent for home sales and rentals. His business was still young, and the staff consisted only of himself and an office clerk.

At the moment he was standing in the corridor of a small house in London's Cranbourne Grove; 48 was the number. The house, a real country house, stood a little secluded within a walled garden in South Kensington, near the museum, the bus, and the subway station.

As always, Mr. Armstrong applied his old business trick: he pretended not to care at all about renting the house, while in reality he was very much interested; there were five pounds to earn, and five pounds would be a tidy sum for a young house agent.

For this reason, too, Mr. Armstrong emphatically brushed his mustache while trying to impart a look as indifferent as possible.

And the bird he wanted to catch had actually started flapping into the net. It was dirt cheap for such a house! Three and a half guineas per week!

The bird, who was a Dane, converted the sum into Danish money.

"Three and a half guineas are more than three and a half pounds," he said to himself, because a guinea, according to an ancient tradition—God knows why—is as much as a pound and a shilling. Three and a half guineas are thus three pounds, thirteen shillings, and sixpence, that is, sixty-five Danish kroner.

That was more expensive though than Holger Nielsen had intended. But there was also a studio in the apartment, and in general it was a lovely little house. In addition, Holger Nielsen was not planning to live in it alone, for he had arranged with a doctor Jens Koldby to rent an apartment in London together—and not a floor in one of those enormous apartments, but a real clean, old English cottage with a garden. And Madame Sivertsen, who spent fourteen years as an attendant on an Atlantic steamer and spoke perfect English, would be in charge of their household during the three months they intended to spend in London.

Doctor Koldby was a painter, and therefore the studio was needed.

Holger Nielsen also stroked his small, light-brown mustache and made an effort to negotiate prices.

"Let's say three pounds ten shillings," he suggested.

"We always count with guineas in London," replied Mr. Armstrong. "It's really dirt cheap! You can believe me! The house is not my own; it belongs to an officer who went to Burma. And I have my specific orders. Actually, it should be four guineas. I can go down to three and a half, but not half a penny less."

And Mr. Armstrong tried to look superior but failed because of his thin yellow mustache.

"It's really too much," said Holger Nielsen.

Mr. Armstrong shrugged. "Then let us go," he said. He didn't want to give in, because at three and a half guineas he would get five pounds. And so, he stuck to his demand.

Holger Nielsen, who liked the house, hesitated. And Mr. Armstrong grew hopeful again.

"Show me the house again," Nielsen said finally. And they went in again.

The entrance was small and narrow; it turned into a corridor about twelve feet long and four feet wide, from which a staircase led upwards. Behind it, the corridor narrowed and led to the kitchen and the basement. On either side of the corridor was a door to the two living rooms, each with a window as high as the wall. Toward the back, a door led from the corridor to the small garden with its two elongated grass lawns and a few fig and laurel trees. The two rooms on the ground floor were large, richly carpeted and decorated with old-fashioned and carved furniture. From the room on the right a door led to a corridor running to the rear, at the end of which lay the very spacious and high-ceilinged dining room; it was rather a hall, but quite dark, as it received light only through a window in the ceiling. The old oak furniture was heavy and dark, and the floor was covered with new linoleum, which Mr. Armstrong seemed to fancy.

"It's pretty dark here," said Nielsen.

"Oh, it's always dark on the ground floor of a London house," the agent told him. "It's much lighter up there."

The upper rooms were indeed bright and friendly. The windows of the two bedrooms, which were next to the stairs, looked out onto the sunny side of the garden, and the sun was kind enough today to support Mr. Armstrong. It shone in through the cute little windows with all its might, and the studio with its large skylight was literally flooded with light.

This sunshine put an end to Nielsen's hesitation; it gave a considerable advantage to Mr. Armstrong, for the sun is a rarity in London, especially in South Kensington, which is so close to the Thames with its mists.

"Shall I sign the contract right now?" Nielsen asked.

A sigh of relief sounded in place of the yes. The bird in the net had stopped fluttering.

Holger Nielsen signed the contract and paid half a crown for the stamp. Nothing else. "The owner has to pay all the rest," said Armstrong eagerly; now that he had won the game, he let himself be brought to some amiability.

"Who is the owner?" Asked Nielsen, who wanted to know in whose house he would be living.

"Major Johnson," replied Armstrong. "He went to Burma. Just left. It's a real coincidence that you got the lovely house. The major has just lived in it for a week. Yes, just think. He had bought the house from a friend who had inherited it from his mother. I don't remember his name, I have a poor memory for names, but this mister . . . So-and-so had just sold the house to Major Johnson when, on the following day, he was ordered to go down to the colonies. And there was nothing to do, he had to go. He had wanted to get married, but his bride broke off the relationship and he left without her. Yes, this can happen in countries that have colonies. Be glad that Denmark has none except Spitsbergen. But that's what happened to the major. His friends assure me, he almost leapt with joy to avoid an evil mother-in-law."

You see, Mr. Armstrong—happily contemplating the prospect of five pounds—had begun to joke.

"How about the furniture?" Nielsen asked.

"Oh, the major bought the furniture along with the house. As far as I know, Mr. So-and-so, who inherited it, or his sister, lived here until a week ago. Then he sold it to the major and went his own way."

"And what happened to him?"

"I don't know. I don't know him at all. All I know is that he was unmarried."

Nielsen looked at him, scrutinizing.

"The furniture suggests, however, that a lady has been here. Don't you agree?"

"Yes," said Armstrong, "it must have been his sister who lived here with her husband. He had the studio set up by the way, because he painted, I believe. But, as I said, I don't know anything about the

276

family. I know only Major Johnson; he belongs to the Johnsons of Yorkshire. But you understand nothing about that as a stranger to these parts."

In fact, Nielsen didn't know the Johnsons of Yorkshire and quietly accompanied Mr. Armstrong to his bureau where a proper contract was drawn up and signed. On May 1, Doctor Koldby and Madame Sivertsen were to arrive, and both expected to find everything in order. Now that it was already April 29th, it was time to come to a decision, and Nielsen was overall satisfied with the deal.

Chapter Two

Holger Nielsen was, as we already heard, a Dane. He had studied law, was the son of a government official, thirty-two, and had considerable knowledge. He had originally been in a ministry position but had to retire because a certain stiffness in his back prevented him from crawling in front of his superiors. Then he had tried being a lawyer, but also found that job not suitable because his back had been too stiff for the clients. Then he had thrown himself into the study of crime and shocked all of his conservative relatives with his radical ideas. He was an only son; his parents, both of whom were already dead, had left him a considerable fortune. He now lived on his inheritance and devoted himself entirely to his field of interest—criminology. And this interest had finally led him to London, in whose narrow streets he intended to conduct criminal studies. He had received praise for his great published volume, *Crime*; however, as a strong and healthy man, he despised sitting in his chair and gathering his knowledge from books alone. In fact, he avoided books altogether; using only the material that life itself offered for his study. Of course, it was not his way to roam the so-called criminal quarters and spy on the questionable rabble—he had not come to London to carry out the traditional journey to Whitechapel with two or three copper coins in his pocket. No, what he wanted was to observe the population of a big city in their narrow streets and get to know the conditions of their daily lives; that was to be the starting point from which he hoped to explain abnormal phenomena.

He wanted to understand London, and this visit was just an introduction. First, he must accustom himself to the language and so follow the events on the street and the police station until he could progress to exploring more serious problems.

On May 1, Doctor Koldby and Madame Sivertsen reached London on the train arriving at Harwich at 7:35. They had made their way via Esbjerg staying aboard the steamer until morning to avoid arriving in London by night.

Holger Nielsen had already arranged his belongings to be taken from the wretched boarding house where he had been staying to the new home, and now received the newcomers—with the help of the sun—

most cordially.

And he obviously had succeeded.

Madame Sivertsen's chamber lay in the basement near the kitchen; it was a little dark and narrow, but Madame Sivertsen was not difficult to satisfy; she had been used to tight quarters on the steamer, though age had made her quite stout. And now, as she herself had remarked, she had been lazy for a fortnight, she was ready to go to work. And so, she did.

Meanwhile, Doctor Koldby inspected the studio and grunted with satisfaction; it was everything it should be. He immediately unpacked his sketches and paint tubes, set up the easel and adjusted a canvas. He had come to London to make some sketches of the Thames and the docks; he also wanted to study Turner in the National Gallery.

Koldby was a painter of seascapes with the title of Doctor of Medicine; his father—a doctor—had forced him to take this job thirty years ago. Koldby's inclinations, however, went in a different direction, and his father, an old land doctor at Thisted, had scarcely closed his eyes when Koldby threw his stethoscopes and other instruments into the corner and spent the old man's well-earned pennies on paints and canvas. Since he was attracted to the sea, he crossed the ocean to Mexico. From the coast of Florida, where he was shipwrecked, he gradually came, traveling and painting through the country, to New York, later returning home, then traveling to Egypt, where he painted sphinxes and pyramids, and became, as time goes by, an old man of about sixty years. But his back was straight and his spirit young. On a Christmas Eve in Rome, he met Holger Nielsen, and they both took a liking to each other. They became, and remained, friends.

During his many journeys through Egypt, Doctor Koldby had adopted Muslim-like attitudes; he loved the sunrise prayer and abhorred wine. In one respect alone he had not become a good Muslim; the Prophet's teaching about polygamy didn't meet with his approval. He not only detested wine, but also women. And though he had to admit that his hatred of the weaker sex was wholly without reason, since no woman had ever harmed him, he clung to his dislike; he thought that in this way he had been saved from many disappointments.

With his colleagues, the professors of fine art, he lived in constant dispute; he declared them all idiots and treated them with disregard, an opinion which they returned in kind.

Otherwise, he was sensible and straightforward.

And now the sun was shining into the studio of the house at Cranbourne Grove 48, warming the back of the painting doctor and conveniently lighting up the sketches he had made of the stormy sea on the journey from Esbjerg.

For Doctor Koldby, it was everything as it should be.

Chapter Three

The first night Holger Nielsen spent in the new house, he could not sleep. Not because he was not tired, because he was always tired in London. The long walks through the streets, standing in the midst of the cosmopolitan city and following the flow of the people about whom everything individual disappeared, watching the richly dressed, well-groomed crowd that floated past the bright shop windows—always shopping, busily increasing their abundance, and the infinite maze of byroads and lanes in which dirt and poverty lived, where the miserable children of the poor surrounded him while playing, and where the contrast to the abundance of the great streets taught him the elements of socialism—all these walks tired him very much.

And yet he could not sleep.

The noise on the street decreased more toward midnight, the wheezing of the motorcars, and the rumbling of the buses became increasingly rare, the coachmen's shouts died away, and the footsteps on the cobblestones began to sound only occasionally. At last everything fell silent, blanketed by the night; only the clock on the nearby tower announced the hours with dull blows.

It was a dark night—no moonlight—and complete silence had finally arrived. And yet Holger Nielsen thought he heard something somewhere in the dark, something he could not decipher, or explain.

It sounded almost like the cry of a child . . . or a cat. Not like a loud cat howling or meowing, but like a very soft, miserable, helpless crying that seemed to come from far away. Nielsen tried not to notice it, tried to find sleep, but the lamentation grew louder and even more miserable. Of course, he knew that there was at least one cat in each house in London, all very well-treated animals that enjoyed some kind of civil rights, under no constraint, and able to pass their lives day and night as they pleased. On the other hand, this cat, if it was a cat, must have been a wretched, maltreated creature mourning in the cellars of the house; because in this house it definitely sat.

After listening for a while, Holger Nielsen rose, put on some clothes,

281

turned on the light, and quietly walked out into the corridor. Again, he could not find out where the sound came from; it sounded vaguely from the depths.

Now Nielsen walked quietly, so as not to disturb his companions, into the kitchen. Once there, he heard a rustling in Madame Sivertsen's chamber and noticed a strip of light under her door.

Madame Sivertsen!" he whispered.

"Is this you, Mr. Nielsen?" her voice asked. "Thank God."

"Aren't you asleep yet?" he asked.

"No," was her answer. "I can't shut my eyes. I always hear something moving."

There was really something moving, Nielsen heard it now as well. The sound was like a soft scratching or creeping and yet again resembled neither of them.

"There must be a cat in the house somewhere, Madame Sivertsen," said Nielsen in a whisper.

"*That* is not a cat," she replied softly, but firmly.

"What else could it be?" he replied. "Listen, now it's howling— Where could the animal be?"

The old woman stepped out of her chamber in an elaborate nightgown with a huge night cap.

"That is not a cat," she repeated, shaking her head causing the ribbons to fly. "There's something in the house, Mr. Nielsen."

Nielsen had to smile, "Do you think the house is haunted?"

She was silent.

"You don't believe in ghosts, Madame Sivertsen?"

The old woman shook her head, "It's definitely not a cat. Something is going on in the house."

"Are you afraid?"

"Me? No. I have a clear conscience—it will leave me alone. But it sounds so frightening."

Nielsen decided to get to the bottom of the matter. He combed the house, stomping on the floor and knocking on the walls. The sound stopped; but as soon as he left the corridor, the lamentation sounded anew.

Finally, the clock struck one.

"Well, now our ghost is going to rest," he said to Madame Sivertsen with a smile. "And I think we must do the same."

Madame Sivertsen shook her nightcap ribbons and jiggled back into her room.

Nielsen also went to bed, finally falling into a restless sleep and dreaming of a huge black cat, who sat purring on the bed in front of him.

He slept very badly that night.

Doctor Koldby, on the other hand, rested in the true sleep of the righteous, and the next morning he had only a mocking laugh for Nielsen and Madame Sivertsen. He was delighted with the house and especially with the studio.

Nielsen spent the whole day searching all the rooms, but without finding a cat or anything else noteworthy. Finally, he put the matter out of his mind and left for a walk.

The very next night both he and Madame Sivertsen were unable to close their eyes again; the cat was heard again.

This time, they woke the doctor, who had to admit that something was making a noise. The doctor also thought it was more of a cat than a ghost, and the two friends decided to do a very thorough investigation the next day. Such was the decision of their second night, which was to be carried out on the third day.

Chapter Four

"Look, Doctor, there—that's a tiny cellar, isn't it? Nielsen gestured toward a coal cellar with a round iron plate to close the hatch. Can you see anything else in it?"

Nielsen and the doctor were on their expedition. It was bright daytime now and they were determined to find the cat. It had to be in the house . . . it could only be in the basement . . . but the basement, the only one in the house, was empty. The animal was no longer howling and seemed to have retired after the efforts of the previous night.

"We dreamed, my dear friend," said the doctor, "unless Edgar Allan Poe's tale of the cat, walled in with a corpse, is to be realized in this little London cottage. That would be something for you, right, Mr. Criminal Investigator! A cat in the walls calling for justice with its whining and meowing. Then the ghost we heard at night would not be so strange. Well, let's go back to daylight."

They went upstairs and around the outside of the cottage again. The wing that housed the dining room had been rebuilt and had its own roof; it was built like the rest of the house out of brown bricks, while the pedestal was made of cement bricks. To allow for air circulation small gaps had been cut into the pedestal, which were protected by iron bars. Nielsen walked around the outside, poking at the gaps with a stick to see whether they led to a cavity.

Suddenly he paused.

"Doctor," he said, "look, here's a low room only tall enough to give shelter to a cat. Look, there's the cat inside!"

"Wriggle in," replied the doctor sardonically. "Make yourself thin and crawl through the bars. There is no other way."

"Well, the floor of the dining room, which must be here, is covered with linoleum."

"Are you going to rip it open?" cried the doctor in horror.

"Well, now," said Nielsen, "I want to get to the bottom of this, because I want my night's sleep—and otherwise we would be acting cruelly toward the cat."

"How on earth do you think the beast got in there? The bars are barely wide enough to let a mouse through."

"Oh, for example, through a trapdoor, perhaps hidden under the linoleum," replied Nielsen, who was already hurrying toward the corridor door.

The doctor followed him—almost annoyed. As always, he was the more stubborn of the two, though he had to admit that Nielsen's guess could be the right one.

The linoleum was removed, and lo and behold, there was indeed a trapdoor in the floor looking down into a cellar-like room that had no steps leading into it. And no sooner had the light penetrated the small square opening into the cellar than a long, thin, gray cat leaped out, fleeing, half-alive, full of fear, with stiff, awkward movements, through the corridor into the garden, where it vanished.

"That was the cat," said Nielsen.

"That was it," said the doctor, "but how in heaven's name did it get in there?"

"Let's get a lamp and a ladder," said Nielsen. "Then we'll climb down. I mean, there's more to it."

It was a very low cellar to which the air had access only through the narrow, barred gaps. It appeared to have been a wine cellar, but at the moment it was empty. But in one corner stood a big long box with a nailed lid.

Nielsen stepped toward it to take a closer look.

"Watch it, it's going to explode," joked the doctor. "You know what? A Russian terrorist lived here and kept his stock of dynamite in this cellar . . . By the way, it looks like lime has been strewn there. Right, it's lime."

"Wait a minute," said Nielsen, "I'll fetch a crowbar."

The doctor stood with the lamp in his hand and waited, whistling until Nielsen returned with a chisel and crowbar. "You will see, Mr. Criminal Investigator, finally, there's a corpse in the box. Just like in Edgar Allan Poe!"

Nielsen tore at the lid. "Shine the light here, Doctor," he said, a little excited.

The doctor—still whistling—came up with the lamp. Suddenly he fell silent. "It really looks as if . . ." he said, still joking, but suddenly his voice cracked hoarsely—"There under the lime—lies a cloth—Holy God—there really is a corpse in the box!"

Want to know what happens next?

Visit www.kazabo.com to get the ebook,

or visit amazon.com for digital and print formats.

Made in the USA
San Bernardino, CA
18 December 2019